THE GUNSMITH'S DAUGHTER

•

Also by Margaret Sweatman

Mr. Jones

The Players

When Alice Lay Down with Peter

Sam and Angie

Fox

THE GUNSMITH'S DAUGHTER

MARGARET SWEATMAN

GOOSE LANE

Edited by Bethany Gibson.
Cover and page design by Julie Scriver.
Cover illustration adapted from "Yellow Eucalyptus" fabric by Honoluludesigns.
Printed in Canada by Friesens.
10 9 8 7 6 5 4 3 2 1

Library and Archives Canada Cataloguing in Publication

Title: The gunsmith's daughter / Margaret Sweatman.
Names: Sweatman, Margaret, author.
Identifiers: Canadiana (print) 20210289813 | Canadiana (ebook) 20210289821 |
ISBN 9781773102399 (softcover) | ISBN 9781773102405 (EPUB)
Subjects: LCGFT: Novels.
Classification: LCC PS8587.W36 G86 2022 | DDC C813/.54—dc23

Goose Lane Editions acknowledges the generous support of the Government of Canada, the Canada Council for the Arts, and the Government of New Brunswick.

Goose Lane Editions
500 Beaverbrook Court, Suite 330
Fredericton, New Brunswick
CANADA   E3B 5X4
gooselane.com

In memory of Jake MacDonald.

PART ONE

June 1971

Just before sunrise at solstice, Lilac Welsh jumped into her boat and yanked the cord on the twenty-five-horse Evinrude to make her way back to her family's log house at Rough Rock, taking the deeper, wider channel where there were fewer reefs.

That night, at her high school graduation party, she'd drunk an entire bottle of strawberry wine. Jimmy had asked her to be his girlfriend right in front of everybody, he was so sure she'd say yes, and when Lilac said no, her classmates called her "a fish" and gave her the cold shoulder all night long. Apparently, she was supposed to marry him and work at the marina and live in Minaki her whole life. She didn't give a damn. Jimmy got drunk too and fired his shotgun out at the lake, laughing his head off till somebody took the gun away from him.

All night, Lilac had hung out alone at the edge of the light from the bonfire. When she was fairly sober and the mosquitoes woke up and the sky glowed in the east, she headed for home, tracking the shores of white granite, ghostly in pre-dawn light. The lake was glass.

She made it to Rough Rock in less than an hour, record time, and was cleating the lines when she became aware of her father's scent and a pair of boots on the dock. And here he was. Kal Welsh, glaring down at her. She clambered out of the boat to stand facing him, explaining how she'd waited till the sky lightened before going out on the lake. "I took the long way, so it'd be safer," she explained in her reasonable adult voice with a slightly boozy slur.

Her father said, "Well, that's just swell. You made sure you'd be safe." Then his arms darted out and he put his rough hands around her neck, a loose necklace, his strong, familiar smell. "What would you do if somebody grabbed you like this?" he asked.

"I'd kick him hard in the balls." She watched his eyes flicker, and she added, "Dad."

Her father's gunsmithing tools, the belt sander, wrenches, his brass hammer, the brass trimmers and deburring tools for his ammunition, the saw, the hatchet, the tools he used every day, had made his hands so strong, Lilac's mother, Ruby, often joked that he should need a licence to use them. "You'd better let me go," she told him.

He dropped his hands to her shoulders and gave her a squeeze that was half-angry and half-affectionate. "You remind me of myself," he said, with grudging admiration. It was his version of a compliment. At that moment, Lilac felt generally sad about the futile universe. She also had a hangover. She was eighteen years old.

Her mother emerged in the grainy dawn, wearing her flannel dressing gown. Ruby's wild red hair and pale face made her look fierce and beautiful. Her Scottish blood was up and she was mad. "You said you'd be back before dark. I've been up all night, waiting and watching for you, thinking you'd drowned." Then she saw, as she always did, into Lilac's heart, and came close and wrapped her up in her arms. "Jesus, darling, you scare me halfway to death when you pull stunts like this." Then she sniffed, probably smelling that pink wine, and asked, "Where were you all night?"

"At Judy's," Lilac said. "I went to her house and we watched TV with her little brother. I fell asleep."

Ruby, with her superhuman vision, observed the lie come out of Lilac's mouth, and she flinched.

Lilac was new to lying. She could have told the truth. Ruby was no fool. For a second, she was tempted to do just that. But the moment passed. Her mother gave a small nod and turned and went up to bed with a curve in her spine, like she was suddenly old. Lilac followed her, dragging herself up the stone stairs to the house, feeling crummy but strangely liberated. A person has to be cruel sometimes. It was time to begin her own life.

She felt the presence of her father stepping quickly behind her, and she had the weird and paranoid sensation that he might pounce. She refused to look back.

1.

It was a couple of months later, on the first cold, blustery day at the end of summer, when a stranger came out of the storm. Rough Rock was twenty-five miles from Minaki. The middle of nowhere. Lilac and her parents weren't accustomed to visitors.

It was so chilly they needed a fire in the fireplace, and Lilac and Ruby were sitting on opposite ends of the couch, sharing the cashmere throw, reading and dozing by the hearth, when they heard a ruckus at the screen door. Ruby muttered, "What the hell—" and she and Lilac rushed through the living room to the verandah, where rain sieved through the screens to puddle on the floor. There they discovered, outside, peering in with his hands shielding his eyes, a very handsome young man. He grinned at them and took a step back, rain dripping off his nose. He was soaked through yet shiny with pride.

"We thought you were a bear," said Ruby.

Lilac caught a breath of cold, wet air. Behind him fell sheets of rain. The wind had picked up.

Her mother asked, "Where on *earth* did you come from?"

He laughed with such cheerfulness in his discomfort, Lilac thought maybe it wasn't earth that had spawned him. He wiped his dripping face with a wet hand and said, "I didn't want to enter the premises without permission." So, of course they brought him inside. He didn't look like an axe murderer.

Inside, he stared at the tall gun cabinet, then upwards to the cathedral ceiling, the logs gleaming with varnish. He gazed up at the massive ridgepole and the pewter chandelier dangling with its candles aslant in cold collars of wax. The granite fireplace was all aglow. The taupe cashmere throw looked beautiful on the grey leather couch. On their cherrywood table sat a big blue clay bowl, the floors were red hardwood and stone tile, and bookshelves occupied the entire west wall. Lilac felt a thrill, seeing her home through his eyes. He silently absorbed so much elegance, here in the bush, far from civilization. Only a moment before, she'd been drowsy and bored. Now she felt like her life was some kind of miracle.

Ruby left for a moment, then reappeared with a towel. She and Lilac watched closely while he stripped off his wet shirt and, wearing only a pair of shorts, towelled himself dry. His shorts rode low on his pelvis, and through the thin cotton Lilac caught a glimpse of the smooth paddles of his hips. She'd been reading some science fiction that summer, and again it occurred to her that he might not be human. "Aren't you cold?" she asked. His tanned skin was perfect, unblemished by a freckle or a mole. Lilac's father strode in from the woodpile out back. He still had his boots on, and his heavy canvas jacket, beaded in rainwater, was scented with the musk that always clung to him, kerosene and gun oil. He'd come to fetch something, but when he saw the half-naked young man standing in his living room, he went still as stone. Embers in the fireplace collapsed and sparked. The lamps were lit against the chill though it was only the first of September.

In bare feet, the stranger stepped toward Lilac's father to offer his hand, saying, "You're Kal Welsh," as if baptizing him. He added, "Nice to meet you, Mrs. Welsh," and only nodded to Lilac. Wolfish, Lilac thought. Saving her for later. Even though he hadn't offered it to her, she imagined his hand in hers, cold from the rain.

"How do you know who we are?" Ruby demanded.

"Everybody knows you," he said. To Kal, "You're famous."

Ruby winced and lured the fellow into talking about himself. His name was Gavin McLean. Thunder Bay was his hometown. He'd hitchhiked to Minaki and borrowed a kayak from the marina there.

"A kayak," Ruby interrupted. "Wait a sec. You *paddled* here?" She looked at Kal in his boots and his heavy jacket, heard him snuffle, sniffing things out, biding his time. "I'll get you a dry shirt," she told Gavin McLean, and left the room.

The bedrooms were on the second level, up a set of pine stairs leading to a balcony that framed the living room. Gavin's eyes followed Ruby up the stairs and along the balcony, where she disappeared behind the big oak door to the bedroom she shared with Kal. She was beautiful, everyone said. Ruby the Red. Long, curly auburn hair, long legs, a stormy disposition. Hidden away with her husband and their daughter in the backwoods at Rough Rock.

"This is some place you got here," Gavin said to Kal. Then, when Kal didn't respond, "They say you built it all up with your own hands."

Kal shook his head. But Lilac was tempted by Gavin's story, his enhancement, a stranger's legend. Of course her dad had help building the log house and the boathouse and the docks and his gunsmithing shop out back. The firing range had been cleared by a guy who'd arrived with a backhoe on a barge. Her father *had* to have help; he was still recovering from his wounds when they came out here to live. Now the bone in his arm, the ulna, had healed, as had the divots from shrapnel in his back and his hands, though the scars remained. The shattered bone in his thigh never really mended because there was still a piece of shrapnel in there; he limped sometimes when he was tired and he chewed Aspirin.

Nine years ago they came to this place, to build the big house. The din of saws and hammers, the drone of a generator. A contractor had brought crews of gruff, indifferent men who arrived and shouted and spat and went away again, leaving the family alone.

Lilac was only nine when they moved here. At first, she believed it would just be a vacation place, but when summer ended, her parents sent her to school in town. Then winter arrived, black ice on a river wide and wild as a lake littered with countless islands, with deep, narrow bays and turbulent channels and broad stretches of deep water where giant sturgeon lived, and soon the evergreens were burdened with snow. Her father taught her at home from Halloween till after the Christmas holidays, when it was safe to travel by snowmobile to Minaki to meet the bus for school. When the ice turned to mush in March, her father became her teacher till they could put the boats in the lake again. Nine years she'd lived here, all the way through high school, and now she loved the place, the river's icy currents and mineral taste, its granite shores with grey lichens and pink ribbons of feldspar, deep creases where the tansy grows, the smell of wildness and purity. Nine years, living out here alone with her parents.

She was vibrating all over. Gavin had green eyes. The light was umbral, but she saw when she passed him close, pretending she wanted the book she'd left splayed on the couch, that, yes, his eyes were green. No. Amber.

Ruby returned carrying one of Kal's shirts and a pair of his jeans. Lilac watched for signs of resentment in her father while Gavin slid the shirt over his bare chest, but Kal's face was softening with curiosity.

Now Ruby said, "Here," and held out the jeans. Gavin warily tried to decline. "Take them," Ruby ordered.

"Don't you have any stuff with you?" Lilac asked him.

"Yeah," he said. "My knapsack. It got soaked. I left it under your front steps."

The wind blew rain so hard it sounded like hail. Lilac went to the window to look out through the trees that thrashed in the wind and down to see whitecaps on the water. When she turned around, Gavin offered mildly, "It got a bit sketchy out there." Her father's jeans dangled from his hand.

With a sudden gust of resentment, Lilac asked him, had he thought to lift the kayak out of the water when he landed? He had. "I laid it on your dock," he said. Then, to Kal, "I hope that's okay."

"It's going to blow off," Lilac declared. He disturbed her.

Kal was silent, but Ruby was saying, "You'll have a hard paddle back to Minaki, even if the wind settles. Awful hard, upstream.

The current's a witch." Ruby always claimed that the Winnipeg River was the *daughter* of the Mississippi; her names for her river were female. Now Ruby said, "She'll be full of deadheads after this storm. Besides, you must be starved. Stay for dinner." She gave Kal a defiant, almost frightened glance and continued, "Stay the night. Lilac will tow your little boat up to Minaki in the morning."

"Lilac," said Gavin, smiling. White teeth against a tan, curly hair at his neck.

Lilac broke out in a sudden sweat. Sweat streamed under her arms and down her back. This handsome guy. A jolt of fear. She was trying to recall a dream. What *was* the dream? She'd been afraid in it. "Your kayak's going to blow away," she repeated more shrilly.

Her father stood up, finally speaking, scolding, "I'll go tie her down, Lilac. Help your mother." He went out through the screen door, limping a little, down to the dock. The young man made a move to follow him, then remembered he was wearing wet shorts and his host's shirt. He stood hesitantly.

Lilac heard her mother's distant voice. "The potatoes are ready to go in the oven. Lilac? Get on with it, please." And she stumbled on her way to the kitchen, tripped over her own feet, and whispered, "Shit." This stranger would be sleeping in the house tonight. In all the years living out here, they'd never once had a house guest. Not once. What if he really wasn't human? He was too perfectly made. An angel. Angels are cruel. They bring *tidings.* Whoever sees an angel will be changed forever. Gavin McLean from Thunder Bay. Angel. Damn.

2.

At dinner, their candlelight beat back the night. The wind died and then, milder rain. Gavin sighed happily, telling Kal, "I never thought I'd be sitting down to a meal with a real-life hero."

Lilac, drinking from her glass of water, choked. "What are you talking about?" she asked. Disappointed. He was so good-looking. But the expression *real-life hero* was something a six-year-old boy with a cap gun would say. She wondered if Gavin was a bit slow in the head. "Real life," she scoffed. Stupid concept. She'd been reading her father's American newspapers forever, especially this past summer now that she'd finished high school and had to figure out what she was going to do next, and she knew that "real life" wasn't heroic. It was soldiers shooting students dead at a university in Ohio.

Ruby reached to put her hand on Lilac's arm and tapped twice, her semaphore for "let it go."

Her father's scarred hands hovered over his plate of roast moose meat and potatoes. And always that scent of oil and kerosene, his emanation, as if he created his own atmosphere. Yet his hands were always clean and smelled of soap.

Gavin looked at his plate and declared, "Kal Welsh is famous." He raised his eyes to Kal. "You were in Nam. In the early days. My uncle told me. He read up on you in a gun magazine. That's where I'm headed. To Vietnam." He boldly flashed those white teeth, spilling his news, laying himself down before his hero. "I'm on my way to Grand Forks. I'm going to enlist in the military. I'm going to be a Marine. Except, it's just, I had to meet you first, Mr. Welsh."

"Why?" Ruby blurted. Lilac glanced at her mother, hearing pain. Ruby's red curls flamed, haloed around her head. And again, "I mean, why on earth would you want to—for godsake, why would you go and do something like that? Enlist? For Vietnam? That dirty old war!"

Kal said, "Don't pester him with a lot of questions, Ruby."

Ruby turned on him and burst out, "I want to understand!"

Gavin said, "I can answer." He held his knife and fork upright in his two fists. "Vietnam is my chance to prove myself."

Kal interrupted brusquely. "Course it is."

Gavin burned more brightly, fastened to Kal, feeding off that dark-eyed figure. "I might not get another chance. There might not be another war, I mean, for my generation." And with a boy's husky voice he explained what must have seemed to him utterly true. "It's my only real chance to see what I'm worth. See if I've got it in me. This is *it* for me."

"Sure," said Kal. "A man needs to test himself."

"Test myself," Gavin agreed, relieved, and he raised his face to the candles in the chandelier, the flames skittish.

Lilac, excluded, was an ordinary lump of girl with a mouth full of moose meat. She studied her father. He had *tested* himself in Vietnam? A decade ago, he'd spent a whole year there as a "hearts and minds specialist" in Psychological Operations, Psyops. He was supposed to just be an adviser in Psyops, but he came home smashed up. She remembered the flesh of him and his broken bones. The small piece of shrapnel in his thigh, embedded too deep for the doctors to remove, had become a part of him. Ten years ago, when he returned from Vietnam, they were living in the city on a normal street. Her father pulled the curtains closed, shutting them all in while he hobbled around the stuffy brick house.

War meant that her father was gone for a whole year and returned bust up, in a bad mood, sitting around in his underwear, grunting while he lifted little sandbags on his ankles. War was the stink of Absorbine Jr., the stink of humiliation and menthol and camphor, which smells like mothballs. She watched the small convulsions in her father's throat when he swallowed his wine.

Gavin was making Kal happy with his hero-worship thing, asking him a lot of questions about the gunsmith business, where he had his guns manufactured, how he managed to run the operation from "up here," apparently wanting to show off to the older man how much he knew about the Welsh Model 70, the bolt-action sporting rifle that had been making Kal a lot of money. Enough money to import the chandelier from Italy and the red hardwood from Thailand. He got a lot of mail at PO Minaki, letters from lawyers and banks and the National Rifle Association.

"Welsh Bullets, too," Gavin said. "You've got a proud reputation, Mr. Welsh." He pushed his chair from the table and stood tall, taller than Lilac, saying, "Excuse me," and went to the living room, returning with one of the copies of *Shooting Times* that always lay around. He put the magazine on the table and opened it to an ad for Welsh X Precision Bullets, a photo of gleaming copper fingers loaded with gunpowder. He read the slogan out loud.

"The future of ammunitions isn't what you expected.

"It's better."

Lilac watched warily for scepticism in Gavin's smile. It was just an advertisement; it's how they talk in ads. It was okay for her to cringe over her dad, but no one else had that right; she'd defend him with her life.

Kal said, "I wrote that," pointing and laughing.

All this exposure. After so much solitude, her father performs for a guest, smiling and posing, rubbed to a shine by Gavin's enthusiasm.

"You work for yourself," Gavin continued. "No boss looking over your shoulder. A free man. That's how I want to live, Mr. Welsh. In the future."

Kal hadn't suggested that the young man call him by his first name, though he'd warmed to him. Lilac jealously watched her father's eyes stray over Gavin's face. Now Kal commanded them all to "stay put" and walked outside, soon returning with rain in his hair. He was carrying his ugly new gun by its handle.

Ruby blurted his name in a deep guttural tone that Lilac had never heard before. Kal almost never brought a gun to dinner. This new one was alien, predatory, its action encased in a solid black exoskeleton, like the thorax of an insect. Lilac couldn't have resented a new sibling more than she resented her father's new gun.

She'd always liked the sleek elegance of his old Welsh Model 70. It was what the magazines called a hunting rifle. It looked friendly, dignified, like a handsome uncle. And she liked the wild taste of game the way her mother cooked it. But this new gun shocked, as it was meant to shock, just the sight of it.

Kal grunted as he placed the big insect on its bipod on a wool area rug on the floor. It was so heavy Lilac thought he'd pinch his fingers. He glanced hopefully at Ruby and said, "Don't want to scratch the wood." He held up a shiny slug, half an inch wide, two and a half inches long. "A fifty," he said.

"Fifty?" Gavin asked, and repeated, "Fifty calibre? For real?"

"Ever heard of the Land War Laboratory? LWL. Weapons contractors, R and D. They put out a call for a sniper rifle." He tossed the slug and caught it underhand. "And I'm giving them my answer."

Lilac could feel her mother coiled, tense.

Kal introduced the thing. "Meet my new Welsh Stalker Model 80. She'll take down a multi-million-dollar jet with a two-dollar bullet. And it takes only one man to hold her." He winked at Gavin. "Just pull her tight and squeeze."

Ruby emitted a disgusted, "Bah!" and dabbed at her nose with the back of her hand.

Kal's eyes darted to his wife. "This is only a prototype." He returned his attention to Gavin, boasting confidentially, "I'll have a few made up at Welsh Firearms, down in Connecticut. My manager there, Randy, he'll do some field testing. This baby's going to give Colt's some real competition. See these springs? Free-floating barrel. Muzzle brake. Brand new concept."

Gavin stared at the Welsh Stalker. Lilac saw him pale a little, but he kept nodding, maybe to persuade his own enthusiasm while he recited a string of admiring phrases. She wondered if he felt overwhelmed by the older man's ingenuity. Or maybe he too felt repelled by the new weapon.

Kal said, "There's a good chance you'll see her in action in Nam."

Gavin nodded and nodded and chanted his praise as if he'd like that, to shoot this malignant machine, as if the Stalker was the great news he'd come to hear.

3.

The poplar leaves clapped lightly. Birdsong, sparrows singing at the lip of dawn. It was still pretty dark outside. Lying in bed, Lilac heard men's voices.

She opened her bedroom door and went to the balcony to look down on the living room, where she saw her father talking to their guest. In lantern light, Kal and Gavin stood before the open gun cabinet, the men talking in daytime voices, not the least bit worried that they'd wake her up.

Her father reached to remove his Welsh 70 sporting rifle from its bracket. He fondled it, speaking about its gauge and how he'd developed it, "trial and error." He handed it to Gavin.

Gavin murmured, "Here she is," and lifted the walnut stock to his shoulder, leaning into the cheek piece and closing one eye to focus down the barrel to a gold front-sight bead. Lilac heard him whisper, "Beautiful."

"Still popular in the war. Mostly sniper use." Kal retrieved his rifle and was turning toward the cabinet when Lilac moved, the floor creaked, and he looked up sharply. Lilac in her white flannel nightgown was pressed against the cool planes of pinewood, a chill on her spine, pinned by her father's glance, his dark eyes with their thick eyebrows and eyelashes.

Kal's attention shifted and he smoothly resumed. "Limited number, with the gold sight like this one. But"—his voice rose and swelled—"there are plenty of my regular models in circulation now." His Welsh Model 70 had a twenty-four-inch barrel and a graceful stock. He grunted as he replaced it firmly in its bracket and removed another. The M16. "But here's what you'll be carrying." A black gun with a blunt stock and hand guard, a rubber recoil pad, the blatant exposure of the magazine. Anger in her father's voice when he said, "It's the big winner. Piece of shit."

Lilac wrapped herself in the afghan from her bed, slipped into her canoe shoes, and walked downstairs. The sun was rising red. She palmed a glass chimney and blew out the flame. A clear morning. Lake water mirrored the trees.

Gavin held the M16 casually. First sun illuminated his face. Yes, amber eyes. Beautiful, the way the light went in. Tiger eyes. She started to sweat again. It hurt to see him. She didn't even know him, but he sure set her into a lather. He was saying he'd better get going. "Storm's over," he said. "I can paddle."

"But stay," Lilac stammered. "Stay for breakfast. Stay, like, for lunch. I'll take you in my boat after lunch, you and your kayak. But later on." He gave her an odd look. She wished it was admiring, and she added, "If I have time." Ack, total dork. But he thanked her.

Kal retrieved the M16, put it away, and took down another rifle. He was showing off his beloved old Mannlicher–Schoenauer. "Hemingway's rifle," he claimed, "from the twenties."

Lilac left them to fondle the old-world charm of the Mannlicher and went to the kitchen to make some coffee. She was surprised to find her mother here, Ruby with her elbows on the kitchen table. It was a rare event to find Ruby sitting down, not doing anything. Lilac asked, "Something wrong, Mum?"

Ruby scoffed and muttered, "Not one damn thing in the whole bejesus world."

Lilac fetched the percolator from the top shelf and filled it, lit the propane stove, put coffee on to heat, then leaned against the counter to watch her mother, who was uncannily still. Whatever was eating at Ruby was building steam. She twitched and peered over her shoulder to ask, "You taking him to the landing?"

Lilac said she was. "I'll use the little boat. I can probably lay his kayak across the bow." The little boat was hers: the sixteen-foot Starcraft with its twenty-five-horse Evinrude. The big boat, her parents' boat, was a broad-beamed, steel-hulled, twenty-four-foot inboard that leaned into any weather. They wouldn't need the big boat today.

The kitchen was warming, and Lilac lifted open the window above the sink. Sweet air rushed in. The ryegrass in the yard needed cutting; insects buzzed in sunlight glittering with dew. Her mother's garden was already going to seed, and beyond that her father's shop stood in the trees, barn-shaped, its windows set in black frames.

Kal and Gavin marched through the kitchen then out the back door. Gavin said, "Morning, Mrs. Welsh," and followed Kal across the yard to the shop, barefoot, tiptoeing through cold, wet grass. He still wore Kal's jeans; the cuffs were getting wet.

The coffee began to boil over, and Lilac turned down the heat to let it percolate. Again, she asked her mother, "What's troubling you, Mum?"

Ruby just said, "Tsk."

Through the kitchen window, Lilac watched them emerge from the shop, her father carrying his new gun by its handle, the prototype he was so proud of, the Stalker. What a stupid name. It must weigh thirty pounds. Who could run with a thing like that in his hands? The two men were heading toward the bush out back.

She heard the crack of a powerful cartridge being fired from her father's shooting range, a long dell extending far into their property. This gun made a huge noise, explosive, much louder than the pretty Welsh 70. They'd be aiming at a plywood moose. Or at one of Kal's blocks of ballistic gelatin in the shape of a man's head and chest.

"Well, hell," said Ruby, "the boys are getting along just fine."

The sound of shooting ricocheted off the rocks, over the trees, over the lake. The noise slammed the air again and again, echoing, fading, then again, a loud bang.

Ruby said, "Why did he come here?"

"Gavin? He wanted to meet Dad."

Ruby nodded. "Lucky boy." She sniffed and wiped her nose, grumbling, "I hate that Stalker thing. It's butt ugly." They laughed. Then, brightening with fresh fury, Ruby said, "And what on *earth* does that child think he's going to do in Vietnam?" She shoved her chair back, stood, took a rag from the sink, and began to scrub at the table. "Play commando?"

"He's not a child. He's twenty. Anyway, he says he has to. Like, to prove himself." Lilac looked down at her own big feet in her canoe shoes. Her unproven self.

Ruby humphed that humph of superior insight that drove Lilac crazy. A warrior-woman, Ruby with her quick temper, keen to charge into enemy lines, driving the boat hard, swelling waves crashing over the bow. "Heroes," she scoffed. She wore the same wool sweater she'd worn last night, and now she took it off, revealing a sleeveless black undershirt, her strong arms. Scrubbing, she enunciated each syllable. "At any rate, he can't go off to do battle against the villains in Vietnam because *we* are not at war in goddamn Viet-*nam*."

"We" meant Canada. Lilac's dad was different from them; he was an American. The Americans had a revolution and a civil war, all of it more exciting and easier to remember in History than John A. Macdonald and the railroad. Kal came from Lansing, Michigan, where he went hunting with his father, who would die in a plane crash along with Kal's mother. Then Kal went to university and became Dr. Welsh and moved up to Canada to be a professor.

Back when he was Dr. Welsh, professor of sociology, Ruby had enrolled in his course called Conformity, Compliance, Obedience. Ruby was only nineteen years old at the time. She liked to tell Lilac that she'd enrolled without even knowing what sociology was, and took the course because it started at 8:30 a.m., early; Ruby always liked to start things early. "I even married your dad early. The day I turned twenty." She'd imagined that the course would treat conformity, compliance, and obedience as something to avoid. Like capture. But Kal had taught the course as a life skill, to learn tools to control and dominate others. Though, Ruby declared, he'd better not try any of that obedience training with *her*.

Kal's old university in Michigan had arranged for him to go off to Vietnam to be an adviser, what they called a "policy analyst." Lilac had imagined him wearing a suit and teaching obedience in that foreign place.

But he came home different. Right away, before he was even off the crutches, he quit his job as a professor. That was strange, because he no longer wore suits and left the house with a fatherly leather briefcase. Instead, he holed up in his workshop in their crooked garage outside their red-brick house, working all the time on the designs for his Welsh Model 70 and his Welsh X bullets. Her parents stopped having smoky cocktail parties. Then they moved out here. Where nobody ever visited. Till Gavin came, from Thunder Bay, or maybe from Mars.

Lilac asked, "Do you think Dad should try to talk Gavin out of it? Enlisting in the Marines and all that?"

Ruby stopped to consider this before shaking her head no. "Not possible. The boy's in love with Kal. And Kal wouldn't want to put a dent in that kind of adoration."

Her words surprised Lilac into silence.

Ruby continued wistfully, "Besides, Gavin must have family, people of his own. They should be the ones to talk some sense into him." She looked sad again. Lilac preferred her mother's fury to her sadness. Ruby had been sad often these days. When she was tired, the shadows under her eyes were violet. She stared at the table, then seemed to remember Lilac and made a smile. "Why? You *want* Kal to talk him out of it?"

"I don't care."

Ruby twisted the rag tight and snapped it at Lilac's backside. Lilac leapt out of the way. "The boy's a looker," said Ruby, chasing her around the table. "He's a real good-looker. He should stay and marry the gunsmith's daughter." The sound of gunshots boomed and cracked the fresh heat.

4.

That afternoon, Lilac borrowed Gavin's yellow kayak, slipping away when she thought no one was looking. Deer flies stung her ankles in the cockpit of the tippy little boat. Under a blue, windless sky, a lid sealing her in, she skimmed the surface of the channel like a water spider, aiming at a tall cumulus cloud on the horizon, a cloud full of lightning. If she stayed out long enough, Gavin couldn't leave, it would get too late to take him to the landing. She could probably stall till it was getting dark and he'd have to spend another night.

She heard the drone of her Evinrude and paddled harder. Someone was coming to get her. The back of her neck prickled. Her father. She surged forward. Above, the cloud grew taller and more God-like, towering over the far shore, her destination a yellow smile of beach on an island in the channel.

The noise of the Evinrude grew close at full speed then suddenly decelerated, the way Kal liked to drive, so the wake would come right over the transom. She hadn't asked to borrow the kayak. She'd broken a golden rule: you never took someone else's boat without asking. Her kayak slid over slime on the three boulders that sat just below the surface, and there was the crunch of sand on the hull. She twisted around, prepared to behave angrily, tell her dad that she needed time alone, doesn't she ever get a chance to be alone in this bejesus place?

He'd cut the motor and was bent over to lift the prop out of the water while his wake drove the Starcraft onto the beach. Gavin. His smooth bare back. He turned and stood in the stern while the boat beached itself then leapt out to haul it up over the margin of seaweed and black beetles at the shoreline.

He came to kneel at the bow of the kayak. His face was friendly but unsmiling. He steadied the boat while she climbed out, then he lifted it like a toy and placed it among the driftwood.

Lilac confessed, "I borrowed it without asking."

"That's okay. I didn't ask to borrow it either." He nudged the kayak with his sandy foot.

"You mean you stole it?"

He smiled vaguely and gazed around, not listening to her. Through stunted birch trees, the water glistened on the other side of the small island. White cloud kept piling up in the south, but here the sun bore down from a deep-blue sky. A horsefly boomed in her ear and buzzed over her head when she swatted it. If she'd let it land, she could've killed it. Horseflies are slow. But it dodged and manoeuvred.

The beach was framed by white granite sloping into the lake. "I'm hot," he said. "I'd rather swim off the rocks than the sand." She heard the grey-green lichen crumble beneath his bare feet. He shrugged his shorts over his hip bones and, naked, slid on the green, wavering algae into the water, splashing and whooping in shock at the cold.

He swam out far from shore, ten then twenty yards, even into the grip of the current, and she watched with some concern and interest, catching glimpses of his bum, like turtles. She was uncertain about going in. She still had her period and didn't know how to take off her clothes discreetly. But it was really hot, and heat like this was ever more precious in the new gold slant toward fall; within a week or so, it would be impossible to swim. She slid out of her clothes and down the slime on the rock, gasping, ducking her head underwater, a trick that oddly made the cold more tolerable, and swam, watchful, imagining that she would have to save him, the lake was so cold and the current so strong.

She treaded water till he returned to shore, then watched him grip a crease in the granite to haul himself up the slippery rocks before she made her own way up and out of the lake with white, numb hands. She tried to dress quickly, pulling her clothes over wet skin, but not before he noticed her underwear with its pad, and he gave her a quick, complicit glance.

They lay flat on a warm rock to dry in the sun. There was a big splash of sienna-coloured lichen, like an orange star, where they lay. He explained light years to her, explaining that if they went into space at the speed of light, they'd get younger, and she said, "I know."

Right now, Lilac felt abundantly glad to watch him breathe, his rib cage visible under the smooth tanned skin, the hair on his legs sun-bleached. But then he began to talk about her father, even here, with just the two of them. Her first instinct was to oblige him, to talk about whatever pleased him, and this irritated her too, her instinct to serve his fantasies. He was saying that her dad was "amazing" and how cool it was to hold the M16 last night, so she explained the problems with that gun, reiterating what her father had told her, why the M16 was a "dirty gun."

Lilac had always helped her dad, spooning gunpowder from a brass cup into each small case, running her finger over the top to wipe off excess. While they worked, he would extol the advantages of his Welsh X bullet, how it fired clean and was superior to the M16's cartridge, with its propellant ball powder that fired fast and burned dirty, increasing the likelihood that the rifle would jam in combat.

Kal had trained her, shown her how to scoop the gunpowder and pack the lead bullets into the brass shells he'd modified for his own use. For this she used a hand-powered lever. Precise, decisive work. He told her, "Move smooth. Never hesitate." She would always love the green scrim of tarnish on brass. Her father stood close, a constant presence smelling of gun oil and then, washing his hands at a basin before leaving his shop, the scent of soap.

"Lilac Welsh," Gavin said. He raised himself on his elbow to look down at her and spooled her drying hair around his forefinger. "What's it like, having the same name as a weapon?"

"I'm named after lilacs," she told him. "Born in June." He seemed distracted, tracing her collarbone, idle yet with a gathering focus, but she wanted him to know her, and went on. "And Welsh is a nationality. Not just a gun. Lilac Welsh. Like Huckleberry Finn." She watched his perfect face. He didn't laugh. It was a family story; it was supposed to be funny, her parents' whimsy when she was born.

She wanted him to kiss her. The sun filled her with sweetness she wanted him to taste. She arched her back, yearning for his hands on her breasts. "But anyway, it's like Shrapnel," she said. "Henry Shrapnel. He invented bullets that spray out and kill a lot of people all at the same time. Then he died." He kissed her. "I think he died in bed"—her blood felt as if it was carbonated—"in 1842"—as if bubbles were popping under her skin, millions of tiny explosions. "Or Colt. His first name was Samuel."

He said, "You like to talk." He told her that she couldn't get pregnant when she had her period and again she said, "I know." He was gentle, but it hurt anyway. It was like letting in the sun.

They went back into the lake to wash away the blood. While they stood on the beach in the freezing water, Gavin asked her, "Do you feel good?"

Maybe he was hinting for some kind of flattery, or gratitude. With a flicker of anger, she answered, "I feel fine. At least nobody's going to want to sacrifice me on an altar or chuck me into a volcano or set me on fire. I'm ruined, but I'm also out of the woods." She showed her teeth in a smile.

Gavin seemed startled. "You're a virgin."

"Was."

"Why didn't you tell me?" He walked up onto the beach and picked up a flat stone and skipped it about ten times across the lake, which was now corduroyed by wavelets. "You should've said."

But she was glad to get rid of her virginity; she was on her way to living her own life. In Minaki, they called her "a cold fish" and "a cock tease." That was all over now; high school was way in the past. She told Gavin, "This doesn't give you any kind of power over me. If you don't know that, you'd better figure it out real quick."

"I don't want power over you or anybody." Gavin turned to stare at her as if he could actually see her.

It was happening again. She was vibrating. Something about Gavin really shook her. He seemed so clean inside, crystalline.

"Seriously," he continued. "You're a beautiful girl. And what happened here, it means a lot to me."

She was tempted to believe him. But she said, "Yeah. I bet."

"Don't," said Gavin. "Don't be cynical. Just because you're smart, you don't have the right to scoff at me."

Lilac, stunned, said okay. The sun slid behind the thunderhead and the lake water turned purple, bruised by the approaching storm. She added, "We've got to head back." He briefly touched her face with his cold, sandy fingers then went toward the boats. She watched him in all his perfection.

They managed to jam the kayak on an angle inside the Starcraft, and Gavin stood on the beach to push the stern straight out toward waves that were growing choppy, splashing over the transom so it was difficult to keep the boat perpendicular to shore. He waded out so far, he had to swim while she unhinged the tilt then pulled the cord to start the motor. His hands gripped the gunnel and he heaved himself into the bow. There was barely room for him. She had to speed up because the wind was pushing her boat back to shore. Gavin jolted on the seat, nearly falling backwards, then, finding his balance, he turned away from her to face the wind.

5.

They reached the dock just ahead of silver brooms of rain. The kayak fought like a kite in the wind while Gavin struggled to pry it out of the Starcraft and carry it ashore to secure it to a balsam. Lilac put spring lines on her boat and then on the big steel inboard. The gale was smashing waves against the rock cribbing. It was so blustery, she didn't dare try to dock either boat in the boathouse.

They ran up to the verandah, closing the door against sheets of white lightning. Panting, soaked, they entered the living room. A bed of ashes in the stone fireplace. The only light came from the kitchen. On a spindle chair at the entrance to the house, her mother had left a stack of towels she'd torn from the line ahead of the storm, stiffly sun-dried, and Lilac handed one to Gavin. They hurriedly towelled off, but they were cold, drawn to the heat in the kitchen. The house smelled of roasting venison.

Warmth and the smell of food drew them to the wide doorway to the kitchen, which they entered together, they might even have been touching (later, Lilac would relive this, a forensic recollection), their shoulders touched, drawing what heat remained between them. It must have been visible, what had transpired in the afternoon.

Ruby and Kal sat at the kitchen table, bare of everything but a kerosene lamp, a slab of cheese on a stone platter, a bowl of apples, and Kal's hunting knife, the stag handle emerging from its leather sheath. Kal was drinking bourbon neat from a crystal tumbler. Ruby held a tulip-shaped glass of port. The sweetness of deer meat and liquor. Lilac was hungry.

Her parents regarded them remotely. Their attitudes seemed in tandem, an illusion that would soon dissolve. Ruby spoke. "Do you know how long you've been gone? For godsake, Lilac, it's nearly dark! You left at two! I saw you head out, and I was just astounded. Why didn't you tell me where you were going? What if something went wrong? I've said this *countless* times. How on earth can I find you if I don't know where you are?"

Ruby noticed Gavin come forward, ostensibly for his share of the blame, but, despite the fact that she must have known he'd taken the Starcraft without permission, she ignored him and directed her fury at her daughter.

Ruby's anger always burned white-hot and she never played dirty. It was true: Lilac normally did tell her parents where she was going when she took a boat out. Accidents happen; they only had each other. Kal was rigorous about his family's safety, always lecturing on the subject of their isolation and necessary dependence on him even while he drilled Lilac on self-sufficiency. Years ago, he'd taught her how to apply a tourniquet and how to stitch a small wound.

Ruby downed the port in one gulp then came around the table to embrace her. "Honestly," she said, "honestly, darling," and held her. The peppery smell of Ruby's red hair.

Lilac looked through her mother's curls at her father, still seated with his glass of whiskey. Kal had the stiff-necked, slow-eyed glaze he earned with a third drink. She noticed his hunting knife, and his left hand pressed flat beside it while he held his drink with his right. Her father's square, scarred hands were always clean, unless he'd been dressing an animal. He kept a bristle brush by the kitchen sink to clean his nails.

He caught his daughter's eye, and with the fingers of his left hand he snapped open the sheath and withdrew the steel blade.

He drank off the whiskey, then took an apple and began to peel the skin thinly into a red-and-white spiral he let fall to the floor between his feet, his boots, unlaced as always, the soles sloppy, a result of ankle pronation. Lilac felt a certain revulsion for her father's feet. Other than by accident, by virtue of his strength and his distracted willpower, Kal had never hurt her physically—he'd once given her a nosebleed by smacking her in the face with his elbow while he was starting a chainsaw—but he appeared to be more than a little drunk and angry. She wondered if he was going to stand up and stride toward her. It seemed as if he knew what had happened with Gavin that afternoon, and she resented her own sense of shame.

Ruby hugged Lilac for a long time, swaying, and Lilac let it go on, listening to her mother's body and the sound of her father's teeth when he bit into the apple. She was aware of Gavin standing nearby and sensed that he was calm and watchful, the way her father was calm and watchful when he was hunting.

Ruby murmured in her ear, "Take it easy tonight. Don't let him get you riled." She pulled away and announced more gaily, "Let's take it easy tonight!" She went to the propane oven and opened it, permitting a warm wave of roasting meat. With her back to the room, Ruby said, "Gavin, you go on to the bathroom upstairs and make yourself tidy. Lilac, you get the salad out of the fridge."

Gavin didn't move. Lilac had to squeeze around her dad in his chair, "S'cuse me," to open the fridge door. She was chilled and wet and trying to put aside her resentment that she had to help out before she'd even had a chance to change her clothes. Gavin just stood there, disobeying her mother. The salad was on the bottom shelf and she leaned over to pick it up. She heard her father move suddenly and shove his chair away from the table. His voice made a strange sound. The chair tipped and fell backwards.

Lilac held the salad at the open fridge door. Diced beets and blue cheese with vinegar, a family favourite, an awful salad that they were all loyal to.

Kal moved quickly toward Gavin, moving so close he bumped him, chest to chest, saying, "So this is how you repay my hospitality?" Gavin faced him, unblinking. Kal backed off. "Is this what you do?" He righted the chair then slammed it into the floor—the stone floor he'd procured from a quarry near Vermilion Bay. He seemed to like the sound of it because he slammed the chair into the floor again, harder. The chair splintered, dismembering the legs from the seat. Now he held the back of the chair before him like a shield. "You fuck my daughter?" Kal said.

Lilac had never in her life heard her father say *fuck*. It was an especially disgusting word next to *my daughter*. The bowl of beet salad was cold in her hands when she looked over his shoulder into Gavin's unreadable amber eyes. Gavin stood stock-still.

Kal went on. "You show up at my house. You make yourself comfortable. And you betray me."

Lilac returned the salad to the fridge and closed it. Kal was now charging into the living room toward the liquor cabinet, which just happened to be beside the gun cabinet. From the doorway, she watched him pour bourbon with an air of personal grievance that made her heart freeze. She wanted to get far away from him. He'd come too close, he'd invaded her privacy. She looked to Ruby.

The oven door remained open. Ruby was always stern when Kal was "feeling his oats," she called it. He generally claimed to be a man of routine and measure, but there were times, twice or maybe three times a year, when he went off the rails like this, and he'd been more domineering lately. Ruby's jaw was set hard.

Kal poured himself another drink and was about to down it when he stopped, staring into the booze, weighing it against something in his own mind. "Kind of old-fashioned, isn't it? A boy shows up and deflowers the landowner's daughter. Like a goddamn fairy tale or something."

Ruby said, "That's enough," and closed the oven door. Without even looking at Kal, she said clearly, "If you drink that, I'm leaving you."

Lilac found it painful to witness her father's humiliation. He didn't wear humility well. He was listening to her mother as if he'd like to inhale her. He winced and said gruffly, "I overspoke."

"Yeah," said Lilac. "Well, anyway, I'm going up to change." And she went upstairs.

6.

Alone in the bathroom, Lilac saw that she had blood on her shorts. Her father had sensed something between her and Gavin. But it was the blood that had really set him off. She washed with hot water, wrapped the soiled clothes in a towel, placing them deep in the laundry basket, where she found a semi-clean pair of jeans to put on, then she leaned over the sink to peer closely at herself in the mirror.

She would never forgive nor forget his ugly language. His words were stamped into her mind like his goddamn Welsh patent. *Deflower the landowner's daughter.* He'd choke the life out of her if she let him. But she'd show him. She was going to travel the world. English was her best subject, and she loved how a sentence can make life seem coherent, and now she was thinking she could travel and write and find her own way in the world. In the bathroom, she gave herself a steadying look and walked downstairs.

They sat down to dinner. Beet salad and venison. Her father obeyed Ruby and put the bourbon away, but now he was drinking quite a lot of red wine. Lilac had quite a lot of red wine too, even though it tasted like rubber.

Gavin surprised her by talking as if Kal hadn't said those things. He and Kal were doing man talk: hunting, what kind of cartridge best brings down a moose, the quickest way to dress a kill in the bush. It was so stupidly obvious that her dad had wanted a son but got a daughter. Who would be *deflowered*. She hated him.

Yet just a week ago they'd gone fishing together, the two of them in the canoe on a warm evening. She caught half a dozen good-sized pickerel, whereas her dad only got a couple of puny ones. He kept whooping and laughing when she'd set the hook and yank another two- or three-pounder into the canoe. He was paddling in the stern, and he mellowed out and let them drift and got distracted, taking photos with Lilac's camera, something he'd never bothered to do before.

And then he'd said, "You're lovely, Lilac. Do you know that?"

She'd turned around and smiled at him while he took her picture, and she told him, "You're lovely too, Dad. I'll even let you fillet my fish."

He was laughing. "Fillet your *own* fish!"

They filleted her catch together on a rock, swarmed by gulls, before going home and frying the pickerel for dinner.

But now her father had driven a knife through her heart, staked her to her chair, and she was forced to listen to him talk around her as if she didn't even exist, as if she were a reef that he should steer clear of, while at the same time he was claiming her, claiming his own power in her blood. How could Gavin be so unaffected? She looked at the meat on her plate and put down her fork. It was impossible to eat. Everything was impossible. She drank the rubbery wine.

Ruby sat quietly. She hadn't eaten much either. Lilac reached across the table to clutch her hand, but her mother seemed startled by the gesture and got up to clear the table, muttering wryly, "Sometimes it's just kind of nice to do the dishes."

Gavin and her father had switched from hunting to war. Her dad launched into stories about his time in Vietnam ten years ago. Now, well into the wine, he was telling Gavin that he "got roughed up in '61." Making it sound like something he was proud of. He didn't give the details of his injuries. He didn't mention the divots of flesh that the grenade tore out of his back, didn't talk about how hard it had been for him to recover. Lilac had learned in a comic book how Wild Bill Hickok was shot to death when he turned his back to the swinging doors of the saloon. An enemy can shoot your guts out, but it was sordid treachery to shoot a person in the back.

Her father also failed to mention the strange Mr. Thanh from Vietnam, a boogeyman in Lilac's imagination.

Mr. Thanh was the tall Vietnamese man who tossed that grenade at her father, wounding him and some other American man who happened to be standing nearby. An outrage, her dad said, a total betrayal, because Thanh was supposed to be working as his translator, his important assistant in combat with the enemy Viet Cong. His translator had turned on him out of the blue, with no warning. Kal had often talked about Mr. Thanh over the years, compulsively when he was drinking. Thanh was her father's cautionary tale: trust no one beyond your family.

Kal was now forty-six years old. Ancient, especially tonight. He went on and on about the wars he'd known, drifting to his earlier experiences in the Philippines in World War II, stories that an old man tells when he's in his cups, an old warrior who has lost his balance, who is stumbling over himself. Gavin prompted him politely, feeding him questions, inviting the yarns. Her father was overly jovial, trying to erase his embarrassment. He'd revealed weakness, he'd let Gavin, an outsider, see him lose his temper. And worse, Gavin had witnessed Ruby scolding him, and now Kal tried to cover up with false jolliness.

They seemed stuck beneath the chandelier. The candle flames reflected themselves in Lilac's crystal wineglass. She raised her glass to the flames and saw her own face, shattered yet confined.

7.

Lilac left the next morning with Gavin under an overcast sky, a flat pan of cloud. The air was lukewarm. All the sounds were muted—their voices, their feet drumming on the dock, the scrape of the empty jerry cans that Kal shifted around at the stern of the Starcraft. She tossed two garbage bags and her cotton purse into the bow, refusing to look at her father as he stepped up and out of the boat.

Ruby was very quiet. She still seemed upset about Kal's tantrum the previous night. She looked as if she might burst into flame, like a cup of butane.

Yet Kal occupied his normal self, telling Lilac to take the garbage to the dump, telling her to fill the jerry cans with gas. He even told them all what the weather was like and where the wind came from. Lilac jumped into the boat. How she loved to do this, to spring from the grey pine dock onto the nubby hull, to land lithely, to yank the cord of her Evinrude, how it would always start first pull, the puff and scent of oily smoke, a throaty turmoil from the prop underwater and, on a grey day such as this, the wide green river, islands hovering in the pale distance.

On the dock, Ruby shoved her hands into the pockets of her gold-coloured corduroy jacket and gazed off toward the channel marker a mile away. Then she suddenly jumped and said, "Wait a sec," looking at Gavin. "Lilac is taking you to the highway. Then what'll you do?"

Gavin said he'd thumb, "no problem."

"Hitchhike?" Ruby shook her head. "This doesn't feel right."

Lilac announced, "I'll drive him to Winnipeg." It had just occurred to her. To Gavin, "You can take the bus from Winnipeg down to Grand Forks."

Her mother was talking. "It'll be dark. You'll have to spend the night in Winnipeg."

Lilac agreed, yes, she'd go for the night. "I'll get my stuff." She left the engine running and climbed back up to the dock, running up to the house, up the stairs to her room, her hands trembling while she crammed some clothes into her father's old army bag—a canvas knapsack with *U.S.* stencilled on the flap. She hesitated, looking around her bedroom with all the familiar things, her books, her photographs pinned to the bulletin board, her typewriter on her desk, all her stories and poems tucked away in a cedar box. She realized that she didn't have any money. She had two credit cards, Master Charge and American Express. They were part of Kal's security plans: she'd always have access to money if something went wrong. Good. Let things go wrong.

She rushed out from her bedroom and bumped into Ruby, who had followed her up from the dock and was standing on the balcony.

Ruby tucked two hundred dollars into the pocket of Lilac's shirt. "For a hotel. And whatever."

"Are you going to be all right?" Lilac asked.

Ruby, surprised, answered, "Of course."

"Don't you want to get away from him sometimes?"

"Only when he's being an asshole." Ruby laughed, but then her voice became more hesitant and she embraced Lilac. "He's not like other men," she said, holding so tightly Lilac couldn't break away and see her face while she kept talking. "Sometimes I forget. He's actually a foreigner. I mean, an American." Now she pulled back to look at her daughter. "He really is different, almost his DNA or something. It's always been one of the things I've liked about him. It's made him seem more exciting. As if his being an American could make him super-strong."

Lilac scoffed lightly, tense. Hearing her mother's confession was like looking into a room in her own house she'd never known was there. And again, an inkling, a trace of that dream that had scared her.

Ruby went on. "I know, I sound silly. But in many ways, he really *is* super-strong. It's just, sometimes I worry. Sometimes he seems to act like—I don't know. He seems to feel *God*-like, or some damn thing." Ruby laughed ruefully. "Sometimes I worry that he might be completely nuts." Her eyes weren't laughing, and Lilac wondered if her mother was afraid.

Lilac said, "I'm mad at him for what he said last night. About the landowner's daughter. He doesn't own me."

Her mother's face hardened. "No. He doesn't."

"I don't get why he likes his new gun so much. The stupid Stalker."

"Because it's powerful, darling." Ruby gave a little shake, and sighed, "Ah well," and turned, and Lilac followed her downstairs. But outside, on the steps leading down from the verandah, Ruby stalled a moment, to ask quite idly, "Do you know Kal's middle name?"

Lilac, surprised, told her mother that her father didn't *have* a middle name.

"Yes, he does. It's Strange," said Ruby. "His middle name is Strange."

"So, what's his middle name?"

"Strange. I mean, it's actually Strange."

"Are you serious?"

Ruby was laughing, girlish now, happier. "Dead serious! It's an old family name. He dropped it because it was too—"

And they both said it. "Strange!"

So they were laughing when they arrived at the dock. Gavin was in the boat talking with Kal, who stood above him holding the bow line. "Yeah," Lilac heard Gavin say, "a Ranger. That's what I'm hoping for."

"Rigorous training," her father said. "You're a pretty good shot."

"Thanks. I'm ready for anything." Gavin took Lilac's knapsack from her, offering his hand to help her, but she jumped down on her own. Kal threw the bow line into the boat so it wouldn't drag and get snagged on the prop. It was all routine, Lilac untying the stern and pushing away from the dock while she accelerated because the current would push the boat under the cribbing, and she was twenty feet away when she looked back. Across the distance, she met her father's eye. He waved and turned toward the stone stairs leading up to the house. His posture showed no shame.

8.

They were in her mother's car, a Chrysler station wagon that still smelled of new car, especially since they'd taken the garbage to the dump. It felt great to be on the road, just the two of them. Gavin was fooling around with the radio, trying to find some music, when Lilac gave a start. "We left the kayak at Rough Rock."

Gavin didn't look up from where he was twisting the dial; he didn't seem to register what she'd just told him. Then she remembered that Gavin had stolen the kayak. A sin in Minaki terms, stealing somebody's boat. Jimi Hendrix came on the radio and he turned it up so loud the speakers in the dash started to buzz. Staring out the window, he looked bored or disappointed or just not there, gravel dust boiling up in their wake. *Hey Joe, where you goin' with that gun in your hand.* Hard music, going to shoot his lady 'cause he caught her messing around with another man. Caught her and shot her: it rhymes. Gavin's face was a blank. What did he have in mind? Probably not going down to shoot his old lady. Was he planning to shoot up some Vietnamese bad guys? He didn't seem very aggressive.

That dream had been haunting her. She was at her house, but with rooms she'd never seen before, on a dark night with white light from outer space striking through long windows like they had at home in the verandah but longer, bigger. Way at the end of this long room there was a figure of a man, her father, and not her father. He walked toward her, accompanied by many images of himself reflected in black panes of glass. A cold man, this dream version of her father, cold at his core, he walked with relentless confidence that he'd catch her. She was a done deal. Caught and shot.

Gavin shouted, "Hey!"

She woke up, driving in the centre of the road to the top of a hill. A car zoomed down toward them. She braked and steered to the right, the car passed close, blaring its horn in blinding dust while she gripped the wheel. "Sorry," she muttered.

Thirty miles later they reached the end of the gravel road and met the highway, west toward Winnipeg. They rolled down their windows to blow out some dust. The radio faded and returned, faded and sputtered out into static, and Lilac switched it off. They were still in the Precambrian Shield, the pink granite sheered off by dynamite. It was like the land around her home, rock and pine but with intervals of bog and fallen timber.

They approached a hill torched by fire, black ruff on charred pine. Gavin asked her to pull over, but she said they should wait for an intersection with a country road; the highway was narrow and weather-damaged, with sandy shoulders sloping into ditchwater. He was insistent. "C'mon, Lilac, just pull over."

When she stopped, the car aslant on the shoulder, instead of getting out to take a leak as she thought he would, he said, "I'll drive."

She protested. She liked driving, was used to it because she often had to take the car to get supplies. "It's my car," she said. "My mother's, anyway."

He smiled. "Okay, Miss High 'n' Mighty. Let's get high." He reached into the back seat for his knapsack, bringing it into his lap and digging around till he brought out a plastic bag and, from this, a fat reefer. "You ever tried one of these before?" he asked.

"Of course," she lied. She'd never made friends with the stoners in school.

He lit it, took a deep draw, and handed it over. It was a greasy thing with a smell like fungus but nicer, like mulch, or peat moss. She took a drag and a ball of fire lunged into her chest. "A real hippie," he observed, and showed her how to take smaller tokes without coughing.

He said it didn't always work the first time you tried it, but Lilac took to it right away. She wanted to go explore the burned forest. Cloud cover that had seemed so ordinary a few minutes ago now was fine tissue, "a loving light," she told him, and he said, "Wow, you just discovered your mother's milk," and neither quite understood the other, but she envied how calm he was, whereas she was agitated. He agreed to go explore the forest.

A rusted white half-ton rumbled past, going west, and then they got out and crossed the highway to jump through the cattails on the far side, landing in ruddy grasses, and up into the woods. Here they walked through black ash. The pines were integers, vertical, diagonal, a foreign alphabet. A scarred silence, then a woodpecker, high up, digging for insects. The burn extended several hundred feet till the trees fell away to marshy lowland. Long shadows, it was late in the day.

She'd walked she didn't know how far, and when she turned, she saw him back at the edge of the woods where they'd come in from the highway. He stood facing a tall, scorched pine as if in close conversation. As she drew near, she heard him talking. His hands were in his jeans pockets, he stood so near to the tree his T-shirt was smudged with ash, and he was speaking fast, urgent. It was hard to make it out, but he seemed to be explaining something, explaining himself. "My old man, you see," he was saying, "I love the guy, but he's just a cog. A fucking cog in a sawmill. So you know, I've gotta do this thing. Because if I don't go, I'll be nothing. If I stay in the bay, I'll be nothing but a cog for my whole life. But, like, Kal Welsh, he's the real deal, he's a free man. Kal's free…"

Lilac coughed.

He turned and without embarrassment told her, "I'm just talking to this here tree." He laughed. "Good shit, huh?" He had black ash on his nose.

She told him he was crazy, but her heart felt wrenched. She liked his attention shining on her, but she also felt encouraged by his selfishness, his impartiality, his lack of attachment—to her, to the life he was gladly leaving—his urgency toward his own unknown. She envied him, and this envy felt like desire. It made sense at the time.

They returned to the car and she drove stoned for about a mile before he pointed out that she was going twenty-five miles an hour and took over the wheel. With her in the passenger seat now, they talked, talked the whole way. She tried to get him to tell her about Thunder Bay, but he seemed bored by the subject, saying, "It's okay," and his parents, "They're nice," and did he go to school, "I'm not ignorant, if that's what you're asking." He'd finished high school, hated it, but liked to read, especially stuff about science, astronomy, "the universe and all that."

She wanted to discover how he might feel about her, and how he felt about the way she lived at Rough Rock. His sudden arrival had made her more acutely aware of her family's unusual isolation. Her whole body was a charley horse, a muscle cramp from being in one position for too long. She felt as though she had a box, like a small locked safe, square in her middle, in the solar plexus, her own little prison she was carrying around. Gavin had said Kal was "famous." Why'd he say that? Famous where?

"Where did you learn about guns?" she asked.

He shrugged. "Hunting with my old man. I don't know that much. I know about the Welsh, of course. Everybody does. Guess I'm going to learn." He was happily ahead of himself, already in the army.

"Did you actually paddle all the way from Minaki to our house so you could meet my father?"

He said of course that's what he'd done, and called it "a pilgrimage."

"You know what it's like?" he asked. "When you see something beautiful. The Welsh 70. My uncle has one. We never. My old man could never afford one. But I got to shoot it sometimes. Then I find out, Welsh is actually a person. A war hero. And he lives not all that far from where I live. And then I think, I'm going to make a pilgrimage. I'm going to war. That's a big deal, it really is."

He looked at her briefly then back at the road, and she murmured, "Yeah, it really is," watching him, loving the way he looked and really confounded by him.

He resumed. "I ask around about Kal Welsh. Find out, not only does he live in these parts, he's built a horking big house out in the wilderness. And he's holed up there while his guns and bullets are off in the world getting famous and making him lots of dough. I never realized just how much dough till I pulled up to your place. And, wow."

"Wow, what?" Lilac demanded.

Again, he glanced at her, warily this time. "It's a nice house." He drove quietly for a few minutes before adding thoughtfully, "It's pretty amazing, actually. Something so big and fancy way out in the bush. Must've been hard, just getting the lumber and stuff out there. The stone floors—" He shook his head in wonder. "Like the Taj Mahal."

She admitted, "It's pretty nice in the winter too," seeing winter light in her mind, the absolute peace of deep snow when they had everything they needed, the glow from the fireplace reflecting off the hardwood. "And it's beautiful in the fall. Spring's great too. Summer is amazing."

"You poor little thing!" He had a generous laugh.

Her high school friends thought she was stuck-up, but nobody had ever suggested that her family was rich. She was an outsider. She'd missed a lot of school because of the weather, but her dad taught her more than she would have learned in class anyway. Lilac didn't have close friends; it seemed like too much work, and she didn't understand how everybody got so comfortable with each other, bickering and teasing, knowing the same jokes, the same TV shows. They didn't have a TV at Rough Rock. There were girls like Judy, who really was nice and tried to make friends, and who would probably be Jimmy's girlfriend now. She remembered when Judy called her one time on the radiophone to ask her to come to Minaki for a sleepover, and Lilac had said politely and loudly over the static, "No, thank you." Her dad, overhearing, asked Lilac if she wanted to go and she said, "No way! I'm too busy!" How gratified she'd been to feel his approval, to hear him laugh.

Gavin reached over and touched her thigh. "I know you're pissed at him. I guess I don't blame you. But—"

She interrupted. "Do you still think he's worth making a pilgrimage for?"

He nodded. "Yeah. I do." Solemn as an oath.

She asked him how he could still think that, after last night, the broken chair and all that stuff her dad had said. But she also wanted her father to be worthy of a pilgrimage.

"You have to take a man on his own terms," he said. "It's easy to judge somebody who shows his passion. But what if he's right?"

"Right about the landowner's daughter?" She put her hand on the car door with a sudden desire to hurl herself out, even though she knew she wouldn't do it. She felt like she was meeting a stranger who happened to be herself.

"I was out of line," he said.

For about three miles, she chewed on this. Then, "You were out of line, how? By getting close to me?"

"You're his daughter. I should've showed more respect."

"What the hell. What the goddamn hell. Stop the car."

He did. And she got out. He remained seated. He even tried for a radio station, fiddling with the dials. She stormed around to the driver's side and opened the door. They were closer to the city now and the traffic had increased. A car blew by close enough to muss her hair. "Get out," she told him.

"No," he said. "Get back in the car. You're stoned. You're angry. Get back in the car and we'll talk."

"You actually think it's a fairy tale?"

"C'mon, Lilac. You're the most beautiful girl I've ever seen. Your dad got mad at me. Now you're mad at me. What's a boy supposed to do? I'm sorry." He saw her soften. "You're something else," he said. "I didn't count on meeting you."

She got back in the car.

9.

He drove on. He'd found a Winnipeg radio station. It was playing Bob Dylan. "Lay Lady Lay."

"Oh Jesus," Lilac said. The song was making her feel sick.

He grinned. "It's a creepy song."

"It's a goddamn vomitous song." Telling some lady to lay.

"I think it's about a dog." He turned it off. They drove in silence past blue fields of flax. Driving into the setting sun, his eyes were tearing up. She found a pair of her mother's sunglasses in the glovebox and he put them on. They were white. "Hey," he asked, glancing quickly at her. She liked that he didn't mind looking stupid. "Do you write poetry?"

She said she didn't. Or she did. "But it's crap."

"Tell me a poem," he asked her and laughed when she brought her feet up under her on the seat, as if she'd rather crawl out the window. She wrote a lot of stuff, writing down the things that went on around her, illustrated with her photographs. She was going to be an actual writer one day. But she'd never tell a poem to someone sitting right beside her.

"Okay," he said. "I got one." He was suddenly bashful. "Naw, never mind, I'm just stoned."

She begged him to tell her his poem. He had a hoarse boy's voice.

> I went fishing in a fishing hole
> Caused by a meteor crashing into Earth
> Smashing up the rocks and
> Killing all the animals in the neighbourhood.
> A hole the rain filled up with water and later

Fish.
All winter the fish swam under the ice but
It was summer when I went fishing
And the fish swam deep
So I took it on faith that in the dark water
Under my boat the fish were thinking
About that meteor and saying
Thanks for the catastrophe.

"That's all I got so far," he said. "It's about a catastrophe. And fish. Obviously."

Lilac stammered her praise. She thought it was a brave poem but like something a kid might write.

When they got to Winnipeg, they went to a pub he'd heard about (he said it was "famous") and he sneaked them in through an iron door in the alleyway. He brought her a beer, and while she peeled off the gummy label, he asked her for a pen and she handed him her favourite Sheaffer from her purse and he wrote the poem down for her on a cardboard coaster and showed it, shy but with what she was learning was his innate pride.

"See?" he said, pointing with his finger at his neat, square print. "*Water* and *later*. *Winter* and *under*. I like the sound of that." She agreed and he pressed further. "*Crashing* and *smashing*. That's interior rhyme. *Caused* and *crashing*. That's alliteration."

He'd had a high school teacher, he said, a guy who'd been in the army in the war, "the old war," he explained, "the one in Europe. He taught us all about it. A very cool dude. Alliteration." He placed his beer on the coaster and wiped off the condensation before drinking it.

Lilac watched the blue ink spread and fade into gibberish and asked him, "Are you sure you have to go to Grand Forks? I mean, are you sure you have to go to Vietnam?"

"Hey." He smiled at her. "You really like me."

10.

They had a night together in a nice hotel on Portage Avenue in Winnipeg. Lilac thought that Gavin deserved a night with a girl he found appealing, a girl who would respond to him, her yang to his yin—or the other way around? She discovered that she could create desire to match his desire at the same moment; she learned that if she hesitated even for a few seconds, he'd get shy or even mistrustful, so she kept rhythm. This was generous. And passive, temporarily. She acted, her mind seemed to move in sync with his, she danced him. Yet she was apart, watching. Her body, close, her mind, remote.

How did her body know how to do all this, move like this, as if it were choreographed? They were lit like some old movie, through the slats of the venetian blinds. He was very finely made. Nothing coarse about him. And strong enough to snap her spine if he chose to. She had to trust him to restrain his strength. He was, she believed, mostly ruthless, instinctively selfish. She liked him, she encouraged him, she gave to him.

He had happened to her, was happening to her right now. His arrival in her life was like a depth charge. But this wasn't a romance. This wasn't a World War II romance with people getting married just before the soldier is killed or loses both legs. That story got broken. Nights at Rough Rock she tuned her transistor radio to Windy City Radio Chicago FM, where she heard Country Joe and the Fish. *One two three, what are we fighting for?* Lilac would sing while she zipped around the lake in her quick little hydroplane.

> *There's plenty good money to be made,*
> *supplyin' the army with the tools of its trade.*

Last spring, just over a year ago, when the US National Guard in Ohio shot to death four university students protesting the war, she'd read everything she could find in the American newspapers that arrived for her dad at the post office in Minaki. She took special interest in the weapons they used. The dead student in the famous photo in all the newspapers and magazines was named Jeffrey Miller. Shot in the mouth from an M1 Garand thirty-calibre semi-automatic from about 250 feet away. Jeffrey Miller was twenty years old. His friend Allison Krause, also twenty, was with him at the protest against Nixon's taking the war into Cambodia. Allison Krause was shot in the chest from about 350 feet away. With the same weapon.

Lilac had memorized the students' names during the lazy days of summer, a project that kept her occupied while she stewed over her future. The other two dead students were Bill Schroeder and Sandra Scheuer (twenty and twenty-one). They'd been hanging around between classes, standing 400 feet away from the protest. It took less than thirty seconds to kill those four people and injure nine others. The Garand leaves a big exit wound. Dean Kahler, twenty, shot in the back by a National Guardsman from 300 feet away, was paralyzed from the waist down. The inventor of the M1 Garand thirty-calibre semi-automatic, Mr. John Garand, was a dual citizen, Canadian-American. Lilac was Canadian-American too. They shared that distinction.

Gavin would fight to prove himself, he'd show his worth. Why? Because he thought he was a blank slate, a zero. Just like a lot of the bored kids back at high school. Gavin imagined that her father, the famous Kal Welsh, would bestow heroism on his joining the US military. Now he was turned away from her, curled up on his side with his hands tucked between his knees, breathing deeply. Vulnerable. Even when he was fully awake, he seemed to be sleepwalking, living in a fantasy. Maybe it was just the marijuana still in her system, but she felt as if they were both sleepwalking. Even their dreams came from outside themselves.

In the morning, she walked with him down Portage Avenue to the bus depot where he'd board the Greyhound that would take him to the United States. "Do you have a passport?" she asked, over a sugared doughnut in the coffee shop.

"I got what they call a 'letter of acceptance' to the army. I can even become an American citizen if I want to." He held up a ragged envelope with a fancy seal.

"How do you get one of those letters?"

"It was easy. I thumbed to Plattsburg and asked for a letter of acceptance. So they gave it to me. Plattsburg is in Missouri."

"I know."

"It was a long hike, but it was worth it."

"They're looking for young men to go fight their war," she said, then shut up. She wouldn't interfere. He needed to make himself grand and epic. Broken bones carried her dad home from his year in Vietnam, the ulna, the tibia, shrapnel in his thigh, holes in his back, wounds that would never completely heal. Something important to her dad had been hurt when he was betrayed by Mr. Thanh. A fragmenting grenade tossed at close range would naturally affect a person's attitude to other people. She didn't bring this up because Gavin knew the risks. He was a fantasist, a Boy Scout. But he wasn't stupid.

She'd paid for everything except his bus ticket — their hotel room, room service, the doughnut — using her credit cards. She was saving the cash her mother had given to her, though she hadn't yet figured out why. The credit card companies would send the bill to Kal Welsh, PO Minaki, Ontario. Kal would pay. She didn't want to feel indebted to him, but she needed his money for a while, till she could figure out how to make her own.

Since 1961, when her father came home and quit his job and started to sell his Welsh Model 70 and his Welsh X Precision Bullets to the US Defense Department, or whatever government department buys lethal weapons, her family had had plenty of everything. The steel-hulled inboard was shipped from Alaska six years ago to replace the old Chris-Craft they'd started out with. The steel boat had a shovel attachment, an icebreaker that Kal would hook onto the bow in late fall and early spring when the lake water grew slushy. Around the same time, he'd built the big boathouse (with help). The boathouse had a hydraulic lift. She hadn't even shown Gavin her eight-foot hydroplane boat with a mahogany deck, which had been a gift from her dad for her sixteenth birthday and which she kept in its own small shed around the shore, not visible from the main dock. Five years ago, her father ordered the red hardwood from Thailand, replacing the regular broadloom he'd installed when the house was built. There was the stone floor from Vermilion Bay. The pewter chandelier had come from Italy three years ago. She wasn't in any position to lecture Gavin on the war in Vietnam that was making money for her family, money she'd inherit someday, even if by then she was getting paid to write about the world.

She watched Gavin stuff five packets of sugar and two little plastic containers of ketchup into the pockets of his windbreaker. She'd mostly seen him naked or wearing her dad's clothes. Now, in the stink of diesel and shriek of air brakes, she looked closely at his windbreaker. It was a Large, with the words *Great-West Life Assurance* stitched on the chest. Gavin was a Medium, he'd had to roll up the ragged cuffs. The jacket was teal blue. It didn't suit him. He belonged to shades of green and amber. Beneath it he wore a grease-stained white T-shirt. She looked down at the concrete where they stood and saw that his running shoes were too big for his feet, like clown shoes. She embraced him. He let her hold him, but he was already gone.

He boarded the bus. Ten a.m. and they were both stoned again. Gavin had escorted her into a stall in the men's washroom, where they shared a joint. She didn't know if she wanted a toke or not. She was stalling her own decisions, giving over to what would make him feel happy. She was his last meal. She marvelled over how he could function so well when he was stoned, gathering up his knapsack, his sole belonging, checking for his precious letter of acceptance to America.

He let the bus swallow him up, and it reversed out of the bay and then he was just a pale face behind a blue window.

11.

She walked right past the hotel and kept going, walking toward Main Street, where she turned north. People were a blur on the wide sidewalk. She wasn't accustomed to crowds and it didn't seem correct to look at people directly. In her periphery they looked like ducks. Canvasback, pintail, a bufflehead, a ruddy duck, and a wood duck. She enjoyed the walk. She'd lived in the city till she was nine years old, but in a residential neighbourhood to the south, and this was the first time she'd ever walked alone down a busy city street. She was Lilac Welsh, born in the time of lilacs' blooming, a girl in love with a wild river, growing up on its rocky shore. Now she was paddling down an unknown river without a chart to navigate its strange currents and reefs.

At a narrow storefront stacked with magazines and newspapers she bought a copy of the *Winnipeg Tribune*. It was the first time she'd ever bought a newspaper on her own, from a newsstand. She had to break a fifty to pay for it and the store owner regarded her with disgust, emptying his till to provide change.

At the back of the store was a lunch counter, where she ordered a Coke float and read the newspaper from the front headlines all the way through to the obituaries and classifieds. She'd always liked reading the magazines and newspapers that arrived at the post office in Minaki: *Life*, *Time*, the *Washington Post*, the *New York Times*, and her dad's favourite, the *Wall Street Journal*. And her mother's *Maclean's* magazines, which were published in Toronto. But never before had she read the *Winnipeg Tribune*.

And now while she read the *Tribune*, she suddenly heated up, as if she'd been spotted by some giant power, fried in a sunbeam through a magnifying glass. She had abruptly found her future self, or the person she was going to be had found her. Here was a newspaper with words written by people who *live in this city*. It hit her with a bang: actual writers live here and actually write.

A man in a brown wool suit and a fedora sat down at the counter on the stool next to hers. "Where are the offices of the *Winnipeg Tribune*?" she asked him.

He told her he was a salesman, selling "space" for the *Tribune*.

While she waited patiently for him to answer her question, she looked at the blue tissue of his eyelids and the tiny bumps like grains of yellow sand in the skin beneath his brown eyes. She said to herself, These are the same eyes he had when he was a baby, and when he was four, and when he was twelve. She had just read in the newspaper that 55,849 American soldiers had been killed in Vietnam since 1960. So many Gavins, their deaths blurring into white noise. She loved her nimble little hydroplane with its mahogany deck. Apparently she was rich, supplying the army with the tools of its trade. She should feel decayed, riddled with helpless guilt. But she wasn't helpless, she felt really pretty good. The man in the fedora stirred his coffee with a fork. She prompted him, "I'm looking for the *Tribune* offices."

"Sure," he said. "But I sell time too. FM radio is huge now." He called to the woman working the counter. "Shirley!"

Shirley brought him a toasted cinnamon bun saturated in butter, and he winked at her.

"It's a pretty good living," he said to Lilac. "My old man worked in print. Back-busting work, jeez, printing presses, heavy machinery. Wrecked his kidneys, that's what I think." He looked down at Lilac's hands, blackened by newspaper ink. "You should wash that off." He pried out the centre of the bun, sticky with walnuts and brown sugar, and popped it into his mouth. "I've got three kids," he said, exhaling cinnamon. "You believe that?"

"I'm looking for the offices of the *Tribune*."

"Oh!" he said. And told her the address. She asked him to clarify: four blocks west, make a left, half a block.

Lilac put down a five-dollar bill, went back outside, and walked toward the address given to her by the man with brown eyes. She was wearing a long-sleeved shirt and blue cotton pants and felt presentable enough, if disoriented. She had such an aptitude for marijuana, she felt no paranoia or anxiety, and was inspired to believe that the editors at the newspaper office would penetrate the surface of reality to perceive her true qualifications for a job. She was, or she would be, an actual writer.

12.

Mrs. Mavin, editor of the women's section at the *Tribune*, was rake-thin and varnished with makeup. She smoked while she talked to Lilac in an office crowded with ashtrays—crystal and glass ashtrays, a hubcap filled with sand, clay ashtrays the size of platters, and a small one, painted orange, in the shape of a child's hand.

Mrs. Mavin wore bifocals suspended on a glass bead chain around her neck. She set the bifocals on her nose and, in a voice like a broken muffler, demanded, "Tell me why I should hire you."

Lilac had asked at the front desk for a job as a "reporter" and was disappointed to get this interview with the lowly women's section, but she responded cheerfully, "Because I can write." She paused. "And I'm observant."

"How old are you? Fifteen?"

"Twenty-one," Lilac lied.

"Education?" barked Mrs. Mavin.

"Yes," said Lilac. "Extensive." She paused, then used a word her father liked. "Autodidact."

Mrs. Mavin's painted eyebrows met in a frown, but she seemed amused. "Do you type?"

"I know my way around QWERTY," Lilac answered.

Mrs. Mavin laughed, her face a mosaic of wrinkles, like fish scales, like feathers. She escorted Lilac up a wide set of marble stairs in a limestone stairwell to a noisy room packed with desks and surrounded on two sides by tall, dirty windows with a view of the low yellow-brick buildings of downtown Winnipeg. There she told a man in a checkered suit, "This girl is Lilac Welsh. I'm giving her a crack at the Junior League Annual Meeting."

The man shrugged and relinquished his Olivetti, and Lilac sat down on a wooden seat still warm from his bum. Beside the typewriter on the desk were several sheets of the man's nearly illegible scrawl. When Lilac looked up at him, he winced defiantly. Mrs. Mavin said, "Louise quit last week. Got married. Stewart here has been pinch-hitting on the women's desk. You've come at the right time." She instructed Lilac to "make something out of this mess and give it to me in twenty minutes. I'll be in my lair." She left the room.

Stewart mumbled, "Good luck," and followed Mrs. Mavin out.

Twenty-five minutes later, Lilac was again admitted to Mrs. Mavin's smoky office. With the bifocals on the bridge of her nose, Mrs. Mavin looked very much like the caterpillar in *Alice in Wonderland*, puffing on a hookah from its leafy perch. Lilac watched, fascinated, as Mrs. Mavin pulled a cigarette from a pack on her desk and lit it with a gold lighter, never losing concentration while she read Lilac's single-spaced type. When she concluded, she peered up over the glasses and commented, "You misspelled *hors d'oeuvres*. Otherwise... How'd you know that Mrs. George Lambert was wearing a 'tailored suit of taupe cashmere'?"

"His notes said 'purplish woolly dress with matching jacket. Sweating.' So I guessed."

Mrs. Mavin said, "Taupe cashmere."

"Sorry. I'd do better if I was taking my own notes."

Mrs. Mavin said, "She'll like the taupe cashmere, true or not."
Lilac had a job.

13.

She heard her mother's voice, heard the ambience of the room
where Ruby would be standing, the beautiful gloom of the river
beyond the trees, yellow poplar leaves drifting down. Since it was
a radiophone, only one of them could talk at a time. She told Ruby
about her job, and said, "Over." After each utterance, they had to
say, "Over," so Ruby could use the press-to-talk button.

"Are you going to *take* the job?" Ruby asked, surprised.

"Of course." Lilac paused. "Why wouldn't I?"

Ruby stuttered. She sounded hurt. "It's sudden," she said.
There was the crackle of interference.

Her mother's pain was intolerable and Lilac tried to shut it out,
shut off Ruby's access to her. "I have to," she insisted.

"Well, come home, at least, and we can talk about it."

"No," Lilac said. She heard her father's voice in the background, asking, "Who is it?"

"Darling," said Ruby, "just come home so we can talk this
through."

And Kal, who would be wearing his boots, wafting the scent of
himself, was demanding to know what was going on. Ruby must
have put her hand over the receiver; Lilac heard "she" and "her"
and fought the impulse to hang up.

Finally, Ruby relented (her father saying something indiscern-
ible, the sound of the back door slamming). Lilac would stay
in Winnipeg till Thanksgiving and "try out" the job. She'd go

home for Thanksgiving weekend and they'd talk. They needed her mother's car, anyway. Lilac would return the station wagon, spend three days at Rough Rock, and then, if she still wanted it, Ruby would drive her back to her new job. Over.

Lilac found an apartment in the attic of a derelict mansion within walking distance from the newspaper office, and covered AGMs for women's organizations, reported on fundraisers, school science fairs, a dying tiger at the zoo. The newspaper gave her the use of a Pentax camera just like the one she'd left at home. She got a great shot of the sick tiger. (Mrs. Mavin dryly called it "a tear-jerker.") She interviewed a dietician who claimed that women can lose five pounds in a week if they restrict their diet to bananas. She did a three-page "puff spread" with photographs of Mrs. George Lambert, Mrs. Harry Squire, Mrs. Frederick Cuthbert, sitting on couches and chaise longues and at vanities in the furniture department at Eaton's.

Stewart, the man she'd replaced at the women's desk, told her, "So you're the new superstar." Lilac stifled a small jolt of loneliness at the resentment she heard in his voice and, smiling pleasantly, answered, "I'm a rocket." She got paid. She liked getting paid.

And she used the newspaper's library to read everything she could find about the war in Vietnam. Everything that she read took her farther from home. It was fine to be writing about little things in the city, providing a mirror for well-intentioned women. But she wanted to write about big things. To report on people's actions that are not well-intentioned, that go astray. Farther away. She was thinking about going to Vietnam. The idea appalled and frightened her, but this made it even more compelling. She thought she had to go look at it, to actually *see* this war.

A war story lived in her gut, like a cat in a cage. Blood thirst, anger, trace elements from home—her father's love of the hunt, her mother's red-headed fury. How will Gavin from Thunder Bay prove his worth in Vietnam? What is this hunger to fight? To kill, dominate, destroy. And to profit from it.

14.

It snowed on Friday, October 5.

Mrs. Mavin granted permission for Lilac to leave work at noon so she could get to Rough Rock before dark. Snow fell sideways and spiralled to melt on the ground. It was even colder at Minaki. Her Starcraft was moored where she'd left it, with a lone jerry can full of gas protected under a green poncho. Her parents would have bailed the boat whenever they came to the marina. They'd kept it from sinking, but now it floated low in the water, snow on the seats. She soaked her wool gloves, bailing. Her good old Evinrude started on the third pull.

Snow melted onto the surface of the black lake. It stung her eyes as she drove. Her gloves turned to ice so it was hard to hold the throttle. She was at the first channel marker, thirty minutes from home, when she spotted the dark shape of the steel inboard droning toward her. They met in the channel. It was Ruby, alone. With some difficulty, they tied the bow line of the Starcraft to the stern of the inboard. Lilac climbed aboard and they churned around to head for Rough Rock.

Ruby's face beneath the hood of her rain gear was ruddy and wet. Lilac had quite forgotten how lovely her mother was, grinning and handing over a Thermos. Consommé with bourbon, a concoction the family called hunters' brew. Heavy on the bourbon. Lilac stood beside the captain's chair where Ruby sat to navigate, her arm around her mother's shoulders.

"Where's Dad?" Lilac asked, her lips numb with cold.

Ruby jutted her chin toward Rough Rock. "He'll be in his shop, making love to his Stalker." Then, "Sorry. That was rude."

Lilac watched her mother's face, trying to measure the temperature between her parents. They were always hot or cold, rarely lukewarm, especially this past year, it seemed, since the Stalker came into their lives. They used to be happier. She had a distinct memory from when she was a little girl, of her mother leaping into her father's arms, hugging him around his neck, and kicking, literally kicking up her heels. She used to call him "darling."

Lilac said, "Is he still pretty obsessed with that butt-ugly thing?"

Ruby didn't laugh. "You know how he gets." She paused. "He seems more desperate or something these days." They were half a mile away from the house. She pulled back on the throttle and shifted into neutral. The snow squall, a near whiteout, seemed audible above the rumble of the big engine. "Listen," Ruby said, "don't let your dad get to you. Don't react. Consider what's best for *you*. I know you want your own life. I get it. You might not want to live out here all the time, at your age. But please. Don't rush things."

"Mum," said Lilac.

"Please don't let him push you away."

Lilac, a bit stunned, said, "Okay."

"You could go away next fall. You could go to university somewhere, anywhere you like. I'm proud of you. You amaze me. Your job, it's great, but you've got so much potential, don't you want more time? I mean, more time to get to know yourself?" She retrieved the Thermos from Lilac, took a swig, and handed it back to her. "Never mind," she said, shaking her head. "I guess I'm the one who wants more time to get to know you." She put the boat in gear, and they went on.

Kal was standing in the boathouse when they arrived. Lilac went aft and, with frozen hands, dragged on the soaked line to haul the Starcraft up to the stern of the inboard and climbed down into the bow to paddle the boat to its slip. Without comment, Kal cleated the inboard then helped Lilac dock. The boathouse was dark, but beyond the big doors the light was eggshell in the lush silence of snow. The smell of pinewood and gasoline and wet wool. She took her father's army knapsack and her wet cotton purse and walked behind her parents up the stone stairs to the house.

They'd attached the storm windows over the screens in the verandah. But the house was cold. Kal went out the back door and returned with an armload of firewood, chucking it onto the hearth.

Lilac climbed the polished pine stairs to her room. The beauty of her home surprised her, seeing it fresh, after the dingy functionality of her apartment and the newspaper office. She'd turned on the small propane heater and was changing into dry clothes, still in her undershirt, when her dad tapped at her open door. She pulled a sweater over her head and went to her dresser and brushed her hair. The landowner's daughter had returned to the castle.

He loomed in the doorway. "Did your friend get away?"

He was already talking about Gavin. She blushed and said yes.

"Heard from him?"

She said no, she hadn't heard from him.

"He'll be in training now. Probably too busy to write." Her father entered, sat down heavily on her bed, asked her if she was hungry. She said she was. He slapped his thighs. "Good!" And made as if to stand, but sat down again and studied her. "How are you managing?" he asked.

"Perfectly well."

"You rent an attic?"

She said yes, in a big house.

"How are you fixed for money?"

"I get paid."

"Not much. Do you eat? You're skinny."

"I'm fine. I eat. I like my job, Dad."

He looked quite lost. She felt all tight inside. If she started to worry about him, it might make her feel too guilty to leave. She sought for some kind of personal admission she could afford to make. "It's not a hard job. I write about little things. In some ways, it's quite silly. But it's interesting to be working." She went to sit beside him on the bed. "And how are you?"

He snorted. "You really are grown up. That's the first time you've ever asked me how I am."

"How's it going with the new gun?"

"Oh. Your mother wants you to ask, does she?"

"No. She doesn't need me to do her asking."

He hesitated. "No. She doesn't." He finally stood up. Her bedroom was a good size, but he overfilled it, looming over her. She remembered having tonsillitis, back when she was thirteen, and he'd sat at her bedside all night long, angrily waiting for first light when he could boat her into Kenora to a doctor, furious with Ruby for not being able to fix their daughter, and indignant that he needed outside help. After that, they kept antibiotics in the house, refreshing them regularly. A real field hospital, he called it.

He cupped her chin in his palm. His clean, calloused hand. "You don't like the new gun either." He tilted her face up to look at him. "Well," he said, "that gun is going to make you very rich."

"I don't need it."

"You're going to be rich as Midas."

"I said, I don't need it."

"You can do whatever you like if you have money. Think about that. You could own your own newspaper. A woman runs the *Washington Post*, did you know that?"

"Katharine Graham," she said.

"Autodidact," he said, and his hand chucked her chin just a little too forcefully. "Just for once, I'd like to give you and your mother something that you'd actually be grateful for." He sighed and left the room.

Lilac took a deep breath, surprised to feel her heart hammering. It was four o'clock, and snow, out of season, fell thickly through yellow poplar leaves. She stood at the window of her room, where she could watch the snowflakes disappear into the black lake.

15.

The sun shone on Saturday. Lilac spent some time in her father's shop, helping him load cartridges. This ammunition was for his own use. He wanted the three of them to go hunting together on Sunday, "to celebrate your homecoming," he told her.

His Welsh X Precision Bullets were mass-produced in Connecticut, under the supervision of Randy, his long-time manager, whom Lilac had never met. But they'd initially been developed in the crooked garage outside their brick house when they lived in the city. "Through trial and error," he liked to say. As a child, Lilac had helped him in his experiments, until eventually he'd hit on the design that gave him the penetration and performance that caught the attention of the National Rifle Association. The NRA gave him glowing reviews in their publications ("Welsh slugs really get the job done!") and Kal's bullets became popular among hunters, even for dangerous game, all over the world. He got fan mail. Nailed to the wall beside the door of the shop here at Rough Rock was a photograph of a man in a cowboy hat crouched beside a dead lion.

Today, Kal muttered while they worked, describing what he was doing, talking like the narrator in a documentary movie. He was odd that way—not exactly vain, though he always wore nice clothes, even in the bush; he was self-conscious, aware of himself, as if he had an audience in his own head. He always got mad if anyone interfered with his plans or made him wait. But Lilac had never before been quite so aware of having to pay absolute attention to him. At one point, she got distracted and perched on the stool he used while seating the bullets. Kal shoved her off, firmly, resuming his seat. He said, "You'll spoil my rhythm."

It was always understood: you do not sit in his chair, you do not put your boots in his spot at the back door, hang your jacket on his hook, use his coffee mug or his favourite glass. You never talked if he was talking, never interrupted him, and if you had to disagree, you'd say something like, "You're probably right, but I was just wondering…" Lilac thought about this while she loaded gunpowder into his cartridges.

The other small mishap that day was when Lilac forgot to put on protective glasses. Kal rebuked her harshly. He always got angry when she hurt herself. She couldn't blame him for that; it'd be hard to be responsible for everyone, living out here, so far from a hospital. It was a day that recalled the many times they'd worked together, but now Lilac felt more weighed down than she used to. Kal seemed to sense Lilac's discomfort. "You need to quit?" he asked gruffly when they were only about half-done, his tone suggesting that quitting wasn't an option.

On Sunday at dawn, she and her parents went hunting. Sun like honey on white birch, the forest floor covered in red leaves, the scrub oak already bare. They walked through brush, staying close to shore. Ruby and Lilac each carried a backpack and a .22, while Kal had his big pack with the cotton game bags and his Welsh 70 with the heavy grain cartridges that Lilac had helped him prepare, packed specifically for moose. "I won't take down a bear unless I have to," he told them as they were setting out. "Can't stand the smell of bear meat in the house." Ruby didn't reply. Lilac, listening, wondered why Kal's observation sounded like a reprimand. Her mother refused to cook bear. She made him cook it on a fire outside, and she and Lilac never ate it.

They went quietly through the woods and around marshy bays where trout would be suspended above the silt in the reeds. Ruby bagged a few grouse, and Lilac got a blue-winged teal, a small, quick bird.

Her dad said, "Sweet shot!" And smiled at her. "You remind me of me when I was your age."

Kal took his pack and walked inland while Ruby and Lilac stayed at the shoreline. They sat down to eat hard-boiled eggs with salt and drink hunters' brew, perched on a slab of rock that jutted over the water, swinging their legs in the air. The river was miles wide here, with countless islands on shelves of white granite. The violet shadows beneath Ruby's eyes blended into her pale skin, startlingly pale against her red hair—but she seemed happier today, less pensive, and she and Kal had been amiable. No one talked much; they were listening for game.

The sound of Kal's rifle echoed off the rocks. A single shot.

Ruby and Lilac wrapped up their picnic, slung their backpacks, and turned inland, pausing at the edge of a stand of tamarack, rare, their needles still intact, the colour of white gold. There were patches of snow in the forest. They tracked east, the sun at their backs, and walked for several minutes, Ruby calling out Kal's name before he finally answered, "Here!" When they saw him, he was standing over a dead moose.

He held his knife. He'd already opened her up from jawbone to tail and stripped the hide, which now lay like a bloody rug beside him. The air stank of his sweat and the iron scent of blood. He reached into the guts and pulled out a pale orb like a small moon. It steamed when he laid it in snow. He sliced it open and removed a calf, cupping its tiny head by its throat, and, lifting, dangled it while he ran his other hand down its long, spindly, almost boneless body, rinsing away the amniotic fluid. "So beautiful," he murmured, and nested the calf on the bloody hide.

He quartered the moose, speaking quietly, describing his own actions while he cut the meat off the bone, tenderloins, backstraps, brisket. "I'll take a strap of meat from the neck. Nice bit here." His knife sliced against the esophagus. All this time, Ruby stood a little way off, half-turned toward the woods, averting her eyes. She had, of course, often witnessed her husband butchering the game that he brought down, especially deer, and moose like this one, though never before had she watched him remove an unborn calf from its mother. She stared absently at the long, thin body of the dead calf. Lilac couldn't detect what her mother was thinking; her face was drawn closed.

Kal straightened and, seeing them standing idle, spoke scornfully. "Do I have to do it all?"

Ruby emerged from her trance and bent to the work, bundling warm meat into the sturdy cotton game bags. Lilac helped her, and together they stuffed the bags then wrapped them in strips of loose-knit tarpaulin and filled their backpacks. With his knife, Kal fashioned a travois from pine boughs, rope, and another tarp, and loaded three of the bundles onto that so he could drag it out, but the bulk of it went into his big backpack. Lilac marvelled over how her father was always well-prepared, always had the correct supplies. She could trust his competence. Yet, it occurred to her, there was something theatrical in it all, as if he was demonstrating how to be Kal Welsh, the best at everything.

They trudged out of the tamarack forest toward the sun. Ruby led the way and they emerged at the shore ten feet to the west of the spot where they'd had their picnic. It was heavy going. As they hauled their burdens home, Kal boasted, "That was a clean kill." Lilac understood that he wanted their thanks; they should be grateful for the food he'd provided, and she agreed, "Nice work, Dad." Her mother remained solemn, alert, watching the path, always wary of bears. But more than that, she seemed to be giving Kal the cold shoulder.

Before they'd headed out that morning, while she and her mum were brushing their teeth side by side in the bathroom, Ruby had muttered, "Why'd he pack cartridges for big game? We're already stocked up." She spit into the sink, wiped her mouth, turned away, and muttered, "Just can't stop himself, I guess."

They were quietly occupied that evening. Ruby stripped the fat and the silver skin before wrapping and freezing the steaks and roasts. Tomorrow they would take the refuse away from the house and bury it, but for now she put it in a cooler in the pantry. Kal hovered, watching his wife's hands, saying, "You're quick with a knife." His admiration seemed resentful, as if her casual skills separated her from him, excluded him. He watched her every move, but it didn't seem to make him happy. A surprising thought struck Lilac: What would happen to her father if Ruby were to leave him? He'd be alone. She watched his back as he left the kitchen, heard his heavy footsteps on the stairs.

When he withdrew, it was as if he'd taken away Ruby's script or something, her purpose. Suddenly she threw up her arms and her eyes filled with tears. "Why are we doing this?" She stared at her bloodied hands. "I remember," she said in a breathy, private voice. "Oh, God, how I admired him." Startled, abruptly aware of her daughter's presence, she added, "I still do."

Lilac murmured, "I know."

"I do." Ruby wiped away tears, but then more came. She tried to laugh. "How are we *ever* going to eat all this?" She gave Lilac a bald, helpless look. "Especially if you're not here." The kitchen counter and table were loaded with packages seeping blood. "I'll give it away. I'll take it to Minaki next time I go." She stopped and stood firm as if prepared to take a hit. "Are you going to leave tomorrow?" When Lilac said she was, Ruby nodded, sniffed, and wiped her nose with the back of her hand, nodding. "I'll take the meat to the Sinclairs when I drive you in."

"All of it?" It was a lot, an entire animal.

"Why not? If he complains, I'll lock him in the freezer, with all the shit he's already shot!" Ruby paled, her eyes met Lilac's, they burst out laughing. Ruby said, "That's awful, I'm awful, awful."

"No, you're not, Mum."

That night, Lilac awoke in the dark. Something had touched her chest. The house smelled of roasted wild meat. She lay under the quilt that her mother had sewn for her, in her familiar bedroom among her things — her typewriter and her books; the photographs she'd had developed at a shop in Kenora, pinned to a board above her desk; her scrapbooks and poems and stories in the trunk under the window. She felt loss, and dread. If she closed her eyes, she'd see the moose calf they'd left behind in the woods. That unborn calf. The wolves will find it in its mother's ribs.

Before they left the site of the kill, her father had made a strange ritual. He'd sliced a sliver of the moose's heart and pushed this into the mouth of the calf. Then he'd laid the calf in its bone cradle. He felt his wife's and daughter's eyes on him and he explained, "I was hunting with my friend Peter one day. Saw him do this. Seems to make sense."

Peter was an Ojibwa man. As far as Lilac knew, her dad had been out hunting with the man only a few times. Peter had come to the house once, a few years ago, and never returned. Yet Kal referred to him as a friend. He did this pretty often, laying claim to acquaintances by calling them "friend." He liked to say, "A friend of mine, Peter, an Ojibwa man..." Her father's yearning for friendships that he didn't have the time or interest to actually foster made Lilac uneasy. She'd never be like that. Her mother had often told her, "You're very competitive." Lilac wanted good grades. Who wouldn't? At school, she never cared to be one of the crowd, even though she envied that crowd sometimes. When she was with her schoolmates, she'd sometimes notice she was having a conversation with herself, words running inside her head, things that she never said out loud. It made her feel quite superior. She was alone so much. But in her new, independent life, she would have many friends.

She sat up in bed. She was wearing long underwear and a T-shirt, and now she threw on more clothes and slipped into her canoe shoes.

The house was dark except for the fireplace, where a fresh fire meant that someone, either Kal or Ruby, had recently replenished the wood. She stepped quietly down the stairs and went to the kitchen. Here the wood stove too had recently been stoked with birch, crackling. She returned to the living room, peered into the dark corners, looked at the rocking chair where Ruby liked to sit, nights she couldn't sleep. There were Ruby's books and a lantern, unlit.

Lilac's heavy parka hung on a hook. She hefted it on and opened the back door.

16.

Behind the house, beyond Ruby's garden and Kal's shop, beyond his firing range, stood a dark wall of spruce against a sky punctured by stars. She listened for the sound of big animals. Woodsmoke drifted through the air. An owl hooted in the woods. When she was young, she believed she'd have a happy day following a night when she heard an owl. And when she was young, she believed that the trees were her guides. That the trees were "good." They were indeed good, the trees. But she was too restless to stay and listen to them. It would be lonely in the city and she'd miss the river, she'd miss her mother and even her dad, she'd miss herself as the kid who used to think that an owl would bring her a lucky day. What becomes of the broken magic from childhood? In the morning, she'd leave.

Autumn was always beautiful here, until November's barren interval, before December's snow blurred the edge of things again. But one of her worst times had actually been in summer, a year into their time in this house, during perfectly nice days in early August when she fell into a peculiar state of anxiety, of what her ten-year-old brain called "dryness." She was just a little kid then, listless and bored, and, trying to find the words for this terrible vacancy, she complained to her mum, "My soul is dusty." Ruby winced. "Go for a swim, why don't you." Ruby didn't like people talking about their souls. She always made a sour face when Kal kissed her forehead and said, "God bless you."

There was that time, their first winter here at Rough Rock, when her mum got full-bore mad at her dad one morning when they heard on the radio that the United States had sent a man into space on a spaceship. Her dad became really emotional and said, "God bless America," in a choked voice. Her mum said, "Oh, stop the bejesus God thing!" and slammed down her cup so hard it cracked and hot coffee leaked across the table and into her lap.

That August when she was ten, Lilac's dusty soul had persisted for days, until she grew desperate. Finally, on a hot afternoon, she spread a sleeping bag out on the ryegrass and lay down. Her body felt stiff, she hurt all over. The weight of what she called "everything" hurt so much she moaned. The sky was empty, it yawned with boredom. She might have a heart attack or something, she could barely breathe. But right at that moment, a feeling of kindness floated down on her, and she heard—she heard—a voice. The voice said, "It doesn't matter." It *was* a voice; she didn't make it up. Lilac's dusty soul was suddenly released like a bird and she experienced a wonderful lightness. *It doesn't matter.* All the weight lifted, absorbed, taken up and away by the voice.

She'd been given a gift. What a strange gift, to tell a little girl that nothing matters. But the voice. She had heard it, a calm tone, neither male nor female, or both.

In the dark tonight, the words were reconfigured. *It doesn't matter* became *You do not matter.* An interesting diminishment. It's tricky to take spiritual advice from a voice in the forest. Maybe she'd never hear that voice again; maybe she was shut out from the magical aspects of the world.

The job at the *Tribune* was quite dumb. Interviewing pearled ladies of women's committees for the symphony orchestra, the Dominion Theatre, Friends of the Winnipeg Zoo, the Women's Pavilion at the General Hospital, transcribing her notes, writing wholesale advice on weight loss and furniture—it wasn't where she wanted to end up. But she couldn't stay here at Rough Rock. Already she felt like a guest.

Bundled in her parka, she went toward the shadow that was her father's shop and opened the door. It was nearly pitch-dark, but her hands knew where to find the kerosene lantern and matches. She struck a match to the wick and the room gained a yellow cast. On the workbench where Kal kept his tools sat his new, alien rifle on its bipod, a giant ant.

Lilac wanted a sip of bourbon and comforted herself with the thought of the amber warmth in her father's liquor cabinet back at the house. She leaned to blow out the lantern when something made her stare into the dark corners of the shop. A man was standing on the other side of the bench. Unmoving. He was so still, she wondered if she was imagining him, and she raised the lantern by its handle, the metal hot across her palm. The shadow melted into the wall, and she heard the shuffling of someone close by. The smells of the oil, gunpowder, soap gathered into his presence.

"What are you doing here?" she asked.

"I live here," Kal said. "What about you?"

"You scared the hell out of me."

"You're up late." He moved till his face was revealed in the lantern light. He looked sober. "Almost early. What's on your mind?"

"Nothing. I couldn't sleep. I didn't mean to freak you out or anything."

"Who's 'freaked'?" His body was relaxed. He leaned back against his workbench and with his palm he lightly rolled the small brass primers to and fro. Lilac thought she could see the tiny shadow of each bead. "Were you looking to talk to me?" he asked.

She stretched her back as if suppressing a yawn, though her heart pounded and now a headache jabbed at one eye. "I'm pretty tired." He'd scared her, standing in the dark like that.

"Here." He struck a match and put it to another lantern hanging from a bracket on the wall. In the brighter light, she studied him. Yes, he was sober. He moved languidly, as if enjoying the feel of his own strength. Without comment, he reached beneath his workbench and effortlessly, with one hand, lifted something, a funny-looking machine. "Clear this away, will you?" He motioned for Lilac to shift the Stalker over to one side. "Make some room."

She touched the gun then, that obstinate steel body. Kal was holding a film projector. "Where'd that come from?" she asked, startled. She lifted the Stalker out of the way and he set the projector down in its place.

"I bought it," he said. "Sixteen-millimetre. Stay put. I'll be right back." He went outside and there was the sudden drone of the generator that he kept in a shed behind his shop. He returned and flipped a switch on the projector. A bright white light shone on the wall—he'd nailed a sheet there. "I was going to show this to you and your mother tomorrow, but—since you're leaving..." The projector's fan blew loudly. "Sit down."

"How'd you get that running?" she wondered. She meant, how was he drawing so much power?

"A couple of marine batteries." He motioned and she saw the cables connecting the projector to two big batteries. He pointed at another, smaller box. "That's the inverter. An inverter changes DC, direct power, into AC, alternating power. Good to know?" he asked. This had been one of his refrains when he was her teacher. He'd finish a lesson and ask, "Good to know?" She always said yes.

17.

With the rat-a-tat-tat of sixteen-millimetre film rolling through the machine, the room filled with an eerie blue wash while she sat, stunned. The long, restless pan was jerky; the cameraman must have been walking over rough ground, through a grove of trees, their white trunks dimly visible through blue shadow, white trees like ghosts, a weirdly menacing effect. Then a low, slow moaning, a lament in an incomprehensible language.

It was an unearthly song, sweet as rainwater, filled with longing. Voices, male or female, she couldn't tell, voices twining around themselves. She felt her father glance at her. The room rippled with stark white limbs. Mesmerized by the film, she asked him what was going on.

"Just a film I made for Psyops," he answered with boyish pride.

She asked him why he'd make something like this.

"We were in the Mekong River delta. Trying to warn the locals that they'd lose everything, their families, their lives, if they supported the Viet Cong." He affected a humble tone. "I was saving lives with this film." And continued, "Day for night. That's the technique. I used film stock intended for indoor light. Underexposed. Gives it that mushroomy look."

She stared at the flickering images. "What are they saying?"

"That's one man speaking. You'd never know it, eh? We recorded him three times then made a final recording of all three tapes running at the same time. Sounds great, doesn't it?"

"Well then, what's he saying?"

"It's an old story. A husband, a father and so on, is killed in a war. His body isn't buried. The peasants think that if a corpse isn't buried, his spirit will wander forever. They call it a hungry ghost. He has to spend infinity searching for his family." He shuddered. "Imagine. Infinity."

"Who is it?" she asked. She wanted to know: Who was singing this strange song? The amplified sound of feet in dry leaves and a tone, a single note, was rising, very low to high, and higher till it reached a screaming pitch. And now, here in the room with her, Kal began to sing in a high voice, "Where are my wife and children? No one comes to bury me. I wander through this vapour. Where are my loved ones? We can't find each other. We're lost."

The projector's fan started clacking. When he switched off the machine, the room got quiet and he stared hard at the dark screen. There was the drone of the generator outside, and a harsh scent of vinegar.

18.

He went out and killed the generator, and when he returned, he took a bottle of bourbon from the cupboard above the sink and poured them both a drink.

She took a good sip and held it out for him to top it up, which he did.

He sat close beside her. His Stalker crouched insistently, and he nodded toward it. "I am making your mother unhappy."

"I guess."

"I've got to get this gun into the field."

"Why?"

"Because young men are dying, Lilac."

She hated it when he "taught" her like that, as if she'd asked a stupid question.

He went on, pontificating. "The M16 is a shitty rifle. My Stalker will save young lives."

The daughter of the gunsmith laughed.

He was solid, square, owning the place, declaring, "It doesn't matter whether we like it or not. War is a necessity."

"Says who?" She knew she sounded like a sulky adolescent and took another good gulp of bourbon.

But Kal lit up as if this was exactly the question he'd hoped she'd ask. "God," he said, "as a matter of fact. God says war is a necessity."

Lilac took the glass from her lips and sputtered, "Yeah. Right."

"That's funny? You think God is a deer? A lamb? A chipmunk?" He looked down at the floor, as if speaking only to himself. "God is a wolf. A wolf king. And the wolf is lonely. But severe." He raised his head, his chest, the professorial inhale, yet he didn't seem to care if she couldn't understand him; his convictions went far beyond her understanding. He looked satisfied and assured of his own value.

"You think all this"—he waved vaguely, and she thought he was indicating his shop, their home at Rough Rock—"was created by *me*?" Now he gave her a friendly wink and bumped his shoulder against hers. "Come *on*."

"You had those guys here, helping you. That contractor—"

"Contractor." He nodded, as if she'd helped him to a revelation. "Contractor. Now *that's* a good name for him."

Lilac was thirsty, the bourbon made her thirsty. Her tongue clacked against her palate. "Name for who?"

"For whom." A quick grammatical correction. "No words. No words can speak his name." He smiled to himself. Lilac envied his self-assurance, even if it was also a bit creepy. His voice sounded low and warm. "But listen, kiddo. You're more fortunate than you know. Not by luck. Not by riches. No. Not by ordinary riches, darling."

He had never ever before called her "darling." It was her mother's word and didn't belong to him. "What exactly are you going on about, Dad?"

"The power and glory of God," he answered quietly, studying his bourbon then tossing it back. He rose to his feet. "Ready?" And offered to help her stand.

She let him lift her to her feet, leaning away from his solid chest. But she couldn't help it, she wanted to fold herself into him. He seemed athletic, sporting, happy, certainly indifferent as to whether this blind puppy, this *girl*, would ever comprehend him.

He grinned and took her empty glass from her. "I guess I haven't talked to you about my—convictions. You went away. But yeah. Him. The—contractor. That's what's behind it all."

"I only went away a month ago, Dad. You weren't talking about the wolf king last summer."

"My faith has been constant. You know that. Your mother doesn't approve, but I can't change myself for her. I can't change something as fundamental as my faith in the Almighty."

She was wary of pushing him, but curious. "It *is* new," she asserted tentatively. "Except for 'God bless America,' I've never heard you talk like this before."

"Maybe I'm finally growing up." He turned away, smiling at his own joke and, setting their glasses down beside his gun, he blew out the lanterns. In the dark, he touched her elbow to guide her to the door and outside, to the cool air, the seeding garden with a quarter moon's light silvering the curled stalks and bean pods, where he stopped to grip her arm more tightly and speak closely in her ear. "Your—friend, your—Gavin."

She interrupted. "He's gone. He went." The moonlight, she thought, it's rushing over him, flushing out his scent, the moon in the lax folds of his jacket and jeans, his face almost handsome in relief.

"He could die unnecessarily," Kal continued. "Die stupidly. A sacrifice of no value. Because we gave him a bad gun. Do you really want him to waste his life? Do you? Lilac? You're—close to Gavin. What if he gets killed because we gave him a shitty gun?"

She grunted. "You already said. You're going to make a ton of money with the Stalker."

He chuckled something like *hey hey hey*, then, "Talent plus necessity equals success."

She heard the owl again.

He assembled his patience to speak low and close in the dark. "The Land War Lab wants a powerful sniper system and I'm the one who knows how to build one. In the right hands, the Stalker 80 has a two-mile range. I created the first, the *first*, fifty-calibre shoulder-fired sniper weapon. I arranged the Starlight scope. I assembled the system." He paused and added, "I know how to make us—great." He leaned back to view her, taking in her length. "You've gone through quite a lot since you finished school. Your job. And your—"

She quickly interrupted. "Not really." If he said anything about "becoming a woman," she'd vomit. It wasn't his style. Surely.

"Your—"

"Friend."

"Gavin, yes. Do you know why Gavin joined the military?"

"He needs to fight. To be a guy."

"You make it sound almost arbitrary."

"He decided to go. He didn't have to. It's not his war. That's arbitrary."

"You could show him some respect. He'll make something significant of his life."

"A significant tombstone."

"To die with God is richer than living out his days in wages."

She heard the first birds, the ones who sing in the dark. A lamp glowed in the house now; Ruby always woke up early. "It's really kind of funny," she observed uneasily, "the way you're talking, Dad." She wondered how her mother would continue to put up with this alliance between God and Kal.

"It's hard," he went on, in that maddening, confidential tone, "to speak the truth. It's hard to fight for what's right. Gavin, all our best soldiers, face an enemy. A ruthless enemy who wants to overthrow our values. Our freedom. Our massive accomplishments. Tricked by guerrillas, bush monkeys. When it started, you know, the Viet Cong were just a gang of thieves stealing our weapons. Now, Russia and China are involved. I don't think you realize, it's a war for world dominance. And I know how to contribute a gun that could tip the balance a fraction, a *fraction* in our favour. How can I not do that, Lilac?" He looked up at the house, at the lamp in the bedroom window. "Even if it makes your mother unhappy."

"Epic," she said.

"Watch it," he said quickly. Then he took a breath and smiled. "You're too old to be sassy."

"I know you think you're right. But what if you're not?"

"Read the newspapers." He laughed to himself.

The newspapers that instruct women to limit their diet to bananas. "I should go to Vietnam," she said.

Kal didn't seem to hear her. He said, "You just try to keep an open mind." He gripped her shoulder a little too hard and gave her a slight shove to make her walk ahead of him through the gathering dew, back to the house. She heard him behind her, his kindly, tolerant tone. "Anyway, kiddo. I love you. I don't say that enough."

"Actually, you've never said it before, Dad. This is the first time."

"Oh, I don't think so." At the house, he cut ahead of her, going inside and adding, over his shoulder, "Get some sleep before sunup."

19.

Ruby drove Lilac to Winnipeg then paced quickly through her attic rooms, absorbing her daughter's new digs. Lilac pointed out the best features, the bathroom that still had the original tiles, her map of the world taped to the wall above an iron post bed that had been left behind by a previous tenant. "Hardwood floors. See? Somebody took the paint off them in here." She indicated her favourite room, the living room, free of furniture except where she'd put big pillows beneath the window. It was her refuge, where she'd listen to music and smoke pot at night. "I found this nice throw for five bucks."

It seemed that every detail hurt Ruby. Lilac tried to see it from her mother's perspective. "It's not like home," she admitted. "But it's nice, isn't it, Mum?"

Ruby nodded. She looked brittle.

Lilac knew that she couldn't help Ruby without taking too much from herself. Her life here in the city was too new, and it cost her dearly in homesickness and anxiety over making her paycheque last the week. She couldn't afford her mother's pain.

She walked with Ruby back toward the station wagon parked across the busy street. The light was red, interminable, and while they waited for it to change, not speaking, Ruby trembled then declared bitterly, "Don't wait with me! You might as well go." She turned to face her daughter and her voice broke. "You've done up your buttons crooked!"

Lilac looked down to see that indeed her favourite lumber jacket was buttoned wrong. She shrugged, who cares? But this almost undid her mother, who cried out, "You look like a little girl!"

"Well, I'm not," Lilac told her sternly. The light turned green, they joined the crowd surging forward. Ruby got into her car and drove away, her hand waving through her open window, maybe crying, her face shielded by her crazy hair. Then Lilac was again at the corner, waiting for the green. She'd smoke a joint, she'd own herself again.

This time leaving home, she'd packed her camera, telling Ruby that she'd use it at work. But she doubted that her future was with the *Tribune*'s women's section. The job was a birdcage. Mrs. Mavin had told her that the newspaper would move Lilac to the city desk. But municipal council meetings would probably be deadly dull. The newspaper was buying her time, buying her life. She hadn't anticipated that becoming a writer would be tedious.

A couple of weeks went by, then a letter from Gavin found its way to her attic rooms. He'd addressed it to the Minaki PO and Ruby had forwarded it. An exuberant letter. He'd "made it to Da Nang" and was with the 75th Infantry. He said he was now "a proud cog in C TRP, 1st SQDN, USARV" and included a photograph of himself with five other soldiers, their faces smeared with mud, looking relaxed and happily unfettered. He signed off, "Peace, Gavin." This was another thing that she liked about him, his willingness to contradict. Proud cog. Peace in war. He hadn't seen any "action" yet and was eager to "get out there and give 'er."

The far-fetched possibility of her own journey to Vietnam now tormented, taunted her. The fantastical distance, the improbability that she could match Gavin's adventure, this uncertain future provoked and alerted her with such force she could barely stand to be *anywhere*. Why did this nice city with its nice people feel so fake? But then she would watch the TV in the newsroom, footage of young soldiers like Gavin wading through jungle swamps with their rifles held high above their heads, and she felt violence running like an underground stream, feeding the complacency, the pleasant optimism of the women's committees.

Her current situation was just a substitute, a delay. She felt at a remove, as if she was already someplace else, as if she'd already gone. There was real life *out there*. In a war. She didn't know how the hell she was going to get there.

20.

Lilac became friendly with a girl named Vivian Bergson, in the advertisement department. Vivian was tall and bony, with a pale, freckled, flat chest she revealed beneath flimsy cotton T-shirts under denim overalls, defiant about wearing fancy clothes or even a bra to work. She had a talent for assembling the photos from Eaton's or Chrysler dealerships with copy that she typeset and spliced onto the galleys. Vivian had professional skills that made Lilac feel small by comparison. She was only a year older than Lilac, yet she seemed ancient, like an old granny, and she had a vaguely Appalachian hillbilly accent, popular in the music they both liked. During their lunch hour, they'd often walk over to Lilac's attic room, where they ate Dare maple cookies and drank instant coffee with a splash of Napoleon brandy, listening to Crazy Horse, *Everybody Knows This Is Nowhere*.

Vivian had a lot of art books in her office at the *Tribune*, and she loaned some to Lilac. Lilac had never seen much art in her life, and she was immensely grateful to her friend for showing her a whole new world. Impressionists and all that. Pop art too—Andy Warhol—whose repetitive images made Lilac feel sick, though it was hard to say why. His replicating Campbell's soup cans seemed to suggest that the creation of the world was complete; there will only be repetitions of banality in Lilac's future.

Viv had books of German art too, some of it disturbing, especially the flayed, bony nudes by Egon Schiele. And books filled with glossy images of commercial design. Vivian laughed at what she called "psychedelic hippie shit." "Revolution makes money now," she said, and scorned the paisley cotton skirts selling at Eaton's to suburban blondes carrying stinking hand-pressed leather purses with thick braided straps. She said hippies were "kitsch."

Vivian's most prized possession was a compass set into what looked like a complicated board game made of ebony and brass. "That's a feng shui compass," she told Lilac. Vivian said that its purpose was to "find harmony in space."

Viv seemed to hate her family, but she sure loved to talk about them, engaging often in intense family gossip. She was a second-generation German with a merchant father who worked all the time in Europe and a "totally neurotic" mother, an anxious "hausfrau" who cleaned obsessively and counted her embroidered linens, convinced that the cook was stealing from them. There was a large, one-legged grandfather (a wartime injury, Viv said, from the First World War, when he'd fought for Germany) who dominated the shady stone house. "He thinks he owns us, mind and body. He thinks he knows when I have my period."

"Really?" Lilac asked, listening intently.

Vivian liked an audience. They began to get together after work. They'd smoke pot, and she would tell Lilac stories. Once she described a hot summer afternoon when she was thirteen. "My opa wheels over to the windows and closes the curtains," she said. "Then he wheels over to me and says, 'Zit.'"

"Zit?" Lilac laughed.

"Zit! So I zat!"

Lilac imagined Viv's gangly body draped over the grandfather's lopsided lap, his hands searching. "Is this where it hurts, Liebling? Here? Unkraut, you must tell Großvater everything now."

At school the kids used to call Vivian "Schultz," with a heil Hitler salute. "But my grandfather hated the Nazis. They were vulgar. Too 'id' for his taste," Viv said.

Lilac said, "Too what?"

"Id. It's Freud."

"I know," said Lilac.

"No, you don't." Vivian took a deep toke. "You're so full of shit." She squinted at Lilac. "What about you? How come you never talk about *your* family?"

"There's not much to tell."

"Total bullshit."

Lilac shied away from talking about her parents or her life at Rough Rock. Thinking of home made her feel guilty and homesick.

She couldn't match Vivian's casual malice, her corrosive, almost cartoonish grotesqueries, but was a bit ashamed of herself for imbibing Viv's tales while not offering any of her own. She told Viv, "My folks are pretty dull. I'm just taking a break from them." She didn't want to tell her about the Stalker, that lethal weapon sitting on her father's workbench, didn't want to talk about her dad's foreign American DNA, or Ruby's precarious faith that Kal was "super-strong."

The idea that she was sleepwalking recurred to her. Her prolonged childhood, which she felt had ended when she was "deflowered," had been shrouded by her father. He was so domineering, maybe she'd always been performing only according to what she hoped would please him, as if she wasn't actually *here*, except as an extension of his wishes. Even homesickness wouldn't make her go back to Rough Rock. Her need for her separate life was a force, a compulsion.

One weekend, she and Vivian went to the pub that Lilac had gone to with Gavin on their one night together. They stood close to the stage to watch the band, which had come all the way from Minneapolis, and then they danced, ignoring the crowd, mostly ignoring each other. Viv's face was expressionless though she danced wildly, swinging her long bare arms around her frizzy head of hair in an exotic manner at odds with her bumpkin attire. She looked so tough and uninterested in being cool, Lilac loved her.

The place was full of buffed football players standing with their plastic cups of beer, their eyes filing through all the girls with sardonic shoppers' smiles. Vivian flipped them the bird and she and Lilac were immediately branded "lesbos" and treated with hostility, which was fine, Viv said, "as long as nobody wants to beat us up and rape us."

Lilac was dancing in her own world when Viv's cold hand gripped hers and brought her close. The music was so loud, Viv just held out three small pink pills and mimed: put these in your mouth. And Lilac did.

She and Viv danced till the band packed up, then they stood with their arms around each other, talking as fast as they could get the words out. The bass player picked up his amp and, walking past, observed, "Did a bit of speed, did we?"

It checked Lilac, who'd forgotten the source of her ecstasy, and she asked Vivian, "Is this speed?"

Viv laughed. "Pink churches. Bennies. Benzedrine. Good kick, eh?"

They couldn't find a conclusion to the barrage of ideas that flowed out of them, ideas that bifurcated and multiplied and shredded into shavings. They danced to silent music in their heads, somehow hearing the same beat, making whispery jazzy noises. Viv did a soft-shoe polka, like something she must've seen at a Lutheran church fundraiser sometime in her past.

The janitor finally came for them, wearily, kindly, an old guy with a nicotine face. Lilac and Viv called him "melting man" because the drug made his face look like melting wax. They hugged melting man as he ushered them to the back door and out into the alley. "You look like a pair of raccoons," he told them. "Go home."

While they walked over the bridge, they sang the song by the Animals, "We Gotta Get Out of This Place." Viv said she didn't want to go home. She said that her grandfather wore a heavy cashmere bathrobe with a lamb collar, and he'd be waiting for her in the dark kitchen when she unlocked the door at the back of the house, not far from where they stood now, his large, sloping property and the stone house with a great belvedere that overlooked the river—what Vivian had once described as "folly architecture," a fake turret that gave the house the theatrical appearance of a medieval fortress. "His wheelchair is huge," she said. "Big enough for two."

"Why don't you get your own place?" Lilac asked.

Vivian's body hummed. She bristled, wide-eyed. "I can't."

"Don't go home tonight. Come and stay with me."

"No," Vivian answered curtly.

"He's a monster, your grandfather."

"No, he's not." Vivian gave her a hostile, resentful look. "He's old, that's all. Don't you know any old people? He loves me."

"That's what they say. They say they love you."

Viv stopped, confused, and suspicious. "Who does?"

"Nobody," Lilac answered quickly. "Everybody. It's how they own you." *. She doesn't want to be owned.*

A cab was approaching. Vivian waved and it slowed to a stop in the middle of the bridge. Lilac didn't want her to leave, she grabbed her arm. "Come and stay at my place," she insisted.

"My opa will be up all night, waiting for me."

"You don't owe him anything."

"Yes, I do. He's my—he's *mine*."

"Come on, Viv. We can listen to music." Lilac had never before in her life made a bid for a friendship the way she wanted to now. She felt humiliated.

"Poor Lilac. You don't understand anything," Viv said. "I tell you things that you just can't understand. And you tell me exactly *nothing*." She hugged Lilac hard then said, "I'm not your friend anymore," and got into the cab.

Lilac, alone, swallowed the words that had been babbling from her throat. She was mad. It was unfair of Vivian to cut her out so suddenly. She stood alone on the old bridge. Two a.m., and she had to cover a meeting at City Hall at eight that same morning. November. A cold wind from the east made an eerie bowing in the elms. She looked into blackness and could sense but not see the muddy river forty feet below. Over there, on the south bank, in clay and willow, a small bonfire burned. She made out the figures of two people, three, seated around the fire. Hoboes. Or young people stealing purchase on the sleep-abandoned city, a camp-out.

Yesterday (was it?) she'd covered another meeting of the Women's Auxiliary something-or-other. *Auxiliary* meant supplemental—the helpfulness of women to the men who run things. A young lawyer had attended this meeting, handsome in a dark suit and persuasively knowledgeable in his speech about the constitutional mandate of the women's service club. Lilac had never witnessed such an ideal specimen of reliable manhood. When he saw Lilac with her camera and notebook, he stared at her, startled, and she guessed that he found her attractive.

As it turned out, he was the grown son of the chairwoman of the board, and when the meeting broke, Lilac watched him escort his substantial mother to a racy little Italian sports car. The chairwoman wore a mink coat, and her hands were latched in front of her in a mink muff, so she couldn't open the passenger door without his help. Lilac watched the lawyer guide her furred rump into the leather bucket seat, the woman's broad shoulders overfilling the small car. The sound of the engine, of gears smoothly shifting, this alerted a desire in Lilac. Like melting butter, the seduction of security, the lure of genteel status provided by a reasonable man in a dark suit. She could pursue him or someone like him; she could marry and live in this city and have children and become chairwoman of volunteer organizations raising funds for charities and amateur theatres. In her loneliness and confusion over losing her only friend, the prospect seemed quite plausible tonight.

She would never be lonely if she became a wife and mother. Ruby was sometimes freaked out and furious, but she'd never feel lonely, Lilac was pretty sure of that. Maybe Lilac should join the Women's Auxiliaries, all of them, Symphony-Theatre-Church-Zoo, and dash around in a handsome lawyer's sports car wearing a taupe cashmere suit and a mink muff. A mink handcuff. She would never end up like Vivian's mad mother, the hausfrau scrubbing her porcelain sink with bleach. Vivian Bergson was imprisoned in an enormous wheelchair in the dark kitchen of her grandfather's mansion. The Auxiliaries play golf and bridge and make sandwiches without crusts. They write intelligent annual reports and stand tall in church basements to deliver them to an audience of alert, like-minded ladies. They are kind to those who are less fortunate; they do not take their privilege for granted. Lilac liked these women. She admired their kindness. And their good posture. And tonight, frazzled by Benzedrine, she envied them their place on Earth, the centripetal force of their conformity to what everybody believed was the common good. These women's families would embrace and secure them like a bucket seat in a neat little car with a powerful engine.

It hurt to lose Vivian's friendship, but Lilac would be okay on her own. Maybe friends aren't the solution anyway. She thought she'd better get out of this place, before she succumbed to its Italian sports car charms. Loneliness was the price she'd pay for freedom.

21.

That afternoon, she stormed past Mrs. Mavin's office in a foul mood. She'd been up all night in a buzz of pink churches and by dawn, as she tried to get ready to go to work, she felt acidic, as if she'd swallowed Drano. She'd covered the early meeting at City Hall and now she was on her way to attend a budget announcement by some politician, when Mrs. Mavin cawed from her smoky office. Lilac stopped, and went in.

"I find it interesting," said Mrs. Mavin, "that you can make such a racket in *those*," and pointed at Lilac's feet in their size ten canoe shoes. She lit a cigarette. "You're cranky. Why? I'm giving you stories for the city page."

Lilac gathered her frazzled nerves and tried to boil down the cause of her irritation in a way that would intrigue Mrs. Mavin. "I got a letter," she said, "from Da Nang. That's in Vietnam. It was from my friend who went down to the US and joined the American army."

"Why?" asked Mrs. Mavin again, with greater interest. "Why did your friend do that? Is it a *he*? I'm assuming it's a *he*."

Lilac ran through the list: Adventure. Romance. Boredom. Poverty. Desperation. She understood desperation. When you run into an idea that nearly swamps you, it's a terrible, terrifying idea. To Mrs. Mavin, she answered piously, "He felt it was the right thing to do."

Mrs. Mavin said, "I thought this was the Age of Aquarius."

"My friend is too smart to fall for all of that."

"All of what?" Mrs. Mavin raised her chin, unfolding the paper fan of her throat.

"Propaganda, pro and con. It's all manipulation. Both sides manipulate the story."

"Really." Mrs. Mavin considered this for a moment and rose from her chair. "Follow me."

Lilac trailed the bright chirrup of Mrs. Mavin's black heels down the marble stairs then through a steel door she'd never noticed before and descended another set of wooden stairs painted battleship grey, onto the concrete floor of the basement. There was no ceiling, but they could look up and see daylight through the cracks in the hardwood of the main floor and hear footsteps creaking.

Fluorescent lamps hung from long chains drilled into the floor above, illuminating countless rows of grey filing cabinets. At a desk at the entrance sat a thin man with an Adam's apple that reminded Lilac of the bump on a pelican's beak in mating season. Mrs. Mavin instructed the fellow to "dig up that *Post* article on the female war correspondents."

He did. And Mrs. Mavin withdrew, leaving Lilac alone with this Ichabod who warbled, "The light's bad everywhere but here," and gave over his seat. "Never mind," he said when she protested, "it's my dinnertime anyway," and took a paper bag from a drawer and disappeared, wafting egg salad.

The article from the *Washington Post* was already a few years old, from 1968. It focused on several women who were covering the war in Vietnam. The women were from the States and from Australia. In their early twenties. It said that the female war correspondents "ask no favours and want none," that they "dress and act like men" and "refuse to be classified as hawks or doves." It said their newspapers made them "stringers" and kept them on a "retainer."

Lilac sat bolt upright. She could send stories to the *Tribune* from Saigon and get paid from Winnipeg. She ran back upstairs and told Mrs. Mavin, "I've decided to be a war correspondent in Vietnam."

"A war correspondent in Vietnam," Mrs. Mavin repeated. She kept her eyes steadily on Lilac while she knocked a cigarette out of its pack and, *click*, lit it with her gold lighter.

Lilac said yes. "I want Vietnam." In her effort to sound cool, her tone turned sulky, as if she were ordering the lobster thermidor. I *want* Vietnam? Even the name scared her. For no reason, the word evoked images of trapezoid cells, bacteria, V for virus. She didn't *want* to go; she had to. "The newspaper should put me on a retainer."

Mrs. Mavin barked a laugh-cough like a backfire, and in a thin voice she observed, "My, you do pick up things quickly." The pencilled eyebrows frowned. "What will your parents have to say?" Lilac had told her a bit about her family when she was hired. She had to give a home address for HR and that led to some vague descriptions of the log house at Rough Rock and the parents who still lived there: the gunsmith and his wife.

"My parents can't make a fuss about it," Lilac said.

"Why not?"

"My father is building a fifty-calibre sniper rifle he plans to sell in Vietnam. I mean, if the gun is going to make money for my family, I should definitely see the war for myself."

As if something had suddenly become clear to her, Mrs. Mavin announced, "Your father is a warrior."

"Not really."

"He is," Mrs. Mavin asserted. "He's of the warrior class." She was spinning a scene in her head and wanted more colourful yarn. "And what of your mother? Such a life she must lead, so far from civilization."

Lilac warmed, thinking about Ruby. Now that she'd made up her mind to be a war correspondent, she felt quite sentimental toward her mother. "Ruby has crazy red hair. She says she's got a Scottish temper. She *does* get pretty mad sometimes. But she's smart, and nice." Lilac hesitated. "My friend came to our house for dinner and told my whole family that he was on his way to Vietnam. Ruby was kind of upset. She'll be glad I'm going to go find him." She paused for a second and added, "Eventually."

An interesting sound emerged from Mrs. Mavin's ornately wrinkled face, a girlish trill. "You're a couple of Valkyries! Your mother and you," she announced. "The lover of heroes. And the escort of the dead." She saw Lilac's face. "What's wrong?"

"Nothing." Lilac had seen Valkyries in an Avengers comic book that Judy, her almost-friend back at Minaki, brought to school one day. She and Judy had laughed about the padded bras on the "Lady Liberators" riding winged horses to slay bad guys. "What does that mean, the escort of the dead?"

"Oh, it's an old Norse saga. You should read it sometime. The beautiful Valkyrie roaming the battlefield, choosing who shall live and who shall ascend to Valhalla."

Lilac had never heard anybody talk so grandly. It made her squeamish. "At any rate," she said, "Kal and Ruby can hardly complain about me going."

"I wonder." Mrs. Mavin lit a cigarette while one already burned in the little clay ashtray in the shape of a child's hand.

Lilac was considering what she would do if Mrs. Mavin said no. She'd have to go to Vietnam without a retainer.

Mrs. Mavin looked torn. "It's too dangerous," she declared. Lilac reminded her that female journalists were already there. Mrs. Mavin's head began to shake indecisively. She sighed and gave Lilac a surprisingly tender look. "The decision has to go *up,*" she declared. Lilac asked what was "up," and Mrs. Mavin sighed again. "Oh, Lilac. It's not my call. You'll have to talk to the managing editor. Do you know who that is? Mr. Fred Wiley." She raised a manicured finger with a knobby knuckle. "Take it upstairs."

Lilac was almost out the door when she heard Mrs. Mavin mutter, "God help us all."

22.

The staff called him Wiley the Fox. In the few weeks since Lilac had started working here, Wiley had grown a greying auburn moustache with matching sideburns, which was confusing because jet-black hair grew like a pelt on his square head. When she tapped at the frame of his open door, she found him posed with one haunch on the corner of his messy desk. She had an alarming view of canary-yellow argyle socks beneath blue pinstriped bell-bottoms. Behind him, a colour TV flickered with images of a soldier touching a cigarette lighter to the roof of a thatched hut amid tall grasses. The camera backed away to reveal smoke billowing from several huts and a tiny old man pleading with the soldier.

Mr. Wiley saw Lilac and announced, "There you are!" He turned around, switched off the TV, then faced her again. "The tall girl from the country."

She thought he had her mixed up with someone else, and offered her hand, reminding him of her name. "Lilac Welsh."

"Oh, I know who you are. I've heard great things about you. Top-notch on that tragedy at the zoo."

But when Mr. Wiley heard Lilac propose that the *Tribune* pay her for stories from the Vietnam War, he went very still before rising slowly to make his way to the chair behind his desk and sit cautiously. "Where'd you get that idea?" he asked in a solemn voice.

"Mrs. Mavin showed me an article in the *Washington Post*. About women covering the war from Saigon."

"Mrs. Mavin did, did she?" He looked unnerved, almost guilty, just like Mrs. Mavin.

Lilac figured it would be a tough sell. "It's the big story for my generation, Mr. Wiley."

"You can call me Fred. I don't know about 'your generation,' Lilac, but you're right. It's a big story." He was studying her warily. "What makes you think you can handle it?"

"Well. I have an idea. A focus. For starters." And she told Wiley about the young man from Thunder Bay who had travelled down to Grand Forks and joined the US military to go fight the war in Vietnam. "It's important," she said. "Everybody's talking about the hippies, and the student protests, and Woodstock and all that. But did you know, fifteen thousand Canadians like my friend have joined up and gone over?" She didn't know the correct figure but took a chance.

"Of course I know that. It's my job," he answered quickly. (Lilac observed that some people's pupils get small when they lie.) "It's also my job to look after our employees."

"Mr. Wiley. I have to go to Vietnam. It's the story of my—"

"Generation. Yeah. I know. Then maybe you should stay safe right here and read about it in *Rolling Stone*. Am I right or am I right? You been reading the *Stone*?" He smiled. "Smoking a little" —he made a toking gesture—"doobie?"

"I read the *Washington Post* and the *New York Times*," she answered politely. "And *Canadian Dimension. Maclean's.* The *Montreal Star.* The *Toronto Daily Star. Life,* and *Time.* And the *Stone.*"

He stopped smiling. "You're dead serious."

"I am."

He put his elbows on his desk and leaned his head in his hand. "Christ." He looked down at the green felt pad on his desk and blew away a trace of pencil shaving, muttering, "Send a girl to goddamn Vietnam…" He scratched his jaw, speaking low, as if to himself. "You've got the paw."

"Pardon?"

He picked up a pencil and mimicked writing. "The paw. You write well." Resentfully, he added, "And you've got an eye. That tiger…" He sighed and shook his head. "Christ."

Lilac saw that he was tempted, that he felt guilty over such temptation. She held her breath and gently pushed. "It would be great for the newspaper."

"I know," he answered sharply. "It's just—How old are you, anyway?"

"Twenty-one." So far, no one had called her bluff.

He dug his finger in his ear, muttering, "Twenty-one."

"Age of majority," she told him. But stopped. He mustn't feel coerced, she knew that.

"Have you talked to anyone else about this?"

"Mrs. Mavin."

"I know that," he said sharply. "What I mean is—have you talked to any other newspaper?"

The question surprised her. Her heart began to race. She had him. "Not formally," she lied. He would be thinking about the *Winnipeg Free Press,* his big, and more successful, competitor. But another idea sprang into Lilac's head. A different kind of newspaper. She would cinch this deal and then go to the *Loving Couch,* an alternate rag with ads for head shops and interviews with rock bands, a mimeographed folio drenched in ink and patchouli oil. War stories in the *Loving Couch*. The local *Stone*. The idea amused her so much she smiled.

Wiley saw the smile and said, "It's got to be exclusive."

"I won't sell my stories to the *Free Press*, if that's what's worrying you."

He sighed. "Jesus. I must be out of my mind." Then he slouched, and gave in. "Okay, kid."

Lilac's mouth was suddenly dry. She thanked him, trying not to be effusive. He said, "This is lunacy." And pointed at her. "No battlefield stuff." He jerked his thumb back toward the blank TV. "No jungles, no burning huts, no executions. Hear me? You stay in Saigon. Get an interview with your friend from Thunder Bay. That kind of thing. What the women are doing, you know, the... the peasants. Survivor stories. Right? Lilac? Agreed?"

She agreed.

He stood up and walked her to the door, where he shook her hand. "Scares the hell out of me," he said.

She told him she'd be careful. He seemed so defeated and conflicted. "It'll be all right," she told him.

He shook his head. "Be very careful. You've got a future. Don't lose it."

23.

In a celebratory mood, Lilac grabbed her parka and marched the few blocks to the offices of the *Loving Couch*. Their offices were much like the rag itself, baroque and scrappy, a dazzling mess of Warhol, Klimt, 1930s German kitsch, and Russian *nyet* in red and black. Where the mechanics in Minaki would hang *Hustler* centrefolds in their shops, these guys went for Pre-Raphaelite ladies in lace with huge hair and snowy shoulders, swooning over themselves in a mirror, very soft porn.

She discovered the staff of four passing a spliff between them. Two of them lounged on a futon loaded with Indian print pillows while the other two were upright, playing an edgy game of foosball. They all said, "Hey." She declined a toke because she didn't want to be stoned when she returned to the *Tribune* to get her camera and say goodbye to Mrs. Mavin and negotiate her pay. They said it was "heavy" that she was on her way to Vietnam but didn't seem particularly surprised, and if she wanted to send them stories from "the fascist war," that was totally cool with them.

When her eyes had adjusted to the design chaos of their digs, she saw that they were each of a specific type, as if drawn for a Marvel comic anniversary issue. There was one fat guy in a black T-shirt, one ultra-skinny dude, a nerd in thick glasses, and a bearded sybarite with limpid Paul McCartney eyes who found a way to sit close to her on the futon and stare at her legs.

It soon came time to bargain. She was arguing for the industry standard of thirteen cents a word against their counter-offer of free copies of her own stories when the black T-shirt felt compelled to tell her that he was "a Trotskyite." She didn't know what he meant by that except that she wasn't going to be paid scale. She started to laugh.

The nerd gave a clear-eyed half smile and in a concise, robotic voice asked her what was funny. "Us?" he guessed good-naturedly. He had a laugh like a staple gun.

She waved, hoping to indicate cosmic merriment, but the nerd was lucid even if he was stoned. "You're really going to Vietnam?"

he asked, coming to stand before her. When she said that she was, he considered this seriously. "You know you're going to hell, don't you?"

She laughed again, thinking that he was speaking of her ultimate fate.

"What are you seeking on your pilgrimage?" he asked.

Lilac looked into the nerd's bottle-thick glasses. He was sustaining her gaze into his kaleidoscopic eyes for as long as she liked. But finally he blinked and backed off and said, "We'll pay you fifty bucks for four hundred words, a hundred for eight, hundred fifty for a thousand, can't go any higher than that."

She breathed out. "Thank you."

"Make it good," he said.

The black T-shirt protested, "Where the fuck do we get that kind of bread?"

The nerd reached into his jean pocket, withdrew a tormented black leather wallet, and handed her two twenties and a ten. "A retainer," he said.

He accompanied her out. They stood at the doorway in the damp November chill with a view of a back lane behind Main Street. An Indian man in rags lay passed out on a piece of cardboard outside the brick building. The nerd's gaze was dispassionate, but he seemed puzzled by the world beyond his funky office. He said, "It's fucked up everywhere."

Lilac liked his bewildered, disappointed clarity. He was of this world the way the decimal system is of this world. She thanked him again and told him she hoped he would enjoy the stories she would send.

He shook her hand. "Keep it together," he advised. "Don't go crazy in Crazyville. Stay away from the shit."

She promised that she would stay away from the shit. And walked back to the *Tribune* to tell Mrs. Mavin that things had gone "smoothly" with Mr. Wiley. She was saying that she'd need a bit of extra cash for the plane ticket when Mrs. Mavin interrupted her.

"So you're going?" Mrs. Mavin asked, paling a little beneath the pink pollen of her face powder.

Lilac said yes she was, as soon as she could get a plane ticket. "I might need—"

Mrs. Mavin interrupted again. "You're sure?"

"Of course." To lighten the mood Lilac told Mrs. Mavin about her conquest of the *Loving Couch*, thinking it might amuse her. "Winnipeg's *Rolling Stone*," she added.

Mrs. Mavin shook her head. "Potheads. Communists."

"Trotskyite," said Lilac.

"Write for *us*, Lilac. Write about the war, write about what it does to people. Make the writing good. Send me the story of your young soldier. Go find him. Focus on that. It'll help, you'll see, if you have a focus." And with her sharp red nails she opened her black patent leather purse and removed five one-hundred-dollar bills. "Take this. It'll get you started."

It was marvellous and dizzying how quickly her boss assumed that Lilac was actually who she said she was: a writer with the chops to become a journalist in a war zone. Lilac took the money, thanked her, and was turning away with a bit of a pang when Mrs. Mavin said, "Wait a sec." She lifted a quivering hand to tap Lilac's chin with her lacquered fingers. "You're brave."

"I know," said Lilac.

"But I can't let you go." Her eyes reddened. She governed herself and gave a tight smile. "Not without some kind of assurance that you're going to be all right over there."

"I'll be careful."

"Yes. Do. Be very careful." Her handbag, gaping open, hung from her elbow and now she fished her gold Cross pen and a small pad of paper from it. "I know someone there. In Saigon. He's a photojournalist"—she looked up to smile brightly (if a little condescendingly, Lilac thought)—"like you. He's with UPI. He's actually my nephew. The son of my *much* older sister. Whom I don't see anymore. We're 'estranged.' Isn't that a terrible word? But my nephew is grand. Just *grand*. His name is Larry. Larry Donovan," she said, writing it down.

"Larry Donovan," Lilac repeated. "Larry Donovan? Isn't he—famous?" She'd seen his work in *Life*, in *Time*. "Didn't he win a prize?"

"A Pulitzer." Mrs. Mavin flushed with pleasure. The smiling wrinkles looked decorative, like antique silverware. "I come from an old newspaper family, down in Chicago. Larry's our big star."

"Wow. But—would he have time to see me?"

Mrs. Mavin tipped her head, staring, as if taking Lilac's picture. Her eyes reddened again and she blinked hard, smiling tightly. "You'll find him at the Caravelle Hotel in Saigon. Now, you'd better run along, before Wiley and I come to our senses."

PART TWO

1.

Lilac arrived in Saigon at midnight on a flight from Hong Kong filled with foul-smelling, hungover soldiers returning to war from a few days of R and R. She emerged from the plane into hot night air and descended to a tarmac still radiating the day's heat, where hundreds of grey metal containers were stacked like mailboxes. She'd seen photographs of scenes like this in *Rolling Stone* and knew that these steel boxes held the remains or the partial or substitute remains, a best-guess assembly, of dead young men. The coffins evoked a tense silence in the screaming commotion of aircraft. Someday, Gavin might be parcelled up like that, postage paid, and mailed back to his father at the sawmill in Thunder Bay.

The airport buzzed with healthy boys newly arrived from America, and dazed survivors waiting to be traded home. The currency exchange was open, and she swapped her Canadian money for a leafy pile of piastres. Vietnamese money was a pretty colour and improbably abundant.

Through her journey from Winnipeg to Minneapolis to Los Angeles to Honolulu to Hong Kong to Saigon's Tan Son Nhut airport, Lilac had developed a strategy: she would let the man (it was always a man) do the talking while she listened attentively, spurring him with questions but never appearing to judge whatever he said. Eventually he would get uneasy, perhaps even suspicious that she wasn't really interested, that she was playing him, and then he'd ask, "Where you headed?" No one asked her where she'd come from, only where she was going.

"Saigon."

"Yeah? You got a boyfriend there?"

And Lilac would answer yes, a boyfriend, yes, the war will be over soon, yes, the war is futile, yes, the war is winnable, yes, the war is honourable, yes, the war is a farce, yes, the war is criminal. *Yes* was her mask. She was modest, demure, disinterested, and knew exactly when to feign sleep.

Such interactions changed colour as she travelled farther from home. Right off the hop, at the airport in Winnipeg, waiting for her flight at dawn, she'd sat with three hippies headed for a music festival near Minneapolis. New to the travel game, she told her alarming truth like a magic chant or incantation of her future: she was going to Saigon to be a war correspondent. "Piss on those fucking Americans," said the hippies.

And Lilac said yes, piss on them; it's way better to be a Canadian. Pure as lake water. But as she flew south then east toward the rising sun, being Canadian was no prize. In fact, she saw how quickly her nationality bored her interlocutor, as if she were admitting a personal weakness.

Her passport indicated her dual citizenship, and it was easy to pass through borders. Countless people were flying around the world in the anarchic patterns of startled, hungry birds. Flocks of travellers reminded her of seagulls, pelicans, cormorants, geese, roosting in airport lounges.

The Minneapolis and Los Angeles airports were Lilac's first visits to the US. On the red-eye out of Los Angeles, she had a window seat beside a man in his fifties, built like one of her father's blocks of ballistics gelatin, wearing a dark suit and a very nice gold tie. Breathing heavily, he comforted himself by sweeping his hand over and over the copper-coloured buzz cut on his head. As the plane took off, she became aware of him as a container—or contained. Which? She thought of her father's sociology course: Conformity, Compliance, Obedience. Was this man powerful in himself, or merely obedient to some bigger power? For forty-five minutes he stared at the seat in front of him, not reading or sleeping, but she was aware of his steady breathing and imagined that she could feel him thinking. A mind like an idling generator. Finally, she remarked, "I don't know if we're ever going to get breakfast."

He relaxed, he dimpled. She figured that he must have a wife and daughters at home; he seemed to be the kind of man who liked to chat. "They're sure taking their sweet time." He turned the clear blue whites of his eyes on her—with one tiny red blotch, a broken blood vessel in the left eye.

She felt like a bird, a sandpiper, beside his solid mass and asked agreeably, "Are you a military man?"

He was pleased. "Is it still obvious?"

"You have excellent posture."

He dimpled again. "My whole life's been devoted to the military," he confessed with sentimental pride. "My daddy, my granddaddy, my great-granddaddy, my great-great-granddaddy." He was shaped like a missile. But friendly. "Since the War of Independence," he added, offering a warm, square hand. "Albert Perry." He said it as if it was a name she should know.

"Lilac Welsh. Like, Huckleberry Finn." She figured he'd appreciate a literary allusion.

He did. His wind-burned face lit up. "General Albert Perry," he added. "I guess I might as well own up."

He began to teach her about himself. Not war stories, his education. "USNA," he told her. "That's the naval academy in Annapolis, you know."

"They make generals in Annapolis," she mildly observed. He liked that, he liked a bit of spunk in a woman. He twinkled.

General Perry was retired from the navy, "but not from life," having taken on corporate responsibilities with a company that made computers and electric razors. "And a fine pistol," he added genially. "I'm a VP." But he frowned, as if she'd led him into dark waters, and turned the questions onto her. "Where you headed?"

Destination Vietnam carried specific connotations for General Perry, and in a strained voice he asked, "What takes you there?" Then he suddenly snapped his fingers. "By golly, I knew it. You're a nurse."

"Yes."

"We need young gals like you." He thought that she belonged to him somehow. *We.* She didn't correct him. For several minutes General Perry admonished her to be careful in Saigon, to take a few days to get accustomed to the heat, to the strangeness of the place, before "digging in at a field hospital, somewhere inland, I'm guessing. It'll be hot as Hades, young lady," he added, implying that such an idea wouldn't have entered her head.

"Thanks for the tip," she said.

He was no doubt a nice man. Was it simply his size that seemed so oppressive? His confidence somehow diminished her, as if he absorbed her energy for his own purposes. Maybe General Perry hadn't killed anybody, at least not in person. It wasn't a crime to leave the military with a big pension then make a lot of money in computers and electric razors and "a fine pistol." He probably painted toy soldiers for his grandson, Albert Perry VI. She felt anxious about finding her way to Saigon, and her nerves made her mistrustful. Everything she'd read about the war indicated that it was something freshly lethal—napalm wasn't new (it had been "useful" in WWII, her dad said), but the new defoliant, Agent Orange, had improved the US military's use of starvation as a weapon. This war, bolstered by lies too numerous to count, was wildly profitable for certain people—herself, for example.

She said goodbye to the general at the airport in Honolulu, where he collected a leather golf bag the size of a coffin. He watched her sling her father's army knapsack over one shoulder. "Do you know how to find your flight to Hong Kong?" he asked her, carefully enunciating each word as if she were a little girl. She lied and said she did and marched off as if she knew where she was going.

Somehow, she made it to Hong Kong and from there found her way to Saigon, with the still-drunk soldiers. When she emerged from the last flight and onto the hot tarmac, she'd been travelling for five days, or something like that, she'd lost track, with only catnaps in airplanes and lounges, drinking apple juice, eating peanuts and four Spanish omelettes.

Saigon's lush night air was like chlorophyll. What was she doing here, with her notebooks and her camera? How could she write about this wild scene? The screams of aircraft landing and taking off drilled into her painfully. She lurched from the airport out to the curb carrying her knapsack in one hand, with her camera around her neck, stumbling toward traffic so intense she wondered if there'd been an assassination or a bomb. There was a war going on somewhere nearby. She had no clue what to expect other than violence.

A burly man burst out from the pandemonium and yanked the knapsack off her shoulder. Lilac gripped her camera and yelled, "Hey!" The man opened the back door of an idling taxi, tossed her bag inside, and gestured for Lilac to get in. She did as she was told. He slammed her door and walked around to slide behind the wheel, then drove fast into a stream of cars and motor scooters that zoomed like tropical fish with electric eyes.

"Downtown hotel!" she blurted, trying to sound tough and worldly. "Not too expensive," she added, studying his face in the rear-view mirror. Graphic eyebrows met at the bridge of his nose to rise in a sharp V. His attitude was angry, contemptuous. His radio was loud, a female voice in a snaky melody, like cowboy music but with no consonants, like warm oil.

Night heat. Not even in the thrust of summer would it ever be this hot at night at home. Through the open taxi windows the smell of food, of lovely food, drifted in. Lilac was very hungry. On wide sidewalks riddled with scooters and American soldiers in fatigues, the shop owners — thin men wearing white shirts with their hands locked tightly behind their backs — eyed the giant Westerners who dipped their fingers into the dresses of the Vietnamese women whom they seemed to ride, like bears on tricycles. So many people. It was after midnight. Old women, grandmothers, sped by on scooters with toddlers standing on the seat between their legs. Children, seven, ten years old, rode enormous bicycles on the roundabouts, passing a hair's breadth from other bikes, yet never colliding. The children didn't even look at each other.

The cab braked in an alley crowded with two-way traffic, and the driver waved impatiently toward a narrow three-storey building. He took several bills from her then pushed her hand away, saying disdainfully in English, "Too much."

She'd arrived at a small hotel. Another man with the same V eyebrows escorted her to a room that overlooked the noisy alley. The room was clean. Lilac was alarmed to see that there were sheets on the bed but no blankets. She still expected to be cold. The man switched on the bathroom light, showed her the bathtub, and, scolding in Vietnamese, left her alone.

A bare room, except for a chair beside the bed. Lilac pulled the chair up to the window to watch the noisy street. She had travelled eight thousand miles, and every inch of the journey was roaring inside her, molecules at a boil. She felt like she'd become a baby, selfish and ignorant. With a sudden leap of joy, she permitted herself a dose of pride at surviving the journey to the other side of the world. Here she could almost forget about being a Welsh. Here she'd be no man's daughter. Just before dawn, the commerce in the alley subsided, and into this lull she fell to sleep.

2.

She had a crick in her neck. It seemed that all her weight was on her left ear on the windowsill. A dream was shredding now: she'd fallen off the stern of the big steel inboard and was being sucked into the boat's double propellers, surging like electric egg beaters. The noise of propellers came from above. A helicopter hovered over the hotel, slapping the pebbled roofs in the vicinity with its rotary rap, an unbearable racket that would soon become familiar.

She took a bath, put on clean clothes, brushed her teeth, and went downstairs, where the scowling hotelier took her key. She loudly said, "Caravelle Hotel," repeating the words until the hotelier waved his arms and shouted the words back at her. "Is it close?" she shouted. The clamour of the street invaded his sunny lobby.

He replied, "Close!" so emphatically she decided that it must truly be very close. The way out was blocked by an emaciated man asleep on a scooter, draped as limp as a silk scarf along its seat. She squeezed around him then looked back at the hotelier and pointed to the right then to the left down the alley. Which? He pointed, and again he shouted, "Close!" Or it sounded like "close." It must be to the right. He was waving his arms. It must be really close.

Bright, hot day revealed countless American soldiers with their Vietnamese women. Young, Lilac realized when she got a closer look, teenagers. Girls. Daylight displayed the hunger and disfigurement of the people on the street, their amputations, scabs and scars and burns. Except for one tiny girl with shiny black hair, maybe four years old, in a clean pink dress, carrying a live bird, like a yellow warbler, calmly cupped in her hands, unafraid in its supple cage. US Army tanks were parked like cars at the curb. Heat radiated from green steel. Lilac had trailed the little girl in pink for several blocks when the child darted between the tanks and vanished.

Lilac was so hungry she thought she might faint and be trampled by the crowd. The heat imprisoned her, inescapable. Lost, armed with cash and two credit cards, she could take a taxi and find a decent restaurant with air conditioning. But she kept walking. She wore a short denim skirt with a navy-blue T-shirt and her canoe shoes, clothes that felt like a snowsuit in this heat. Her cotton purse had a big ink stain from when her Sheaffer pen exploded as the airplane touched down in Saigon. Now the purse was slung over her shoulder (Gavin's letter tucked inside); the Pentax dangled from her neck.

She was in a market that went on forever through a maze of alleys crowded with stolid women wearing shapeless pyjamas and broad straw hats. Periwinkle snails lurked in sloppy buckets of dark-green fluid. How bizarre, what we will eat. She thought of the sliver of meat her father cut from the esophagus of a moose and stewed in beer. Eggs in shades of brown and blue nested in grass baskets, and starfish bigger than Lilac's hand were splayed out to dry on seaweed in the sun. So much *stuff*, American stuff, stacks of *Penthouse*, *Playboy*, and Winston cigarettes, Tide soap, Colgate toothpaste, the drenched bold colours of the West. She urgently needed to eat. Black poppies blurred her vision, her eyes stung with sweat. A horn, a ship's horn, sounded through the market and she followed it, trolling through the food stalls to emerge at a green river.

Wide, brackish, Sông Sài Gòn was lined with beamy merchant ships flying mysterious flags. The river was littered with tufty grass islands and wooden boats, low in the beam, decorated with pots of yellow carnations, and barges loaded with pineapples and open baskets of glittering fish and barrels of grey shrimp. Grim old women poled sampans ferrying soldiers with their Vietnamese girls. Ships with guns like porcupine quills were moored at the docks, flying the American flag. The shouts of men, crews of longshoremen unloaded heavy equipment.

Lilac sank down on a bench to watch. So much equipment. Caterpillars, road rollers, excavators. She took some photographs.

Shiny new machinery. Millions of dollars' worth. The familiar ribbed shell of her Pentax reassured her hands.

She grew mesmerized by the slow movement of a green canopy on a tour boat piloted by an old man, a long, rickety affair with an inboard engine that blew thick purple diesel smoke. He had only two passengers in a boat about thirty feet long: two men in what seemed the Vietnamese uniform for civilians—short-sleeved white shirts and dark trousers. To Lilac's inexpert eye, one of them appeared to dominate, to bully the other; he was older and had a proprietary arm around the younger man, gripping him while he spoke urgently into his ear. The young man averted his head and pulled away, as if trying not to hear whatever was being said, and as his beleaguered eyes scanned the shore, Lilac lifted her camera and he looked directly into her lens. She pressed the shutter.

The next instant, the boat exploded into a ball of fire, a brilliant peony of flames and greasy smoke. The concussion struck like a giant oar across the riverbank and slammed into Lilac, flinging her off the bench in a sun-bright flash. When she looked next, the boat was only burning wreckage in an oil slick.

She kneeled, vomited, then wiped her mouth on the hem of her skirt. A searing headache, pain in her ears and in her right shoulder. On the river, an arm floated, an arm in a sleeve, a hand, a torso, pieces of flesh that revolved in the water. Remnants of three men. Grey foam eddied and sank and rose to the surface again.

In absolute silence, solid and factual, Lilac crawled to her purse and her camera, wondering how her camera had fallen off her neck. Her face bled onto the sandy grass, drops of blood splattered. Her shoulder hurt like crazy. She stood, crookedly. Here was an oasis, an elegant restaurant across the street, and she weaved through the traffic toward it.

The restaurant's windows were open, no glass, just iron bars. It had a yellow awning with *L'escale* in green paint. Three large wooden fans rotated slowly from a pink plaster ceiling. She stumbled past patrons who flinched from the sight of her and raised their glasses of wine and peered through the iron bars at smoke lisping over the river. She went directly through to the back as if she knew the place, knew there'd be a washroom behind a mahogany door, to find small chairs with chintz padding staged before a bank of mirrors.

Her nose was bleeding, she was deaf, heard nothing but a mosquito whine, and couldn't move her right arm, the shoulder hurt *like a bitch*, an expression that cheered her up a little, *it hurts like a bitch*, a Minaki expression. At the sink, she tipped back her head, making herself sick again with the taste of blood, but gradually it subsided till she was able to wash. She had blood on her blue T-shirt, so she took it off, turned it inside out, and put it back on, gingerly; something was terribly wrong with her shoulder.

She was leaving the washroom when a middle-aged woman, maybe the restaurant's proprietor, approached, shaking her head angrily, behaving as if the explosion and Lilac's nosebleed were breaches of etiquette. Very dimly, echoing in her skull, Lilac heard the woman berating her in French, and felt so grateful to hear anything that she said, "Merci." She felt unwelcome to dine in the angry woman's establishment and returned to the street, at a loss, hoping to flag a cab though her arm was killing her.

A man approached, a slender man in a white shirt with dark trousers, Vietnamese. He was speaking into her roaring silence, and, reading her incomprehension, he indicated that she should follow him. So she did, down a side street with food stalls and bicycles and a three-legged dog with teats lying in the heat. As he urged Lilac forward with gentle pressure on her back, she turned to look into his face. He was as old as her father, serious, nice-looking, she thought he must be a manager of something, and she let him guide her to a cyclo, which began wearily to transport them both over the cobblestones, a jostling that inspired such soaring pain, she yearned to pass out. In a delirium, she considered the experience of a clam on a rock in a colony of birds, she dreamed the dream of a clam pecked to shreds by pelicans. But then it was nice to get some sleep.

3.

Lilac awoke in a narrow alley lined with stylish shops in dusty disrepair. The cyclo had stopped before a small building with double mahogany doors. The man in the white shirt, with a look of compassion, took her bag and camera in hand then helped her climb down and ushered her inside, to a cool room with a marble floor. He led her to a straight-backed chair carved with dragons and wordlessly indicated that she should sit there.

The silence gathered into a high, thin pitch. She was preoccupied by the pain in her shoulder and a deep hum of regret for the three unknown men in the boat, when she felt a hand gently probing her neck and her shoulder and turned to find an old woman in purple pyjamas looking steadily into her eyes. The old woman came around to grasp Lilac's hands and pull her arms forward, stretching her arms then forcing her elbows to bend. The pain cut into Lilac's skull like a can opener, but the old woman's pressure was smoothly unwavering and she brought Lilac's arms up to frame her head, holding her this way for a minute or two, her eyes locked on Lilac's as if to say, "Take the pain." The shoulder gave a soft thud, the agony subsided.

An hour later, Lilac sat alone in the room behind the closed french doors, drinking lemon water. She had been sick to her stomach, but that had been cleared up, and she'd taken two brown pills from the old woman's hand without hesitation. Pain played her entire body till her toes curled in her canoe shoes. Sun was ochre pulsing under the door. The first sound that more fully returned was her own breath. Then a scooter went zinging by in the alley. The throbbing pain became more friendly. And she began to feel curious, an aura of frail delight. The marble tiles were arranged in the colourful design of a marvellous bird with a beak like a rooster, its wings outspread, a snake dangling from its talons. She studied the bird as if it would tell her fortune, and rested for an indeterminate time in a condition of enhanced sanity. Her hunger had vanished.

When the nice man in the white shirt returned, heat and sunlight billowing through the doors, she was almost sorry, as if he were interrupting a fascinating movie she'd have liked to see to its conclusion. She appreciated the man's scent of decency. Despite his slight build, he seemed patriarchal, but she liked him anyway.

He bent down and picked up Lilac's camera. "You are a reporter for a newspaper," he said in English with a French accent.

His voice was boomy, cloistered, but it was bliss to hear him speak. She said, "Yes," and heard her own breath echoing in her head.

"There are many soldiers in Saigon right now," the man said. "You will have noticed." He smiled at his own understatement. "Others, you cannot see." He waved one foot over the elaborate design on the floor. "Do you like our bird? Fenghuang is its true name." Lilac said that it was beautiful, and he continued. "Our fenghuang is very powerful. You might call it the *phoenix*," he said, putting special emphasis on the word, and, clasping his delicate hands, he wriggled his fingers. "The phoenix is a powerful weapon against our enemies. Yes?"

She said, "Yes," and waited, sensing that the fenghuang-phoenix was an illustration of something as yet unspoken.

"The incident at the river." He looked at her searchingly. "What do you make of it?"

"I'm on a learning curve here."

"You are young. And beautiful. Does your newspaper not worry to send such a young and beautiful correspondent? And to such a dangerous situation. Tell me, how did you happen to be so close when the bomb exploded?"

"I was hungry. So I sat down."

He smiled as if forgiving a falsehood, and said, "But of course."

Because she felt she'd disappointed him, she added, "I'm fond of rivers, so I just sort of nosed it out."

"I hope that you are not overly distressed," he continued, "but it is necessary to make sacrifices for the greater good. The phoenix teaches us this. Yes?"

"Yes."

"Those men were very dangerous. Their deaths will save many lives."

It was the sort of logic her father would apply: killing to save lives. But she liked this man in all his dignity and hoped that he wasn't crazy. "I was surprised," she observed slowly, wondering what the hell they were talking about.

"War is full of surprises. It can make one feel small. As if one does not matter. One might even be tempted to believe that life is

chaos and our lives are insignificant. The lives of we who struggle in a cataclysm can be snuffed out, suddenly, on a Tuesday
morning on a pleasant river cruise. You are at the beginning of
your life, your career. You must not submit to nihilistic thoughts.
Events might appear to be irrational, but it is the magnitude, the
immensity of this time in history that will create the *illusion* that
you are small. This is not true. Do not let this illusion capture you."

"Okay."

"Your passport says you are Canadian." He saw her shocked
face, and confessed, "I searched your handbag, it's true. It is my
duty." He smiled conspiratorially. "But even a *Canadian* will
matter."

She was a bit vexed that he'd rummaged through her purse but
didn't want to seem rude, so she said, "Thank you."

"Shall we go forward with the interview?"

"Now?" This was alarming. She guessed that such an interview
might not be with the Ladies' Auxiliary for the Zoo. "Um. The
general suggested that I take a few days to get oriented."

"The general?"

"On the plane."

"Ah. Good." He seemed cheered by this and gave a happy,
almost martial salute. "How is your shoulder?"

"It's still with me."

"Do you have a tape recorder? I can arrange for one."

"Thank you."

"Do you need to rest?"

"I can rest when I'm dead." It was something Ruby liked to say.

He laughed. "I will consider you my daughter." He helped her
to stand. "We haven't far to go. The presidential palace is quite
near."

"I'm going to meet the president?"

He laughed more heartily. "So ambitious! No, no, Miss Welsh, I regret that your *Canadian* influence does not reach so far. I have arranged for you to meet with the Saigon Women's Association."

"Oh," she said. Another Ladies' Auxiliary after all.

He had turned toward the door and did not see her crestfallen expression, but perhaps he sensed her disappointment, because he quietly murmured, "They are *useful* women, Miss Welsh. Friends of the phoenix." He ushered her out to the street, where the heat quickly enveloped them.

4.

A half-hour later, Lilac was seated in a room much like a furniture display on the fourth floor of Eaton's, a dream-world suite of teak and Naugahyde but for a feng shui compass laid out on the credenza. Lilac felt a glad rush of recognition; it was a more splendid version of the beautiful Chinese compass she'd seen in Vivian's office at the *Tribune*.

Beside her on the loveseat was a Sony tape recorder with quarter-inch tape. She was fiddling with it, testing the microphone, when a short, gracefully built Vietnamese man entered wearing a white military jacket with gold braid at the shoulders and a white officer's cap with gold embroidered on its peak. He entered in a hurry, breathing heavily as if from running, or perhaps he was angry, for he closed the door firmly behind him and stared at it for several seconds as if trying to calm himself. When he turned and saw Lilac with her microphone, he was surprised but seemed mollified, for he smiled and said, "I have kept you waiting!"

Lilac started to rise, but the man waved to insist she remain seated while he took the Bauhaus chair opposite and removed the cap, observing Lilac with cordial warmth. "You have come on a propitious day," the man observed. "I am happy to speak my mind directly to the American people."

"Okay," said Lilac, and with her good arm she placed her microphone on the table between them, establishing friendly eye contact. With one delicious *Pip!* her ears cleared completely. She felt confident, whether from the lingering effects of the old woman's brown pills or from the feng shui grooviness of the room. She pressed Record on the tape recorder and winced from the pain.

"But you are injured?" he inquired politely.

Lilac shrugged. "War…"

He brightened. "Yes. We all suffer. My people suffer. My enemies suffer too. But that is their fate, to be on the wrong side of history. You ask what I mean by this. I tell you, Communism will never suit my people. We are Vietnamese. Individualistic." His round, pleasant face assumed a look of bewildered disgust. "We will never be *Communists*."

Tipping his head, he paused thoughtfully. "Mademoiselle, you are wondering how I can be so candid with you when your press treats me with such brutality. Oui! Tiens! Brutal! You call me 'an American puppet.' But you know, I am the man of the Vietnamese!"

Lilac nodded, her eyes darting to the bright-red button on her machine. The fellow saw her attention shift and irritably he removed from an interior pocket of his white uniform a thin gold cigarette case and lighter and lit up, sitting back in his chair and crossing his legs before he continued.

"I tell you, I want peace! Vraiment! Je veux la paix demain!

Tell your President Nixon. You must bomb the North! It is the only means we have to reach a peaceful settlement! Have we sacrificed hundreds of thousands of lives only to have a bloodbath when my allies withdraw?"

Lilac didn't know what to say, so she said, "Nixon." She felt almost fond of the name at this moment because it was familiar.

He nodded, pleased, as if they'd agreed on a difficult point. "You Americans in the press, you claim that Nixon is feigning madness. You say he thinks he can frighten the North into mutual withdrawal. Alors! C'est bon! This is the madness of a genius. This is the madness of a Machiavelli! Let Pham Van Dong think that Nixon is crazy! Mademoiselle, you know very well, if we show weakness, we are done for! That is why I am telling Dr. Kissinger not to relent but to bomb Hanoi."

"Bomb Hanoi," repeated Lilac.

"Vous comprenez! I say to Kissinger, Voilà! You are a giant! We are a poor country. We are nothing but a fly speck on your map of the world. Do not betray us!"

Lilac took a chance and said, "No."

"Nous sommes d'accord. It is rare to meet an agreeable reporter. But I have given you too much of my time." He plucked his cap from the table and seemed to hesitate, as if judging whether or not he could trust her, then he plunged on grievously. "I tell you, voilà le problème, jeune femme d'Amérique. You have no proportion! Me! I am less than ninety pounds. And I do not feel well! I cannot afford your global interests!" With great sadness and conviction, he continued, "Ah, these great powers who buy and sell small countries." He went to the door, opened it, turned, and said, "I do not tell one thing to Kissinger and another thing to Nixon and another thing to the American press. I am one man against chaos!"

"Actually," Lilac confessed, "I'm Canadian? The *Winnipeg Tribune?*"

He laughed. "Charmant déguisement. It is strange to think that one as young as you is part of the slander machine. No no! C'est vrai. You slander! Yet—I am tolerant. This is the game they call democracy, when even an American fille can speak freely to the president. You evoke in my heart the tenderness of a father. Vraiment! Suffering? My poor daughter must live in a boarding house run by nuns in London!"

"That sounds rough," Lilac observed. She had never in her life heard such lengthy declamations. It offended her Canadian modesty. "I guess there's no room for her here in the palace?"

"Ah! You are all ironists! You punch—like this!—with your irony." His small hand had formed a fist the size of a walnut. "But it is not true what you say. I do not have a magnificent house here in Saigon. I have a little wooden villa in the country for when I need to water-ski. I own no house in Paris or Zurich or Sydney, Australia. Rien. I have no gold." This last utterance prompted him to slap his cap on his head, and he turned and walked out without an "au revoir," leaving the door open.

Lilac pressed Rewind and was listening to the recording when her old friend, the nice man in the white shirt, appeared. He listened, staring at the tape recorder then at Lilac. "You met the president!" he said. "You are so wily!" He was shocked but admiring. "To think that you have interviewed President Nguyen Van Thieu! The phoenix will be happy with you, Lilac Welsh." He was listening to Thieu's declamation, *I am one man against chaos!*, and laughed merrily. "It is tragic. But what of the other?" he continued.

Lilac tipped her head to indicate, other what?

"The Saigon Women's Association." He sighed. "Miss Welsh, I fear that you have let personal ambition corrupt your judgment.

What the president tells us, we can learn from the *New York Times*. But the ladies" — he pressed one palm to his ear — "listen to the ground. They hear even the rustling of the praying mantis." Swiftly, he crouched and one leg shot quick kicks while his two hands clawed the air, a kung fu move, Lilac guessed, remembering a Captain America comic book she'd read once. He straightened and solemnly lifted the tape recorder from the table, tucking it under his arm. "If we are to learn the movements of our enemies, we need the ladies."

"We should be close to our enemies, I guess," Lilac said, the notion flowing out of her as if shaken from a silk scarf.

He seemed mildly surprised but nodded wisely. "True." He waved to indicate that Lilac should follow and left the room.

Lilac gathered her purse and camera and trailed behind him down a heavily carpeted hallway painted turquoise with gold leaf on the cornice mouldings. Perhaps it was the lingering effect of the pills, but the hall seemed to bulge as if through a fish-eye lens. She was struggling with a dwindling commitment to this nice man's enterprise, the interview with the ladies that would yield some form of information, or gossip. She lacked enthusiasm, especially since he'd scolded her for being overly ambitious, and thought it might be time for her to take her leave. When the hallway came to a junction where another carpeted hallway offered a path to the right, she took it.

She walked quickly for about ten yards then broke into a run toward a sign that said No Exit and pushed at the door, expecting to hear an alarm, but nothing happened. Here was a parking lot filled with black Mercedes, and, feeling a bit foolish, she crouched while she ran between them until she arrived at a large gate, which opened onto a busy thoroughfare. A taxi was approaching. She hailed it, got in, and said, "Caravelle Hotel."

5.

The Caravelle was ten storeys tall, crisply white, ritzy enough to have air conditioning. She crossed its tiles to join a crowd of men, Americans and maybe British and Australian in wrinkled civvies and tweed waiting for an elevator to descend. Their voices echoed against the marble walls with a concussion slightly out of sync with their lips. She crowded with them into the iron cage and was lifted up to the rooftop, where they dispersed into a bar with tables set under umbrellas. Palm trees stood in enormous jardinières. Strands of Christmas lights and Chinese lanterns were lit up against the evening sun.

Lilac gravitated to the bar. She swung her purse and camera onto a beer-soaked tabloid called *Stars and Stripes*. A pale Asian man with narrow hips and long legs like tweezers, wearing an impeccable linen apron, said, "Bonjour," and removed her things, then pinched the sodden newspaper between two fingers as if it were a urine sample, deposited it in a trash can, wiped the counter, placed her purse and camera on the clean surface, and, without waiting for her order, placed a cold beer before her. Lilac said, "Merci." It was pretty well the limit of her French.

The bartender, unsmiling, produced a laminated menu, pointed with a long crescent nail at a full-colour photograph of compelling but unrecognizable food, and removed the menu. A moment later, Lilac was half-drunk on her first sip of beer while she devoured something lemony and sweet. It was the best food she had ever tasted and she had no idea what it was.

The bar was crowded and festive. Several American women were here, dressed in miniskirts and high heels or in army fatigues and combat boots. Lilac had never seen such happy people. Her ears hurt and her shoulder throbbed. But now she could clearly hear their laughter and their voices, their broad accents. Maybe among them were the women she'd read about enviously in the *Washington Post*. The dung scent of marijuana was promising, the music loud and familiar, that song, "It's My Life." The sound and scent of home.

Another type of character was here too. She wondered if it was some kind of diet club, because the men were all fat, their guts busting through the buttons on their shirts and into their laps. Their thick necks bulged at the collar and their faces glistened with sweat while they smoked cigars and poured whiskey and beer down their gullets. In accents so Texan they seemed fake, they were boasting about the road-building equipment she'd seen unloaded from the ships at the river. Crushers, bulldozers, excavators, a jumping jack compactor, vibrating rollers—the fat men loved these things and the words for these things, and Lilac wondered if it might be the closest they'd ever get to sex. She gaped and eavesdropped till one of them took his cigar from between his wet lips and asked her, "Ya wanna fuck?" The table roared with laughter.

Lilac felt a light touch on her sore shoulder and turned to find a sad-eyed gent with two cameras around his neck seated on the bar stool next to hers. The sad man nodded toward the bartender and commented, "Henri is writing a book in French about American money in Saigon. It's not finished yet, is it, Henri?"

The bartender, Henri, wiped the gleaming counter, set a beer before the gentleman, and answered, "It is not feenished. I wait for the conclusion, la fin de la guerre, so I may feenish my book. Mais c'est une demi-guerre. And half a war is a long maladie."

The sad man took a swig. "Cheers." He glanced at Lilac's shirt where the stains showed through.

"I had a nosebleed," she explained.

"Ah."

"There was a bomb on the river. It blew up a tour boat."

"I'm guessing somebody got killed."

"Three. Three people." She put her hands to her cheeks, stared at her hands, and looked up to the canopy roof. It must be raining, her face was so wet. But they were tears, tears rained from her eyes to drip from her chin. Lilac didn't cry easily. But she'd never before cried with absolutely no effort. The sad man seemed to find this interesting. He handed her a napkin. Henri placed a snifter of brandy before her without acknowledging her merci.

The sad man asked, "Are you hurt?"

She said her shoulder was sore, mopping her face, then asked him why someone would blow up a tour boat. She found that she could talk normally, she wasn't sobbing, yet she poured tears.

"Could be some intelligence gone bad," he said. "Revenge. A sour deal on the black market." He shrugged. He wore a grey cotton shirt, dry and clean. There was a pressed, sandy cleanliness about him. His aviator glasses magnified his mournful blue eyes.

"I'm looking for someone." The tears kept coming, but her voice was steady. "He's a photographer." She looked at his cameras.

"And what do you want with him?"

"I'm a writer." More tears.

"Are you," he said, unsmiling.

"I'm going to write stories for a newspaper back home in Canada. Two newspapers," she added, wiping her face. "I doubt you've ever heard of them."

He lit a cigarette and squinted at her through the smoke. "The *Winnipeg Tribune* and the *Loving Couch*."

"You're Larry Donovan."

"You're Lilac Welsh. Aunt Martha instructed me to look out for you."

"Mrs. Mavin. Your aunt." He looked too old to be Mrs. Mavin's nephew. "You don't have to," she said, and reached for another napkin.

Larry Donovan gave the sorrowing indication of a smile.

6.

"Tell me," said Larry Donovan, "do you feel lucky or unlucky to have witnessed such carnage in the first few hours of your arrival in Saigon?" Lilac must have looked confused, because he clarified, "It's a trick question." He gave another elegiac smile, but he was kind, she thought, he must be kind.

"It was lucky," she answered. The spigot of tears closed shut. She bit her lip, thinking, it's true, she had been terribly lucky in her first few hours in Saigon. Her work was going tremendously well, even though her shoulder hurt like a bitch and she still smarted from the nice man's criticism of her selfish ambition. Larry Donovan asked why it felt like luck. "Because"—she searched his long face—"I met the phoenix."

Larry straightened. His eyes, enlarged by his aviator glasses, furtively cast about the room before coming to rest on her again. Lowering his voice, he asked her what she meant by that.

"The strange bird in the marble, behind the french doors. Where the old woman gave me pills and fixed my shoulder." She flexed, pushing against the pain. "And then I got to meet the president."

"Who?"

"Thieu."

"Extraordinary. What kind of pills?"

"Brown, they were brown pills. Did you hear what I said about the president? I can't prove it. Because the nice man in the white shirt took the tape recorder to interview the Saigon Ladies. President Thieu wants Nixon to bomb Hanoi."

"So he does."

"The genius of the madman."

"That's the popular theory." He studied her. "This phoenix, Lilac."

"Yes. Fong-something. What does it mean?"

He appeared to be relieved that she'd asked. "Fenghuang. It's a symbol. For Phụng Hoàng. The Phoenix Program. They call it 'counter-terror.'"

"Terror?"

"A CIA contraption. Phụng Hoàng targets Viet Cong sympathizers. It's designed to dig at the NLF infrastructure, gather information on people, assassinate enemy civilians, kill them off, or worse, much worse." Morosely, he repeated, "Assassinate civilians," then pointed to her camera where it lay on the bar. "Any chance you got some photos?"

"Not of the nice man in the white shirt. Sorry. I was distracted." She knew this was an audition; she had to prove to be a journalist. "I did get a picture of the man in the boat."

"The explosion at the river?"

"Yes. I mean no. I took it the moment before."

"Give me the film."

A bit stunned, she began to roll the film.

While she fooled with her camera, he asked, "What did you have in mind when you decided that Vietnam was a choice destination, Lilac? Do you intend to compose a searing exposé?"

A famous journalist teasing the cub. "Sure," she said. "I thought

I'd reveal that the US military drops bombs on children." Was he cruel? Would he abandon her to the carnal pigs of Texas? Did she even *want* his guidance? Oh God, yes, she wanted his guidance.

"And how is life in Canada?" Larry asked.

Another trick question. She deposited the roll of film into his hand, watched him tuck it into his shirt pocket, and answered, "Pleasant. Lowest unemployment rate in decades. Sales of nickel way up."

"Are you a lefty?" he asked.

"I'm neither a hawk nor a dove," she replied, plagiarizing the *Washington Post*. "I came here to see things for myself."

"It's the story of your generation," Larry said.

"Oh fuck," said Lilac, and her voice broke. "I have to be *somewhere*."

The sad smile. "Yes. I think I know what you mean." He looked at Lilac's half-eaten meal. "Great food, isn't it?"

She looked. "Could you tell me what it is?"

He peered diagnostically and announced, "Squid. Eggplant. Marvellous. Eat up."

She did, and they didn't speak for a few minutes, and Lilac felt they were listening to each other's silence, and began to feel more hopeful.

"So, Martha has made you a stringer," Larry mused, holding his beer up to the light. "How very *impetuous* of her."

"Well, I wanted it pretty bad." Then, "Can I ask you something?"

"Fire."

"Why did you agree to find me here? You must have a lot of better things to do."

"You mean what's in it for me?" He considered. "Perhaps you will be a story. *My* story. It's what we do, isn't it? Writers must look for stories."

He had said "we."

He continued. "When Aunt Martha contacted me, asking me to watch out for a backwoods Canadian named Lilac Welsh, something twigged. Welsh. A famous name. Kal Welsh. An American gunsmith living in the Canadian bush. Also, a scholar in mass communication, propaganda, I believe it's called Applied Social Psychology in academic parlance. Michigan State, PhD. Creator of one of the most successful rifles in history. The Welsh Model 70. And ammunition to go with it. Genius, to make an integrated system like that."

"She called me backwoods?"

"'Wealthy backwoods' were her words."

"What the hell."

"You have a wealthy stride. I saw it when you first careened out of the elevator among all those men. Money gives such confidence." He added more kindly, "Confidence isn't a bad thing. Especially in Saigon."

The party on the patio erupted into applause. For a second Lilac imagined it was directed at her, that it was ironic, derisive clapping. Larry was distracted by the noise and looked away, to stare at a rumpled, dusty man who emerged from the elevator to be warmly greeted by the stoned journalists.

"It's okay," Lilac said. "You should join your friends."

"The party has gone on far too long," he said. "My liver can't take it." He waved toward the dusty man. "That's Horst Faas. Best photographer in the field. Better than me, truth be told. He has just returned from a place near Hué where there was yet another massacre, thirty-odd killed. He took the photos, sent them to the bureau. And here he is. Death and grief. Our specialty."

"Is he in *Life* too?"

Larry laughed a lonely sort of laugh, the kind that wasn't often shared.

"I mean, the magazine."

"Yes." He gave Lilac a cold look. "He's famous. Is that what you're after? You want to be famous?"

"No. I want to be good." And when Larry laughed again, she added angrily, "I want to do something well."

"So you show up in a diseased old war with your camera and your notebook. Are you a good shot?"

"You mean with a camera?"

"Not many women would hear my question that way, but yes, I was asking about your skills as a photographer. Aunt Martha said you got quite a fetching picture of a dying tiger."

"Yeah," said Lilac. "I got pretty close. It's a good shot."

"And how about a gun? Can you shoot a gun?"

"I like a twenty-two. My father taught me to shoot the Welsh. The famous one. So yes, I can shoot. Can you?"

"Me? God, no. I had to carry an M16 one night when things got a bit creepy, out near Pleiku. Didn't like it. Hope it doesn't happen again. I'm looking for something less fraught."

"Thus, Lilac Welsh, daughter of Kal."

"Thus."

"You'll be bored. And I don't want a babysitter."

"I don't want to *be* a babysitter. There's something funny about you. I've had my fill of sorrow. I need some levity." He turned his sad blue eyes on her.

"But I'm not funny."

"Lilac, I lost a friend. A month, five weeks ago. He was a journalist too. But that night, he carried a gun. And he was killed."

She murmured her condolences and watched his hands, which

were on the bar where he'd rested the smaller of his cameras, an unassuming Kodak. He was fiddling with the f-stops, the focus, his hands with swollen knuckles and pale webs between long white fingers, when he asked her, "Have you ever heard of Mentor? He was the guide for Telemachus in the *Odyssey.*"

"I know," she said.

"Well. I find I am a bit shaken, and rather tired, and I would consider it a holiday to guide you for a little while in whatever it is you think you're doing. I'm guessing that you're making it up as you go along."

"I'm a bit overwhelmed," she admitted.

"We are all overwhelmed."

"I want to find my friend. But I don't know how."

He asked her to explain.

"He's here," she said, "somewhere. He's from Thunder Bay. That's in Canada. He went down to Grand Forks. That's in North Dakota. He joined the US military. He wants to fight."

"Why?"

She answered slowly. "I think that he wants to prove that he can kill people before they kill him." She was surprised at how hard it was to formulate this simple sentence. Larry looked so downcast, she added, "I'm not cheering you up."

"Do you have any clue as to his whereabouts?"

"I had a letter from Da Nang."

"Da Nang." He raised his palms. He had thin, powder-white wrists. His lips were pale. But his clothes smelled of starch. And his hair, she realized, was a bit long, sandy blond. His age was indeterminate. He was the oldest young man or the youngest old man. He said, "Any other clues?"

"Uh. He said he's with the Seventy-Fifth Infantry."

"He's a Ranger."

Her heart leapt. "That's what he said in his letter. A Ranger." She pulled Gavin's letter from her purse and put the photo on the bar. "I have the names of his friends," she said, and read the names out loud. Wolfman. Spider. Blueballs. Spritz. Gibbon.

Larry heard the litany and added, "Stoner, Dink, Day Tripper." He stood. "I suggest that we start in Da Nang." He saw her hesitate. The air was rich with pot and laughter. "Unless you would rather be a toad on a stool and spend your war listening to bullshit in the bar. There's plenty of that on tap." He was walking away.

She fumbled with the pretty money till Henri plucked several bills and dismissed her with a tolerant shrug while she gathered her purse and her camera and pursued Larry Donovan.

Larry said, "We'll have to take the coffin," and pressed the button for the elevator, which began its clanging ascent.

7.

The following afternoon, Larry got them onto what he called "a flying boxcar," a big-bellied turboprop transport plane run by Air America, headed for Da Nang. They waited only an hour to get a flight and then it didn't even cost anything. He waved his press card and called Lilac his assistant and they were aboard, strapping themselves into jump seats bolted either side of a cavernous cabin lit by an arcade of bare bulbs. The entire contraption rattled and vibrated like a huge amplifier, so it was impossible to talk. Among fifty soldiers, there were several journalists who waved or nodded to Larry. Lilac's eyes filed through the soldiers, looking for Gavin.

The plane reeked of a chemical she couldn't name, and something else, a smell like burned toast that leaked from the young soldier seated beside her, tightly gripping his rifle with white knuckles, staring at his boots, apparently snagged on some bad scene on repeat. She leaned forward to peer into his face. He was gone, asleep with his eyes wide open. Looking at him, Lilac guessed that he missed his mother more than he missed his father, and that he shouldn't be here at all.

She'd been awake all night, too excited to sleep, had spent the night writing letters, had written to Gavin at AB Da Nang. "You're not my target," she wrote, and scratched that, for of course he *was* a target in the worst possible way. She started with fresh paper. "I'm here in Saigon on an assignment with a couple of newspapers." But *he* was her assignment. She was hunting him down. Capitalizing on his bravery. That word, *bravery*, it stopped her. She hadn't considered him brave when she saw him off at the bus depot in Winnipeg. Desperate, he was. Short of options. A romantic. Out of necessity, he had to glamorize the dead end of being Gavin McLean, son of a mill worker. Now that she was here, she knew that Gavin would in fact have to be very brave. "I might as well be straight with you," she wrote in her letter to him. "The *Tribune* is interested in a story about you, and I hope you'll give me an interview." Too cold. And she tore up that piece of paper.

Dear Gavin,
I'm in Saigon. Don't worry! What you said about not getting pregnant? You were right!

She tore it up. In the end, she wrote,

Gavin. I'm at this address in Saigon. No pressure, no
worries, everything is cool. I hope that things are fine
with you. Please let me know that you're all right. And
if you come to Saigon, I'll buy you a beer. Your friend,
Lilac.

What was this sandpaper rubbing, rubbing at the thing she had
to carry around all the time?—Oh. It was herself, it was Lilac, this
creature she inhabited, the ambitious one, the writer, girl, woman,
geek who kept a notebook in her purse, a vampire who used the
desperation or bravery of a young man to advance herself, a
calculating parasite who watched, who absorbed nutrients from
the bones of the living.

She'd mailed the note to Gavin on her way to meet Larry, pen-
nies into a wishing well. The machinery of this war, the soldiers,
tanks, aircraft, it was all insanely arrogant and improbable. Yet a
piece of paper, fragile as a bee, might find its way to Gavin in this
mad hive and he'd come to see her. Then she'd have her story.

Last night she had also, reluctantly, written home to let her
parents know where she was. She hadn't told them before she
left, hadn't told them she was leaving Canada. She didn't want to
worry them, didn't want that burden. She'd mailed that letter too
and was troubled over how much they'd worry now. But it would
take weeks for her letter to arrive at the post office in Minaki, and
she tried to comfort herself with the thought that they weren't
anxious about her yet.

Now, in the din of the aircraft, Larry nudged her and wordlessly offered a white envelope, which she accepted, and from
which she withdrew a photograph. A blurry green river, a green
canopy on a long wooden boat, and, at the centre, in crystal-clear

focus, the eyes of a harassed Vietnamese man in the last second of his life.

She stared at it. Pride hit her like bourbon on an empty stomach. It seared, sizzled. This was exactly what she was born to do. She would send the photo to Mrs. Mavin. The caption would sell the daily newspaper. PHOENIX IN SAIGON: CIA ANTI-TERROR PROGRAM TARGETS VIET CONG CIVILIANS. A man at the very moment of his death. A great shot.

They arrived at Da Nang Air Base in the hour before dark. The base looked like a big rail yard or a massive prairie farm with barn-like buildings and long wooden sheds like chicken coops set among roads and trees, except that the trees were scorched black, no leaves, no growth at all. The ground around the tarmac was charred to oily ash. Larry said that a few weeks earlier an NVA rocket had hit the ammo dump and blew up thousands of gallons of Agent Orange and napalm. She and Larry walked across the sticky tarmac.

Lilac wondered if an insidious poison was now working its way into her body. Years would pass, she'd get pregnant, a baby would grow inside her poisoned body, and she would feel fine, happy and well, and then the baby would be born with joints like potato shoots at its elbows and knees, a newborn with the heart of an acorn and the brain of a corn kernel. She wanted to ask Larry if the air was dangerous to breathe. But didn't. She took shallow breaths, nearly hyperventilating. But it had quickly become too late, too late to preserve herself for a long, safe ride through her life. She let go, she inhaled the atmosphere. They walked quickly past rows of helicopters and small snub-nosed jets, several of them hooked to gas hoses, and then through a cool, vacant hangar and out to a road where taxis waited for a fare.

8.

The noise that had been constant and shrill subsided in the cab. Its tires made a squelching sound over the burned poisons. Lilac was wearing new boots — or not new, because they were used, but they were new to her. Men's combat boots that Larry had insisted she buy from a street vendor before going to the airport to fly here to Da Nang, along with a pair of canvas pants and a khaki shirt. "Better dress for the part," he said. Lucky she had big feet. She appreciated the costume, like armour. Though the clothes wouldn't stop the poisons from getting inside her.

It took a half-hour to reach the outskirts of the city. She took photographs of the roadside shacks, the scruffy grasses and palm trees. Larry said, "Never leave the beaten path." He looked at her. "That's not a parable. There are mines buried all over the place. Don't wander."

And suddenly in Lilac's head she was walking across a field and she stepped on a buried mine and her clothes sizzled into her flesh and the doctors had to pluck strands of her nylon underwear subcutaneously with nail scissors.

Larry said, "Here we are."

She awoke from these pleasant reveries to find that the taxi was arriving in central Da Nang. Night was falling.

In twilight, the taxi bumped over rutted mud on a wide road lined with shops, all alight. Tailors and barbershops, a store selling dusty vacuums, GIs hanging on pretty girls. A water buffalo ambled unattended down the middle of the road, and through the open window Lilac inhaled the scent of its oily hide and mud and the tang of gasoline and shit. They drove past exhausted middle-aged women perched on the broad wooden stairs of their shabby homes while GIs stepped around them, heavy-booted soldiers who'd latched onto the local girls.

She was plagued by the feeling that Gavin was dead. An eerie sensation, something like losing a fish, the line going slack in dark water. He could be killed and she'd never know. No one would know about their connection, no one would ever inform her. "Is there some kind of headquarters?" she asked Larry. They called it HQ in the army, she knew. They would go to HQ and ask for McLean, G. C TRP, 1st SQDN, USARV.

Larry said, "We'll look around in the morning," and instructed the cabbie to pull over.

They were at a white clapboard building with dormer windows. Apparently it was a hotel, but it looked depressingly like the Catholic school near Kenora back home. They got a couple of rooms and went back out for a meal of noodles with warm Coke then returned to the hotel. Larry escorted her to her room then pivoted, exiting to the street. "You're going out?" she asked, trying not to sound plaintive. He was. She called out, "I'll be ready for work at 0600."

"Roger that," said Larry without looking back.

9.

Lilac had geared up for danger but was slayed by boredom. The lull, this slow creep of light across the wall, unnerved her. She wasn't accustomed to being bored. She had her notebook and pen but no words, no music, no magic in her head. Her shoulder still ached. The hotel reeked of Pine-Sol. She'd forgotten to bring something to read, not even a newspaper, not even the *Stars and*

Stripes. It was past midnight, which would make this Tuesday, the start of her third day in Vietnam, and she was exhausted and unhinged by futility, by a total absence of imagination. Her soul was dusty.

It rained. The hotel room was hot, and too late she realized that the open windows had no screens. The ceiling of her hotel room was freckled with mosquitoes, their long legs detailed by harsh street light outside. The mosquito netting hung in tatters. She cocooned herself in her sheet with a funnel for air, but they were drawn to her breath and relentlessly stung her lips, her nose, her eyelids. Sleep was impossible, and in the morning she felt exhausted.

It poured rain. Larry tapped at her door and when she answered, he took one look and brightened. "Ah." Prompted by Larry's surprise, she went to look in the bathroom mirror. The insects had transformed her, she was almost unrecognizable, a face like a big strawberry. Larry tried not to laugh. So, she'd entertained him after all. They breakfasted at the hotel and, with a swollen mouth, Lilac devoured a stack of sweet banana pancakes.

Larry took her to an apothecary, a long, narrow, aromatic affair constructed of cypress wood, stocked with ceramic pots and pestles and mortars. The pharmacist too was quietly amused by her strawberry face. His powders and leaves and roots bespoke an encyclopedic knowledge of ancient medicine, but he gave her Polysporin in an aluminum tube. She longed for the mauve powder in a glass jar and took a photograph of it; it would be a beautiful photo, in colour, the violet powder glowing in warm, rainy light. Her dusty soul stirred a little.

When they left the shop, Larry scolded her soundly because she'd taken the photograph without asking the owner's permission.

While they were at the apothecary's shop, the rain had stopped. "Step quick," Larry said.

Puddles in the road glistened with the dull gleam of snakeskin, with paisleys of gasoline that had spilled from the battered jerry cans carried by children whose chore it was to find fuel. Rain clouds gave way to a clear sky without the cloud netting that would have made this heat bearable. The sun sponged up rainwater, the air steamed and stank. It was heat like quicksand. They couldn't walk in it. Larry woke up an old man asleep in a cyclo, a bicycle with a basket harnessed to its rear end. Lilac sat beside Larry in the cyclo's basket while the old man pedalled them out of the mud and onto a wood sidewalk toward a cracked paved road. The improbability of their big Western bodies transported by a frail old man inspired the terrible sensation that she was feeding off him. He was bone thin, and she imagined her mouth full of his skeleton, splintering. Her eyes hurt from sleeplessness. If only she could see something familiar, Jack pine leaning crookedly from pink granite, whitecaps on the lake. If only, just for a moment, she wasn't in Vietnam, if only for a minute she could be at Rough Rock and breathe that sweet forest air, she would remember who she was.

The broken road ran east. And there before them flashed the blue China Sea. The road ran in a half-circle around white sand and sparkling surf. Lilac had read about China Beach. It was famous. The beach was crowded with young men in bathing suits, buffed American soldiers swimming and surfing. Out at sea bobbed Vietnamese fishing boats. Little sampans drifted between huge US Navy ships and cruisers. There were no women here. The men looked happy. Dazzling sunlight eclipsed then elongated their figures into spindly Martian limbs. It was like an ad for cigarettes or Coke or Coppertone. The sun scoured the insect bites on her face. "I don't know what to do," she admitted, not quite sure what she meant.

Larry asked her, had she brought a bathing suit?

She had not.

"Then I suggest you get one," said Larry, tapping the driver's shoulder and pointing to a strip of awning under palm trees between the road and the beach. They climbed out of the basket and Lilac held out a handful of money from which Larry withdrew several bills and paid the driver. Larry told her, "You'll need to learn what the money means."

A few minutes later she was in the surf with some very glad soldiers. They asked if she was a nurse and she said yes. She'd never before been in salt water. It stung her eyes, but she floated almost effortlessly, easing the pain in her shoulder. Close to shore, she stood with the water lapping at her waist. Several guys hung around to ask her where she was stationed and where she was from. This was different from the people she'd met en route who wanted only to know where she was headed. Here, these soldiers existed in the boomerang that would surely zing them home.

She said she'd come from "no-place." Then she asked, "Ever meet anybody called Gavin McLean?" They volleyed the name between them.

Someone said, "I heard he got his."

She whirled around in the water to see who'd spoken. But a wave, bigger than the rest, threw her off balance, and when she regained her footing, the soldiers were already arguing.

Another voice was saying angrily, "You never met the dude. You're just trying to make her."

"Yeah. You're such a dick, Brody."

A guy who looked like the captain of a football team came to stand over her so close she could smell the coconut oil on his wet, tanned skin. In a deep voice he said, "I apologize for my juvenile companions, Miss. Nobody here knows anybody named Gavin MacLoud."

"McLean," she said.

"Yeah. Do you know his unit?"

"He's a Ranger."

Somebody said, "He's out on recon."

"How do *you* know?" said the football captain.

"If he's a Ranger, he's on recon, dipshit."

"Fuck, you're stupid," said another. "You're seventy-fifth too."

"I know that, asshole."

She left them arguing and climbed back up the hot beach to the shade, where Larry sat smoking. Her purse was tucked under his beach chair, her Pentax was in the shade on the chair next to his. Huffing from the swim, she picked up her camera and sat down.

"Everybody takes me for a nurse," she said.

"Could be worse."

"Gavin must be on recon."

"Reconnaissance. That's what they do, Rangers."

"How am I going to find him?"

"You can't. You'll have to make him come to you."

"How?"

"Write."

"I did." Addressed to C TRP, 1st SQDN, USARV, AB Da Nang. "My letter will get lost."

"Write a story. Send it to the *Overseas Weekly*. Your friend might see the byline and seek you out."

She'd never seen a copy of the *Overseas Weekly*. "Would they publish a story by me?"

"They publish the weird stuff *Stars and Stripes* won't touch."

She considered this. "But would they publish a story by somebody who's never written for them before?"

"Sell them a story about nurses."

This seemed plausible. "Where are the hospitals?"

"Everywhere. We could have a look at Chu Lai. It's nearby. There's a hospital there."

"A story about nurses," she said.

"Do you think you're ready for it?"

She said of course.

He turned his sea-blue eyes on her, China Beach reflected in the lenses of his aviators.

10.

Five hundred feet below, waves clawed the sand and stranded yellow froth in thick black ribbons of kelp that looked like cassette tape. Then a fast, deafening descent and the Loach, a small helicopter, touched down on a windy rock overlooking the sea. Larry and Lilac had arrived at Chu Lai. The sea that the soldiers played in at Da Nang was of an entirely different disposition here; the surf roiled, surly and hostile. Larry had warned her there were mines buried here too, in the sand.

The instant Lilac's boots hit the ground, it started to rain, the red dust immediately slick underfoot. Larry shouted, "Keep down!" She slipped, found her footing, ducked under rotary blades that could have sliced off her head, and staggered toward a construction of white tarp on a frame surrounded by steel drums and sandbags. When she looked back through the rain, she saw legs disappearing into the cavity of the Loach as it lifted, and a medevac dropping to take its place. Men and women wearing scrubs rushed out of the white building to take the stretchers as they were disgorged from the medevac.

A wounded soldier with wispy white-blond hair slipped out of a stretcher and ran directly toward Lilac. His right hand had been blown off, and blood poured down in thick globs. He cried out, "Sal! Sally! Oh, baby!" When he was a few feet away, a nurse in bloodstained scrubs caught up with him and put her arms around him, and he let her lead him inside, sobbing angrily.

The sky clattered with helicopters, one medevac replacing another, dragonflies hovering. Lilac followed Larry a short distance to a steel Quonset with a sign that read *Officers' Club*. The rain quit as abruptly as it had started, and everything glowed twilight pink. She distinctly heard a man say, "It's a hundred and ten." And shivered in the heat.

She and Larry found a table and chairs on the club's balcony. Pink air turned red. To the west, two airplanes were spitting flares from their fuselage—flares sparking and trailing ribbons of red light to illuminate the darkening hills to the west. Sand in the wind, and the smell of sulphur.

Larry went off for a couple of beers and a neat whiskey for himself. "Drink up." He began to talk quietly, telling her about a place far away in the middle of the Pacific, a place called the Midway Atoll because it's midway between America and Asia. The US was maintaining an air base on one of the islands in the Atoll. "Sand Island," said Larry, his mournful eyes roving over the hills. "It's where Nixon shared a meal with your pal President Thieu, assuring him that America won't withdraw and leave him all alone to get beat up by the Communists. Very next day, Nixon orders twenty-five thousand American soldiers home. True story." He drank off his whiskey in one go. "Betrayal, Lilac. Betrayal is at the heart of every war."

She said, "I know."

"Every war since Troy." He had his two cameras around his neck and started to fool with the little Kodak. "My friend who died was shot by a grunt stoned on heroin or something. It was dark. There was action. Somebody handed my friend an M16 to defend himself, and this stoned guy shot him. It's what they call an accident around here. My friend was a great poker player. He'd won big that night." He looked up at Lilac and made an apologetic, wincing gesture. "How's your beer?"

They sat without talking for a while. Lilac's hands shook. She didn't know about Troy, she didn't know anything.

Larry finally said, "We'll give them another ten minutes to process the new shipment. Then you can go in and do the interviews."

He meant the new shipment of maimed young men.

Ten minutes was too long. Don't think, just jump in and flail. He watched her fiddle with her notebook and pen. She kept clicking the top of a ballpoint pen, an ordinary pen she had to use now since her favourite Sheaffer cartridge pen exploded. She had a new notebook too. At the top of page one, with the ballpoint, she wrote *Field Hospital in*—"How do you spell Chu Lai?"

He told her and peered at her notebook. "It's an Evacuation Hospital. Three hundred and twelfth."

She scratched out her first line and wrote *Dec. 12, 1971. 312th Evacuation Hospital at Chu Lai.*

"You've done interviews before," Larry said. "Don't fidget."

"I'm not fidgeting." Sulky. Embarrassed, she added, "I'm scared."

"Oh," he dryly observed, "how terribly human of you." But then he touched her arm. "You'll do fine."

Lilac wrote, *Interviews with field nurses and wounded men*. The wounded men would frame the story of the nurses. She drank half her beer, declared that she was "going to work," left the club, and walked through the red sand toward the hospital, leaning into a gritty wind, aware of Larry several steps behind her, but in her memory of this she'd see him bobbing high in the air, as if the wind was throwing him around.

Inside, she followed a path of blood to a large room set up with tall metal hooks from which hung six hammocks. Beneath each hammock was a bucket. Each man was fixed to a bag of blood draining into his veins. The buckets were positioned to catch what leaked out.

There were three nurses, one of whom came forward. Larry said, "Press," and the nurse said, "Okay," and returned to her work.

Lilac approached a hammock. Here was the boy with white-blond hair who had lost his right hand. He was stoned on morphine. Now he didn't call her Sally; he was of another mind. They'd taped his arm tight in a half loaf of bandage, seeping.

The nurse had a cool, neutral voice. "He's in line for the OR." Then, to her patient, "You're going to be all right."

"It's amazing," said the blond boy, "how much better I'd be if I'd stayed in Kansas." Lilac laughed, but then he coughed, and his face was slathered in blood.

"Internal!" the nurse called, and all the nurses gathered around him. A male surgeon appeared.

Lilac and Larry got out of the way and from a corner they watched the medical team rip open the boy's shirt, laying him open while the blood pumped out of his mouth. The nurses tried suctioning. The sound of gurgling, of drowning, his boots kicking while they held him down. Somebody gave him a needle, and when he zonked out, they heaved him onto his side and rolled him away through rubber slats like they have in a car wash. The nurse with the cool voice went with him.

When the nurse returned several minutes later, Lilac hadn't moved. She stood stock-still, staring, her ballpoint poised at her notepad, her camera dangling. She heard Larry Donovan asking the nurse if he could take photographs of the room, then the clicking of his camera's shutter, and she awoke from her trance, as if now she could see through Larry's eyes. Larry said, "Lilac." Then, "Write."

She scribbled, *In the Evacuation Hospital at Chu Lai, there are white halos around the lamps. The halos reflect on white canvas walls. There's so much blood. In the buckets & on the floor. The blood looks like motor oil, it has a rich purl. I could use colour or black & white film, it wouldn't matter b/c the grey faces of these shot-up guys leach all the sound & colour from this cave. There's a beast on the loose, mauling them. A beast that feeds on young men.*

She asked the nurse, "Would you talk to me? I mean, for a newspaper?" The nurse agreed, but the interview would have to wait till she finished her shift. "How long is your shift?" Lilac asked.

"I'm on a twelve with six to go, unless we get another batch, in which case I'll have to stay longer."

"How much longer?"

"The longest shift I ever survived," said the nurse, "was thirty-six hours." She gave Lilac a level look. "Had a drink or two after that."

Lilac nodded toward the rubber exit. "Will he survive?"

"Gonna try," the nurse answered curtly.

Stupid question.

11.

The *Overseas Weekly* would take Lilac's story of a nurse who worked a twelve-hour shift and then stayed another five hours to assist a surgeon. A nurse who continuously pumped blood into a boy with white-blond hair, pumping blood in as fast as it bled out. A nurse who kept at it, pumping blood that drained into the bucket while the surgeon tried to sew the holes in his stomach, spleen, bowel, until another doctor got out of bed in a bad mood and yelled at them to stop. "Let him go!" And they did. And the boy died.

The nurse showered and Lilac sat with her in a small, messy room in the nurses' residence and they got very stoned on grass and together they drank a mickey of vodka and a lot of beer and sang "Respect" along with Aretha Franklin. Lilac didn't write about the marijuana and she eliminated the vodka but retained the beer. She didn't photograph the nurse; she photographed her bloodstained running shoes and socks.

Larry Donovan waited in Chu Lai for all of this to transpire, then accompanied Lilac by plane back to Saigon in the early afternoon, Lilac still drunk. Her notes were difficult to decipher but, she decided, inspired. Larry told her that she'd last another week, max, if she continued to seek what he called "ecstasy" in this war.

"So I should be, what? Objective?" she asked. "Not feel anything? Just see them die and—what?"

"Objectivity is nonsense. I speak of detachment. Detachment requires sobriety. Maturity. Discipline. It's what distinguishes a professional from a clown."

"I'm a clown?"

"You are currently a clown."

Her throat swelled with tears, but she swallowed and asked him how he had managed to work at this for so many years and stay sane.

"As I told you, I am on holiday."

Lilac said thank you for guiding me, and Larry said you're welcome and looked out the window of the airplane and asked, "What of your father?"

She began to stutter. The invocation of Kal spindled threads of anxiety and guilt up and down her spine.

"And your mother," Larry continued. "What does she think of your coming such a long way from home, in the wake of a young man from Thunder Bay?"

Ruby would be worried sick, but Lilac was hoping she'd calm down once she got used to the idea. Especially if Lilac did find Gavin, all in one piece. Ruby would be glad about that, surely. But Kal? He would be angry. And jealous. She'd seen it in him, in recent years, since she was no longer a kid. He resented her sometimes, as if her youth, her potent future, siphoned some precious element from him. It got worse whenever Ruby expressed her admiration of their daughter. Her dad's face would harden before he'd catch himself and agree that, yes, Lilac had done pretty well at school or whatever. Despite that, she wanted her father's admiration. "I wrote to them yesterday," she said. Or was it the day before? Time was a blur. "I wrote a letter, and gave them the hotel address."

Larry kept looking out the window, something wan in his attitude. "What were their feelings toward your travelling alone to Vietnam?"

"They didn't know."

He turned to look at her and said, "They did not know."

"No." He stared. She continued, "I didn't want to upset them."

Larry swallowed hard and looked down at his hands. She was gratified to think that this might amuse him somehow—in a detached way. There existed a possibility that he would dislike her. They were, after all, of different generations.

"Did you *mail* the letter, Lilac?"

"Of course."

Marvelling, he observed softly, "You're so *careful* not to upset the people who love you."

"I have to live my own life."

"And they would stop you?"

"I had to get away."

Larry asked slowly, "Lilac. Were you in any—difficulty—at home?"

She didn't hear the implication in this question; it didn't occur to her that he was asking if she was in any physical danger from her father, or if such danger might somehow be connected to her relationship with a young man from Thunder Bay. She answered, "Yes."

He looked grave, and shy for some reason, and speaking so softly she wondered if he was feeling sick, he prompted, "Go on."

"My mother is beautiful, and I love her. My dad gave me everything. Books, boats, lessons in everything, a life."

"That doesn't sound very difficult," he observed.

"It's kind of hard to breathe around him."

"I see." But his blue eyes were clouded, confused.

"He doesn't mean to be so intense, it just happens. He gets ramped up." Then, with pride, "He's invented a new rifle."

Larry's avuncular pose hardened slightly; he focused more keenly. "Yes?" he prompted.

"It's really new. I don't think anybody's made anything like it anywhere. But it's ugly. Like a huge ant. It shoots a fifty-calibre cartridge. That's normally machine-gun ammo. But he put it in a rifle. And it has a Starlight scope. That's for night vision. He calls it the Welsh Stalker Model 80. It sits on two metal legs. Because it's heavy. But yeah, a sniper rifle."

Larry's long white fingers twitched as if he wanted to make detailed notes but was constrained.

Lilac felt as if she'd given away information that didn't really belong to her. She remembered that Larry had suggested she might be a story for him: the daughter of the famous gunsmith goes on an adventure in Vietnam. She was proud of her father's ingenuity, she couldn't help it. Sweat trickled down between her breasts. The new gun was no secret. Randy in Connecticut would organize field trials; it would, one day, be on the market. The weapon would be her great fortune, according to her father, and she had no reason to doubt him.

"I think my father will follow me."

She saw Larry flinch, as if trying not to look for Kal Welsh behind his back. As if he'd had the same idea, the same sensation of her father's imminence. Lilac was the decoy for the story he'd reap from his babysitting. Clown-sitting.

Back in Saigon, en route to her hotel, Larry told the cab driver to pull over at a black-market sidewalk vendor where he had Lilac pay for a Remington typewriter the size of a lawn mower, and he hauled it up to her hotel room (the elevator was broken), where he chucked the massive thing onto her bed and suggested she take a cold shower and get to work. He wrote down the address of the editorial office of the *Overseas Weekly* and told her to take a cab there and deliver the story in person when it was ready. "Get to work," he ordered, shutting her inside.

She was still standing, stunned and hungover, when he knocked a few minutes later. And presented a card table. "On loan from your hotel," he said. "And you'll need this." He produced a pad of legal-sized paper, plus a box of carbon paper. "It still surprises me," he muttered, "how quickly you can get anything you want on the black market."

He was going, but turned around at the door to say, "Over the next couple of weeks, Lilac, if you get a fever, chills, if you experience nausea and the rest of it"—he waved delicately toward his abdomen—"it might be malaria. The mosquitoes. I should have warned you. So—" When Larry waved his long white hand like a wand toward Lilac, she felt a wave of warmth as if he could heal whatever might ail her, and she leaned toward him, almost a supplicant, a daughter. He finished abruptly, "See a doctor if you feel ill."

She nodded as brusquely as her compromised condition would allow and said, "Sure."

He softened, nodding, "Do," adding, "Don't fool around," and left. She heard him coughing, descending the stairs.

She heaved the typewriter onto the card table, wrote the story, slept for two hours, then woke to edit and retype it. And the *Overseas Weekly* took it. So would the *Tribune* a bit later. She wrote an angry, stoned rendition for the *Loving Couch*, and the nerd with the staple-gun laugh soon wrote back to say that the story had "made him weep." He included a money order for fifty bucks, which Lilac hesitated to cash, knowing he didn't really have "that kind of bread." But then she changed her mind. This was who she was now. Bearing witness. Selling suffering for bread.

12.

The *Weekly* also ran her photograph of the nurse's blood-stained running shoes. Lilac was on her way back to her hotel, hydroplaning on her success, when she realized that she didn't know how to tell Larry Donovan her good news unless she could find him at the Caravelle Hotel bar, her only point of reference for him, so she went, but he wasn't there. She returned the next day, and the next. The *Weekly* took three of her interviews with nurses in Saigon. She wanted to know if Larry Donovan would find her *detached* and went daily to the hotel to look for him.

The thought of Larry's judgment of her work remained constant. A week, eight days, passed this way. She was happy to be working, but she needed Larry to see the results. It was Sunday, one of the loneliest days of the week, late afternoon, and she thought that if Larry wasn't there at the hotel, she would get drunk because she was miserable today, not malaria-sick but empty. Forlorn. But if Larry Donovan would read her interviews, she'd exist, and this dry, aimless emptiness would be filled, she'd feel confirmed.

Henri was polishing the spotless bar top. He put a cold beer before her and declared, "You look for Monsieur Donovan."

"Do you think he might come around?"

"Peut-être."

She waited for more, feeling like a stalker, and said, "I am not a stalker."

Henri's lip curved in a delicious smile. "Non. He is your father." When she vehemently denied this, Henri shook his head. "Désolé, mademoiselle, I am not literal when I speak. Monsieur Donovan advises you."

"Do you think he'll be here today? This evening? At all?"

Henri tipped his head toward the elevator and there, emerging from the iron cage, was Larry Donovan wearing a cleanly ironed grey cotton shirt. "Synchronicité," pronounced Henri with satisfaction.

Larry looked almost happy to see her, a nearly imperceptible brightening as he hooked his lanky frame to the bar stool next to hers. He appeared to appreciate it when she told him, "I'm totally glad to see you."

He admitted he'd been ill, lighting a cigarette and inhaling with a rumbling cough from deep in his chest. "I'm fine," he added tersely. "But this cough is a nasty habit." He said that he had read her interviews in the *Weekly*.

She studied his face, looking for approval or discontent. "Am I—detached?" she asked.

"You display a subtle degree of engagement." He caught her eye. "They're pretty good."

"I'm going to get better."

"Yes. If you keep working."

She breathed. "I'll work my ass off."

Larry winced.

"Are you in pain?" she asked.

"Only my delicate sensibilities."

The *Overseas Weekly* gave her more small assignments, interviews in Saigon with injured American soldiers. Every time she entered a hospital ward, she was grinding her teeth, afraid she'd find Gavin there. She hadn't had any word from him, no response to the letter she'd sent him in Da Nang, or to the stuff in the *Weekly*. The hospital interviews with soldiers were called Profiles, an interesting choice of words, what with the amputations and disfigurements.

Like Ross, a twenty-year-old from Iowa. Both his arms had been blown off. Amputations above the elbow. Lilac talked to him in a ward stocked with others like him, at the 3rd Field Hospital in Saigon. The room stank. She would soon come to learn that amputee wards were especially rank because the men had lost control of their bowels. Their wounds reeked of sulphur, and another dank, intimate smell. Ross was almost well enough to be shipped back to the States to get on with his diminished life. He expressed gratitude for his chance to have served his country. "The sacrifice is worth it," he said.

Lilac asked him what he liked to do back home in Iowa. He liked to play baseball. "I was pretty good," he said. His eyes filled with tears.

The cots were shoved close in the crowded ward. The man in the next bed, a black guy with a thin, elegant face, was missing both feet, the amputations just below the knee. The man said, "Ross played for the Iowa Potato Wedgie Fries." His voice was sweet and husky, like Sammy Davis Jr.

Ross gave him a grateful look. "Yeah. And Joe's the running back for...for the Detroit Oil Pans."

Joe commented, "I was more of a dancer than a runner."

Lilac wrote this down. Ross went on to say that he thought America was doing the right thing, helping the Vietnamese people.

Joe said, "You just wait till they take the drugs away from you, little bro."

A nurse dropped by to check on Ross and Joe and claimed that they were "draining nicely."

The smell was now in Lilac's throat, in the acid draining into the back of her throat. She was starting to heave, to gag, and feigned a cough, packing up her stuff, saying, "I've gotta run." Horrified. "I mean—"

Joe laughed.

Lilac thanked them both effusively and was hurrying toward the wide, sinus-stinging hallway, the broad twin doors to the ward swinging nearly shut behind her, when she heard a voice, heard Joe singing, yes, as sweet as Sammy Davis Jr. She swallowed the bile and turned back, letting the doors swing shut behind her, went as far as the end of the long stretch of beds, till she caught Joe's eye. He lifted one long arm to wave languidly and with dignity, a forgiving and an unforgiving gesture, both. Joe must have been some dancer.

Lilac's photograph would reveal the two men in full, but the *Weekly* cropped the photo to a headshot of two "bros." Ross was trying to smile. Joe's smile should have been famous.

13.

She did a series of Profiles, one after another for nearly three weeks. She simply recorded what was said. If her photos expressed anything darker than ironic resignation or sad determination, if a picture revealed too much pain, it was cropped or deleted altogether. Lilac didn't complain about the photo editing; there are places light shouldn't penetrate. The regular pictures in the *Overseas Weekly* were headshots of soldiers facing court martial, or pin-ups of nearly naked women. The tabloid was an independent medium here on the ground, and it told offbeat stories that wouldn't make it into the *Stars and Stripes*, which was controlled by the US military.

At night she smoked dope and wrote or altered her stories for the *Winnipeg Tribune* and the *Loving Couch*. To the nerd at the

Loving Couch, she wrote, "Young guys with amputated arms or legs, a lost eye or their jaw blown off, or sick with something nobody can name, still claim they're winning the war. They say their country is winning. Or they say, if the US loses, it's because the Generals didn't let them kill enough slants, gooks, dinks. Hate is powerful. The army stole their lives. But nobody wants to admit his life is over." She smoked a joint and added, "The soldiers who look more like me, the sunburnt boys, they sometimes say they're going to get a lawyer. Then they start to cry."

The dark V of the hotelier's eyebrows would deepen as he observed Lilac pass him in the lobby, reeking of marijuana, carrying her stories in their manila envelopes, and she'd leave his hotel to the music of his soft chiding. His children played chess on the cracked marble floor beside the fish tank while his eldest, a teenaged boy, did his homework at the front desk, and Lilac would feel vaguely disreputable in this atmosphere of clear-headed industry.

She mailed the stories to Canada and walked the streets, talking to anyone who would talk to her, Lilac speaking English with people speaking Vietnamese. One afternoon, standing under an awning to get out of the rain for nearly an hour, she learned from a fisherman the beauties and the risks of his life on the estuary, the fisherman making Lilac nearly seasick in the swells he created with his hands. One morning she listened to the raunchy analysis of a witty, toothless woman who argued with great merriment that the American invasion was an expression of the sexual frustration of ugly white men. "Pfffftt, Nixon," said the toothless woman, laughing hard while she pretended to ejaculate rockets. She was a talented mime.

And from a slender old woman (lithe as a dancer, crouched on the sidewalk beside her cart full of pineapples and cilantro, she wore a tunic of mulberry blue; her grey hair was pulled tight from her seamless face, her age evident only in milky cataracts and the onionskin at her shapely collarbones) Lilac heard the story of the death of her husband and two children. "Boom boom boom, America," said the beautiful old woman who lived in sorrow.

Other than her contact with Larry Donavan, her "mentor," Lilac hadn't exactly made any close friends here in Saigon. It didn't seem like a priority. She still stung a little from her failed attempt at friendship with Vivian Bergson, back at the *Tribune*, and never wanted to feel that vulnerable again. Though she was congenial with the journalists she'd run into at the *Weekly*, or sometimes on assignment, even the young ones were several years older than she was—the difference between eighteen and twenty-four years of age was considerable. One evening when she went to look for Larry at the Caravelle bar, she sat at a table with a bunch of very funny female journalists as they recounted wild escapades of Scotch and sex. The women appeared to enjoy the sex. A lot. And though some of the couplings were crazily inventive—in Buddhist pavilions, on sampans moored at night on the river—their stories seemed happy, cheerful, rather than lascivious. Sex and liquor and laughter. They talked about sex as "love," fast love with handsome guys who knocked them off their feet then flew away, leaving them unscathed, apparently.

Now that Lilac had a byline in the *Overseas Weekly*, she wondered whether Larry Donovan had guessed right, that she would lure Gavin from the jungle, that he would contact her. But what would she do if Gavin did turn up in his fatigues from some deep reconnaissance? She fought with the eeriness of his silence, the persistent sensation that he'd been killed, a lax fishing line. She murmured his name while she walked. What would she do if she saw Gavin again? Make him into a story, apparently. She barely knew him, other than in the biblical sense. And would he want to do that again, sleep with her? Did she want that?

Lilac didn't think she'd been changed by her brief time here in Vietnam, and didn't delve much into her new aversion to intimacy. She was extraordinarily stoned when it occurred to her that she really wasn't interested in sex, even with the good-looking American journalists or soldiers smiling winningly. The thought of making love with Gavin, or with any man, seemed ludicrous and, to some degree, repulsive. Amputations and burned flesh, the smells of mutilation, made her wary of the human body as a site of admiration or caress. What made it worse, and much weirder, was that every time she felt attracted to some guy, she'd encounter the image of her father. His scent, his boot step, his sudden appearance at her door, the smashed-up chair that night when he bullied Gavin. She'd travelled far from him, yet he seemed to be lodged in her head at the most inappropriate moments.

14.

Heather Markham, a senior journalist at the *Weekly*, was a plush brunette, a rational adventurer. At thirty-five, she seemed old to Lilac, who resisted an impulse to lay her head on Heather's epaulettes and inhale her dreggy Chanel and buttery sweat. Mostly Lilac was inspired by Heather's pragmatic grit, her "oh dear" ability to comprehend misery in a fine balance of tough inquiry and church-board compassion. Heather never expressed horror or anger over what she witnessed. She always wore lipstick with her fatigues and was ready for any mission. She said she had three younger sisters back home in Illinois, and Lilac figured that might explain why she could edit Lilac's interviews without condescension, never scooting her out the door, though she had a heavy workload. Heather seemed to exist in a time warp, unhurried while Saigon's blurred frenzy went on around her—yet she was a prolific writer and would fly north as far as the DMZ without ruffling a feather.

It was thanks to Heather that Lilac got her own laminated plastic press ID, accreditation granted by the Military Assistance Command in Vietnam (MACV). And, thanks to Heather, Lilac graduated from the Saigon interviews to an assignment in Quang Ngai, a provincial capital just south of Da Nang where there was a hospital for Vietnamese that was partly staffed by Canadians.

"You're Canadian," Heather pronounced. "Why don't you come along? You can be my translator."

They were the only passengers in an unmarked six-seat aircraft—no lettering to identify it as Air America, no numbers painted on its fuselage. A solo pilot. Heather shouted into Lilac's ear, barely audible above the engine noise. "I'll bet dollars to doughnuts the cargo is drugs."

"Like, for the hospital?" asked Lilac.

Heather smiled coyly, put a finger to her lips, *shh*, mouthed the letters *C-I-A*, and squeezed Lilac's arm, as if *C-I-A* made life more luridly exciting.

A clear morning. On the ascent, they cruised over grey smoke from the burning huts of four torched hamlets, then east to a coastline of white sand and blue sea stitched by whitecaps. The pilot twisted in his seat to grin back at them, pointing down to the coast and saying, "When this shit's dried up, I'm coming back here. Gonna build me a motel, sit in the sun, and rake in the moolah!"

The plane circled the airstrip at Quang Ngai three times before making a nearly vertical descent. Lilac braced herself with her feet on the bulkhead. The pilot shouted, laughing, "No dink sniper's gonna shoot my nice ladies!"

The jeep that Heather had somehow conjured to take them the three miles from the airstrip into town was speeding on open road through sugar cane plantations when they came to a sharp curve sheltered by palm trees and high grasses. The driver jumped on the gas and started to zigzag. He shouted, "This here's fucking Sniper's Gulch!" With one swift gesture, Heather raised her left arm, draped it over Lilac's shoulder, pulled her down into her lap, and folded herself on top.

Lilac stared into the camouflage weave of Heather's trousers. She'd literally been taken under Heather's wing, and began to struggle up to see what was going on. The jeep was bucking, and when it backfired, she screamed and pushed Heather away. Bright sunlight. They were back on open road.

The driver still looked scared. "My apologies, ma'am," he said to Heather. "Captain from One Cav got his two weeks ago, just *exactly* in that spot." At the start of their journey he'd provided them each with a flak jacket. But he said the captain had "got his" in the head.

15.

Quang Ngai was a small town, heat-sealed at high noon. Roosters crowed and crowed again, as if dawn never shut off. There was a lot of Viet Cong action here, Heather said. She claimed it'd be safe during the day, but they'd have to get out before dark. "Not much support for Thieu in these parts."

"Thieu?" Lilac stopped in the dust, remembering President

Thieu in his white uniform with gold braid. It was too hot to think, but with a stubborn thrust of childish emotion, she felt attached to this Thieu who had given her an interview. She'd lost that interview, that piece of gold.

Heather Markham regarded Lilac with amused tolerance. "Thieu is no better than Diem was. And look at what happened to *him*. Shot to pieces in the back of a van in '63. Him and his crazy brother."

"I know," said Lilac. She had seen the photograph somewhere, maybe in *Ramparts* magazine: two bleeding corpses sprawled in a van. The picture seemed pornographic, and she felt corrupt, having this image in her head.

She remembered that her dad had been upset about that assassination. Diem had been the CIA's first pick for president of South Vietnam. Lilac's father had told her about an official dinner when he was here in 1961, saying how much he'd liked "that neat little man in his sharkskin suit." Only a few weeks ago, Lilac read a profile of Diem which claimed that in the early days of the war—when her dad was here—Diem would round up anyone he feared for whatever reason and torture them till they named their friends and relatives. His henchmen tortured men and women to death and left their bodies at their mothers' doorsteps. The thought of Diem's sordid end left a sickening taste in Lilac's mouth, like marbled fat in rich meat.

And she'd quite liked Thieu, had found him amusing. He too jailed and tortured and murdered civilians. It was rumoured that both Diem and Thieu had made so much money from private contracts with the Americans in this long war, they'd created their own bank to manage it all.

Heather and Lilac ambled down the main road lined with little stucco houses. Even with a headache from the sun, Lilac enjoyed Heather's errant habit of walking crooked, bumping into her in a chummy way. Beneath the hubbub of children and pigs, chickens and roosters, ran the *brrrrr* of electric sewing machines emanating through wide-open entries to shabby homes where Lilac could make out the prayerful figures of women devoted to sewing Hawaiian shirts to sell to American soldiers in Saigon. The roofs glittered red, white, and blue, formed from Coke and Pepsi cans hammered flat. Lilac shot some colour film.

In her pleasant alto, Heather crooned, "There's been a whole lot of trouble around here. You probably heard about the My Lai shoot-up a few years ago. That was only a few miles from here." Lilac stopped. Heather turned around and repeated mildly, "My Lai? GIs went berserk and gunned down about, oh, I don't know, four hundred women and children and old men, at close range?" She was waiting for Lilac to confirm that she knew about My Lai, and went on, "In the ditches—"

"I know," Lilac interrupted. She'd read about it. The fact that the massacre had occurred only a few miles from here, it swooped her away like a hawk with a mouse.

Heather saw Lilac turn pale and she removed her own camouflage hat to place it on Lilac's head, saying, "What the heck are you doing without a hat, for gosh sakes?"

The hospital was a cluster of white stucco buildings set back from the road, down a long, dusty driveway with grass growing at its centre, bicycle tracks in the dry mud. Heather wore a patient, hopeful expression, as if anticipating a parent–teacher meeting. Her expression didn't even change when the stench reached them thirty feet from the hospital. The air was alive with flies, buzzing; the yard either side of the road moved with metallic blues and greens, flies feeding on large patches of damp human excrement.

The largest building had louvred cypress doors set above a

narrow open porch where people waited to go in, leaning against the exterior wall or crouched near their own rolled bedding. Heather muttered, "I'll bet dollars to doughnuts they walked ten miles to get here."

Two Vietnamese men in their thirties stood in serious, measured discussion, the way men at home would stand outside a hockey arena. But here one of the men held in his arms a naked, emaciated child, dangling limp and unconscious and glistening, polished hard by dehydration.

By the steps, a woman squatted beside two listless children, a boy and girl, perhaps seven and five years old. The woman cradled what Lilac first thought was an infant but was a girl of about three, a huge head on a skeletal, stunted body. The children were starving.

Lilac's blood quickened and her heart spiked. Cruelty excites, she thought, and was afraid of herself. Like pleasure, the pain was visceral, in her heart, her throat, in her sphincter. She asked the woman, "May I take a photograph?" The woman nodded, do, and she did. The electrical sensations didn't stop, the feelings of panicky excitement in her body increased.

Lilac and Heather entered the hot building. The floors were packed with cots and mattresses on the floor where sick and wounded Vietnamese children lay or sat against a wall. The place was almost silent except for the buzzing of flies. Two large rooms either side of the hall were equally crammed, three or four children to a cot. Starvation, tuberculosis, malaria. Wounds and burns from white phosphorus, napalm, TNT.

This was the pediatric ward. No staff in evidence, Canadian or otherwise. A little girl of about five moaned rhythmically, a phosphorous burn eating into the flesh on both thighs, her eyes rolling back in her head, the pain seething in her. The cots, mattresses, scraps of bedding, clothing, stretchers, bandages, the plates that had served rice, all were filthy, buzzing.

A small boy lay silent on a cot, the only one with a bed of his own. Lilac thought he was wearing a mask; his saucer eyes stared out from ashy crusts of what remained of his face. His nose had been burned to a nub. His torso and buttocks, and the bottom of his feet, were charred black. A figure standing above the child was an old woman wearing white pyjamas and waving a piece of white muslin to and fro over his blackened body.

Lilac backed away. Outside, her boots crumbled dry mud as she backed down the driveway till the smells clung more faintly to the breeze. She gasped, kept her mouth shut, tried to force down the vomit, but her mouth filled with it and she threw up into fly-blown grass. Heather had remained inside. Lilac walked back to join her.

16.

Lilac was climbing the stairs to re-enter through the louvred doors when a boy emerged. Eleven or twelve years old. Skin and bones. Grey sweatpants hung from his hips. His lips were lichen green. As he walked away, she saw that his pants were stained with shit. She paused to wonder if she should go after him and lead him back to the hospital, then heard someone say, "It's Friday."

Lilac turned to see a white-haired, bosomy woman in a white nurse's uniform and a white cardigan despite the heat. The nurse said, "He has to. It's Friday. His little sister will be uncared for all weekend if he doesn't go. He'll walk back here on Monday. The neighbours take over then. His parents and grandparents were murdered in an air strike a month ago."

Lilac said, "He's sick."

"Dysentery. Seven miles he has to walk each way. Seven miles."
The nurse was returning to the ward. "You here with Heather?"
She looked at the Pentax. When Lilac said that she was, the nurse
said, "Got something to show you," and Lilac followed her back
down the steps and around, to the rear of the building.

The hospital compound was circular, with a tall tower at its
centre in a sandy yard. Lilac announced, "It's a water cistern."
They had one at home at Rough Rock.

"Right you are," said the nurse. "We got it on the occasion
of a royal visit from Senator Edward Kennedy. The Americans
installed the cistern and Lord Kennedy flew back to his castle. Do
we therefore have clean water, you ask? No, we do not. Why not?
Because Kennedy's toadies didn't bother to lay the pipes to get the
water from the tower to the hospital, and now there's no money."

"Are you Canadian?" Lilac asked. It was the first time since
coming to this country that she'd heard a Westerner say "the
Americans."

Sunshine glinted off the breastplate of the nurse's starched
uniform. She was Canadian.

"Me too," said Lilac.

"Good for you. Take a picture," said the nurse.

Lilac photographed the useless water tower. Difficult: she
wanted a wide-angle lens.

The nurse said her name was Claire. She explained that each
building was a separate ward, though it didn't make much difference since they didn't have any supplies for anything. No supplies
whatsoever for pediatrics, surgery, TB, or emergency. "What's the
emergency?" Claire asked.

Lilac had not seen such restrained fury since leaving Ruby.

Claire said, "I came to this country to work at a place down the road, at what was supposed to be a tuberculosis hospital. But it has no equipment. Zero. The so-called doctor—also Canadian—won't touch his patients. He *literally* refuses to touch them. It's catching, you know, TB. He says, 'I'm a doctor, not a missionary.' So, I work here, where at least there are nurses. The Americans send a search-and-destroy mission in the evening, and their victims arrive at our door in the morning. You know what we really do, with our holier-than-thou Canadian compassion? We provide info." More loudly, "We give the CIA information on their enemies."

When Lilac returned with Claire to the pediatric ward, there were two lovely women in long flowered dresses floating between the beds. Claire greeted them with a few words in Vietnamese, but together they cried, "Claire teach us English!"

Claire. Dark platters of exhaustion under her brown eyes, black eyebrows contrasting with white hair (curled: she must sleep in curlers, an interesting accommodation), a chin like a brass stamp, a broad and prominent nose.

What they saw, when they re-entered the ward, what Lilac saw and Claire dealt with, hands-on, what transpired, and will transpire:

A three-month-old baby hemorrhaging, lifted from a pool of its own blood.

A thirteen-year-old girl with her breasts sliced off and her vagina bleeding (how do you stitch a child's vagina without clean water and antibiotics and anaesthetics?) from a broken bottle (bits of glass remaining).

A woman with a dead baby at her breast.

A boy, six years old, with a hole in him the size of a hockey puck, a rifle shot that had gone right through his shoulder. A heavy cartridge. Quite possibly a Welsh cartridge.

Claire said, "Take pictures. Send the pictures to Trudeau and tell him he's a horse's ass. Write this down. Tell him he's the devil and a hypocrite. Tell him — Oh Christ, here." And she swiped Lilac's notebook and pen from her hands and wrote with such vigour she tore the paper: "Canada is the butcher's helper."

The jeep with the angsty soldier rushed them to the airstrip before sundown, then the unmarked airplane with its entrepreneurial pilot, now sporting a red bandana, flew them back to Tan Son Nhut airport.

In Saigon, Heather kissed Lilac goodbye, asking, "You going to be okay?" and returned to the office. Lilac went to a street vendor and bought a bottle of bourbon and a carton of marijuana cigarettes.

Lilac had skinned her heart, she'd skinned her brain, her nervous system, her name. She'd skinned her name. The one she'd inherited from her father. She had seen, she had inhaled, cruelty, and now she was one with it. She did not know where to go if she herself had to come along. She despised Lilac Welsh, hated every glimpse of her own corrupted flesh.

powerful —

17.

Night had fallen by the time she got to her hotel with her drugs and alcohol, preparing to snuff out at least the present version of her consciousness. She was rushing past the lobby's riotous green plants, the enormous aquarium with its quick neon fish, two love-seats around a low black plastic table, through to a set of stairs that spiralled around the broken elevator, toward room 214, where she knew exactly where the matches were, where she kept a stack of wax-paper cups into which she would pour as much bourbon as she could stomach, though, she reasoned, feeling ultra-mature, she would smoke a reefer and have only a few ounces of whiskey while the pot took effect: she needed to obliterate herself, but she did not want to vomit for the second time in one day. She was afraid of the emptiness of her hotel room, with its white sheets and its blank paper rolled into the Remington, afraid to be alone with "Lilac Welsh," when that was exactly what she heard. Her name. Pronounced flutingly, transformed almost into another language, but recognizable.

It was the severe hotelier, his deep scowl now indicating perplexity. In a tenor voice at odds with his halfback physique, he repeated her name with a variation on its timbre.

Lilac slowed, dragging her heels, wary. Had she failed to pay her weekly bill? If so, she'd have to dig out some money, and piastres still confused her. Their money was like summer lettuce, damp leaves that would spring from her cotton wallet.

For a third time, he called her name, "*Lie*-lah Whay-oo," *Lie-lah* rising hopefully, a query, *Whay-oo* plangent, melancholic. She drifted on the momentum of her desire to be extinguished.

With the tiptoe thrust of a heavy athlete, he overtook her and relieved her of her packages so smoothly she didn't resist. When he assessed the bourbon and marijuana, the V deepened while he emitted his low chiding. In Vietnamese he made it clear that she must follow him, and he tucked the stuff behind his desk, pointing, indicating, See? Your garbage will wait for you, but come, come!

Lilac followed the hotelier through a curtain behind his desk to find herself in a room with soft sconces that created the atmosphere of a goldfish bowl. The scent of cilantro, broth, lemon, a meal spread on a table, and his family seated around it, three children, their mother, and a grandmother, all but the grandmother smiling at her. The eldest son, a boy of about fifteen, said something in Vietnamese, then in English, "Sit down."

Lilac sat with the family at what she realized were two card tables (like the one that she used as a desk in her room) shoved together beneath a padded cloth. The chairs were mismatched, as was all the furniture, and there was plenty of it. A brocade couch sagged beneath rattan shelves. An ornately carved mahogany table had pride of place, bare of ornament. A large mandala embroidered in silk thread, and paper calendars from random years, decorated the walls. The teenaged boy helped Lilac to fill her plate while the family watched in silence. When her plate was full, they resumed their quiet conversation around her, smiling when their eyes met. At the head of the table sat the grandmother, an ancient woman gazing right through Lilac as if she were a trick with mirrors.

When the meal was finished, the hotelier ushered her back through the curtains and placed her liquor and marijuana in her hands. Lilac bowed to him. She no longer needed her anaesthetics, but she took them upstairs anyway, to room 214, where she collapsed into sleep filled with vivid dreams of home, but with strange rooms, fully furnished spaces she'd never entered before, somehow belonging to the log house. A man approaching.

18.

Since Lilac had first written to let her parents know that she was in Vietnam and doing fine—more than two months ago—she'd received several letters from home, all of them penned by her mother. Ruby's first letter, her first response to the news that Lilac had travelled to Saigon without consulting them, was pretty incoherent. The airmail stationery had barely survived her furious scratches and redactions. "Why would you do something so rash, so goddamn dangerous?" she wanted to know. "You're more like him than you think."

But Ruby's subsequent letters were more conciliatory. Lilac loved her mother's handwriting; the voice that emerged from her splayed tendrils of blue ink was candid, even somewhat less maternal than it was before Lilac left home. "We're snowed in," she wrote. "I'll take this letter to Minaki tomorrow by snow-mobile. I might stay with the Sinclairs overnight. See? I'm a traveller too."

Ruby always closed her letters with, "Dad sends his love." It was unlikely that her father would send his love in such a disinterested fashion, Ruby must have manufactured that phrase to protect Lilac from Kal's anger over her leaving the country without his—what?—guidance. His guidance was the same as his permission. Lilac received no letters from her dad.

They didn't subscribe to the *Winnipeg Tribune* at Rough Rock. Even when Lilac had started to work there at the women's section, she'd discouraged her parents from subscribing, and Kal easily agreed that a city newspaper from a small Canadian city was not worth his time. She would clip the occasional story to send home, small articles to amuse her mother, not wishing to display her rookie work to her father. She didn't want Kal's eyes on her. He'd make her feel like an imposter; any embellishments or demonstrations of fledging skill would provoke his condescending smile, a spectre that haunted her at her typewriter.

From Vietnam, Lilac had sent home only a few of her tame interviews published in the *Overseas Weekly*, nothing that would express much more than soldiers' patriotism and homesickness, and even these pieces had upset Ruby. Lilac guessed that Ruby didn't like to see her daughter as someone other than that girl she knew at home. Maybe it was just something families do to each other. It reminded her of high school, where you're supposed to stay the same; to change is somehow pretentious.

Christmas had passed. Lilac spent that day in dialogue with people speaking a language she couldn't understand except when she gave up and simply *felt* the melody of their voices, the music of Babel. At that time, there was a pause of about two weeks when no mail arrived from Ruby, probably because of bad weather at Rough Rock. But one morning Lilac found a packet of four letters at the post office. They'd been delayed till they piled up and came all at once. It was wonderful to see the familiar handwriting, Ruby's impatient feminine scrawl.

Lilac read the letters out of order, then, unnerved, placed them chronologically and read them again. And again. The series began with ordinary observations of weather, symptoms of cabin fever, allusions to a silent house, a silent life. And then abruptly there came references to Kal's departure from Rough Rock, and his travel to Vietnam.

"I pray that Kal finds you quickly in that godforsaken place. Phone me, I don't care how hard it is, if you decide to move from the address you've given us. I have to know where you are, what you're doing, and that you're truly all right. He's my eyes and ears, darling. I can't tell you how frustrating it is that I have to see you through him. As if he's my damn periscope."

Her father was en route to Saigon. Lilac would be "found." She quickly, briefly, considered leaving town. Impossible. She'd never outrun him. But oh, for a quick exit. Why did her father make her feel like a fraud? As if her private life was an expression of treachery against him. But no, he wouldn't call it treachery. Deceit. He made her feel deceitful, weirdly promiscuous and furtive, having stepped out of his sight.

With a jaundiced eye, she viewed her little hotel room that had seemed lofty just a moment ago, seeing it as he would see it — shabby, pathetic. He'd insinuate that she'd come here to chase after Gavin; he'd present this scenario as if with kindness and compassion, a father's commiseration with a jilted girl. He'd belittle her professional ambitions and treat her like a lovesick kid. And his proof was that Gavin *hadn't* searched her out as Larry Donovan had thought he would, and now she was alone in a dangerous city from which her father had come to save her. The scenario seemed so plausible she felt surreal, as if he was writing her script.

In a panic, she snatched up several carbon copies of the stories she'd written for the newspapers. Her name, her authorship. The interviews for the *Weekly* were transcriptions of the young men's words. Yet surely anyone could discern a manoeuvre in her Profiles, a story. She wanted her father to see intelligence reflected in her portraits of damaged young men, her discretion in presenting their pain to the public, to hear the subtle irony in her "opined," her "so-called," her selection of physical details and attitudes, "leaking stitches," "diminishment," "glad sacrifice." She's there, in those interviews, see her name, there.

She'd sent several stories with photographs to the *Tribune*. The photo of a beleaguered man murdered by Phoenix, his eyes in the split second before a bomb blew up the tour boat that first day here in Saigon. And a feature about Claire, the Canadian nurse at Quang Ngai—Lilac called that story "The Butcher's Helper." She'd sent an account of her experience at the Evacuation Hospital at Chu Lai ("A White-Haired Boy Who Lost His Arm"). And a couple of lighter pieces for the women's section: one about Vietnamese women sewing Hawaiian shirts to support their families, and one about the food at the street stalls, with a recipe for banana pancakes. She'd written modified versions of "The Butcher's Helper" and "A White-Haired Boy Who Lost His Arm" for the *Loving Couch*, too. What would her father think of her work? Had she been faking the detachment that let her write about these terrible things? Sure. Yes. Faking it worked pretty well.

She needed to talk to Larry Donovan. Somehow a conversation with Larry might prepare her for the approaching encounter with Kal, as if she could rehearse her lines, reassemble her character. The situation felt worse for her not knowing exactly when Kal would show up at her hotel. She might as well be at home with her bedroom door open. It was no longer private here, knowing that she'd be on display at any time he chose to make his appearance.

19.

Larry Donovan was taking a sip of beer when she blurted, "My father is coming to Saigon."

Henri the bartender, overhearing Lilac's tone of lamentation, half turned, eavesdropping.

Larry's reaction was complex. Immediate interest, and wariness. "You seem overjoyed."

"Oh, for sure, it'll be—great—to see him." Larry looked so sceptical, she added, "He *is* my dad. After all." In the pause that followed, she asked, "How about you?"

"What about me?"

"Do you want to meet him?"

"Yes. Yes, I'd like to meet him, if it's all the same to you."

"Why not? Famous gunsmith. War hero." It was Gavin's worshipful appraisal.

"War hero," Larry repeated.

"He was here, in Vietnam, a long time ago. But I guess you know that. You did your research. Right?"

"Actually, I know a friend of his."

"He has a friend? Where?"

"I most recently met up with your father's friend in Da Nang. When you and I were there. That night. At a popular watering hole. A remarkable individual."

"Wait a minute. That first night? When we were at that hotel in Da Nang? When you went out and I had to stay in my room and get eaten alive by mosquitoes? You went to a bar all by yourself. And met a friend of my *father's*?"

When Larry smiled broadly, his whole face seemed surprised. "Well, it's not quite such a stroke of luck. I've met the man quite often over the years. He's Psyops. A good source of information for journalists such as myself. I first met him way back in '63. And even then he was talking about his brilliant friend Kal Welsh."

"My father got hurt. He came home hurt."

"Yes. Bull told me."

"My dad's got a friend and his name is *Bull*?"

Again, that big smile. An incongruity, it was like seeing a dog smile. "Bull Johnson," he said. "He stayed on with the military. He worked with your father in Psyops, as I told you. Though Bull now runs the PX. The PX is a canteen, like a department store for the grunts."

"My dad had a *friend* in Psyops." She needed to summarize this information, which felt exotic, like ancient history.

"Psychological Operations," Larry explained.

"I know." She cast around for memories of her father's cryptic and often resentful stories about his work with Psyops, where people didn't fully appreciate him. And there was that strange movie he made, the ghostly trees, an eerie soundtrack, the lament of the hungry ghost. *Hearts and minds.* She shivered.

Larry saw her shiver, and he gently observed, "I know that your father was injured in the Mekong Delta in 1961."

"When he came home, he was on crutches. He had a broken arm and a broken leg. His ulna and his tibia. We lived in the city then. In Winnipeg. His back was cut up and he had cuts on his hands. From shrapnel. He still has shrapnel in one of his legs."

"Do you know how it happened?" Larry asked tentatively, as if unsure that he should be probing.

"He still has the scars." Lilac was remembering her father's return. How urgently he struggled to recover from his injuries, his constant exercising in the house, using any surface to work his muscles, knee bends at the kitchen counter, pull-ups on the door frames, the nauseating smell of Absorbine Jr., the sight of him wearing nothing but army-issued shorts, lifting sandbags and then weights, until he seemed more muscular than before he went away to war. But it was not called a "war" back in 1961. It was called a "police action." And he was not called a "war hero" or even a "soldier" when he returned home. He was an "adviser," a "specialist."

Larry was waiting for an answer to his question: How did Kal get hurt? She remembered an uncomfortable sense of shame surrounding her father's injuries. He drew the curtains in the living room. Lilac had supposed that it was just his nature to despise weakness of any kind, especially his own. He sure didn't boast about a "sacrifice" or claim that it had been "worth it." When the casts came off and the crutches had been chucked into the back alley, a For Sale sign appeared on the lawn. They packed up and left town and began their lives at Rough Rock.

Larry was watching her. She didn't like the compassion she saw in his eyes, and stumbled toward an answer, surprised to find herself unwilling to tell the story of Mr. Thanh, the man who had caused her dad so much pain. "Somebody threw a grenade at him and some other man who was standing nearby," she answered.

Larry nodded briskly, as if eager to change direction, and with a lighter tone he asserted, "He'll be glad to see you."

Lilac sighed. "I wonder how long he's staying."

"Lilac, it's quite likely that he'll expect you to return with him to Canada."

"I'm not leaving. I love it here."

"I see the place has done its magic on you."

"He can't pack me up and take me home. I'm not a child."

"Then don't be childish. Talk to him. He's obviously an intelligent man." He reached for the notebook and pen in this shirt pocket, wrote something, tore off the page, and handed it to Lilac. "I have shifted my belongings to an apartment closer to the Caravelle. You can contact me at this address."

Lilac folded the paper into small squares. "I wonder if he'll bring along the Stalker when he comes." She laughed miserably. Alone. Larry seemed distracted.

"Lilac," he said slowly. "I think you know, I'm interested in your father's inventions."

"Yes." She answered him solemnly because he seemed to be struggling with something. "You already know quite a lot about him. His being a professor and all that."

"He's an interesting person. And I look forward to meeting him. And I want you to know, I'd like to write a profile of him. Interview him. When he comes here."

"I think he'd probably like that."

"I hope you don't mind."

"No. I don't mind." She thought for a moment. "I know you wouldn't write anything terrible about him."

"No. Though—it won't be commercial copy for a gun magazine, either. I mean, my portrait would be more objective."

She smiled. "Detached."

"Yes." Larry looked relieved. "Detached. And while I'm not going to write a sales pitch for his Stalker invention, it might not hurt him either. A bit of publicity. Letting people know what he's come up with, his follow-up to the Welsh 70. It'd be a good story. An American scholar goes to live in the Canadian wilderness, where he invents a beautiful hunting rifle and a copper bullet for big game. And now he's created a unique military weapon that nobody's ever seen before."

Lilac heard excitement in Larry's voice. His detached portrait of Kal Welsh probably wouldn't be quite so flattering or simple, but she hoped that he'd treat her dad with respect. It wasn't something she'd ever be able to write. Not with detachment, anyway. Hers would be a misshapen thing, something that she'd never let her father read.

20.

Lilac waited in such uneasy anticipation of her father's arrival that when his unmistakable boot step sounded in the hall outside room 214, she felt relieved that it was finally happening, the reunion. And when she opened her door to see his stocky form in the hall light, she experienced a rush of love that tapped a lump from her heart up into her throat. "Dad," she stammered.

Kal lunged forward to hug her. "I forgot you were so tall," he said in a choked voice.

She ran her hands over his sturdy back, the familiar scent of gun oil beneath the stink of airplane, then she stepped away and said, "Welcome to my castle," a line that she'd prepared in advance.

From the doorway, he quickly surveyed her small room dominated by the rickety card table and her big green typewriter. She looked for judgment, but he just said, "How about we go out for dinner?"

Disappointed, relieved, anxious, she agreed. He had a cab waiting at the front door of the hotel. On the way out, they passed the hotelier, the V now an expression of polite inquiry. "My father," she explained.

"Ah," said the hotelier, then added something she couldn't follow, those sweet Vietnamese vowels, the slippery language that she loved, though she didn't even know how to say thank you. She wanted her father to stop, to bow, to acknowledge this wonderful man, but Kal was barrelling onward, pushing through the front door.

In the taxi, she asked him if the trip had been long, knowing it was a stupid question, wanting him to talk, but his attention was all on the street. He glanced at her distractedly, with a quick, obliging smile. At one point, he looked at her fully, a fast assessment, and said, "You look great. Kind of skinny, but great."

She stuttered and began to tell him about getting her MACV press card but didn't get far before he interrupted. "My friend is meeting us at my favourite restaurant." He peered ahead into the dark street. "I hope it's still here." He glanced again at his daughter. "Bet you're hungry."

The taxi took them to Tu Do Street. From the trunk, Kal dragged a new-looking knapsack with many pockets and a big black leather bag, and they entered a French restaurant where someone was playing a scratchy recording of Erik Satie's *Gymnopédies*. It was one of the few recordings that Ruby owned and played often at night. Lilac slowed, unwilling to interfere with the music's painful beauty. "This reminds me of Mum," she murmured.

But Kal was already at a table in the corner, the pink walls reflecting off his white shirt. He seemed to glow like a struck match, an effect enhanced by the Technicolor giant who had locked him in an embrace.

The giant was wearing a dinner jacket printed with orange-and-turquoise parrots, and blue jeans with brilliant white running shoes of improbable size. He was about two feet taller than Kal and had long yellow peroxide hair tied in a ponytail. He wore a turquoise stud in one earlobe and looked like a pirate, a roughed-up Thor.

"Yo'ol' rascal," said the giant. "Yo'ol' sum'bitch. Honest to gawd, Kal, it's good to *see* you, man!"

The accent was so black, and the giant was so orange, Lilac wanted to say, Come *on*. He had tawny, sun-damaged skin, fine wrinkles compounded by countless small white scars. Even his meaty palms were lacerated by white welts.

Kal pulled out of the bear hug, blushing happily. With his arm around the big man, he said, "I want you to meet my daughter, Lilac. Lilac, come and meet my old friend, Bull."

"Little honey! It sho' nuff is sweet to make yo' acquaintance!"

Lilac looked from Bull to her father, waiting for someone to laugh. Surely the jive was a joke. But Kal was fastened on Bull, inhaling him. Never had she seen her father so demonstrative, especially with another man.

"She's in the newspaper," Kal was saying. "A published writer. Eighteen years old." His praise shocked her and unlocked her hesitancy, and she let Bull pull her into his arms.

Bull's dinner jacket was soft silk, the parrots woven into its fabric, with a shawl collar of bright-blue velvet. The turquoise earring was set in gold. When she pulled away to study the thatching of wrinkles and scars, she was surprised by the lucid intelligence in his eyes.

With one huge hand Bull gripped the ivory handle of a cane, a long, gorgeous thing of black mahogany inlaid with mother-of-pearl dragons, leaning on it while he pulled out a chair for Lilac and settled her at the table. All the while, he was talking like Muhammad Ali, a tumble of accented rhymes and homilies, Kal absorbing him, fond, fascinated. Bull would include Lilac by looking her way and saying, "You'll appreciate this, little honey."

Lilac devoured a plate of frogs' legs, watching the two men, the way her father turned the focus toward himself, and how Bull let him take over the discussion as if Bull's palaver had been purposed to build Kal's confidence, let him become comfortable enough to talk freely. They hadn't seen each other in a decade, yet apparently a deep-running current ran under their codes and shortcuts.

After a bottle of wine, Kal was deep into a disquisition on his bullet, the Welsh X, when he surprised Lilac by squeezing her shoulder then rubbing her back, as if she had somehow helped foster his inventions. His touch made her heart lurch with a mix of love and lingering resentment of his power over her. Her dad had developed the bullet and the Welsh Model 70 in the years since he'd last seen Bull. He needed to show Bull how much he'd accomplished. She would be one of his accomplishments.

"The Welsh *Precision* X," Bull said, relishing its full name. "*Precise*. I like that in a bullet."

Kal pulled one from his shirt pocket—he must have stashed it there so he could reveal it to Bull—and laid it on the white tablecloth the way a jeweller would display a brooch. Its copper jacket gleamed ruddy by candlelight. He lifted the base end of the bullet. "Boattail," he said. "I narrowed the base. No drag. Twenty percent deeper penetration."

Bull breathed his admiration, and said to Lilac, "Your daddio is one smart dude."

"I know," said Lilac. She caught her father's eye before he quickly looked away.

"You mus' love him to bits," Bull insisted.

Lilac opened her mouth but could only say, "It's complicated."

Bull roared with laughter. "Gawd, she's got your golden tongue, Kal. She's got your way of saying nothin' like it's a clue to the universe. That is *gnomic*!" he declared. "You know what *gnomic* means, little darlin'? It means you are a mystery, gal. Just the prettiest little mystery."

21.

Kal emptied his glass, set it down firmly, and asked Lilac, "Did you find him?"

Gavin. It had taken her father two bottles of wine before he thought to ask her about Gavin. Or about anything, for that matter.

"He was in Da Nang," she said. "He's a Ranger. That's all I know."

"Good," Kal breathed. "Good for him." To Bull, "A...close friend of Lilac's...enlisted. He's a Ranger." He called to the waiter, "My daughter would like crepes Suzette," and lofting an empty wine bottle, he added, "Bring us another."

Lilac did not want crepes Suzette. Then she did. She wanted to please him and she wanted to be clear of him. She said, "I don't know if Gavin is still alive."

Bull announced to the waiter that he was switching to beer, but his eyes remained on Lilac. "Friend of yours? They call his number?" He looked to Kal in some confusion. "Now, I might be mistaken, but I thought you been raising your famb'ly up in Canada."

Lilac told Bull, "Gavin's from Thunder Bay. That's in Ontario."

"And he joined up? Of his own free will? This late in the game?" To Kal, in real consternation, Bull asked, "Why would a nice Ont-air-ee-o boy go and do something crazy like that?"

Kal interrupted. "It's exactly the time for serious young men to step up. For the final push."

"The final—" Bull broke off. He ran his big hand over his face.

The waiter brought Bull's beer, and the crepes Suzette, and another bottle of red for Kal, but Kal said, "I didn't order that. Take it away." The waiter almost masked his distaste, and replaced the bottle on the tray. "I'll take a cognac," said Kal. "You want a cognac?" he asked Lilac. She didn't want a cognac. But she asked for a beer. It would clear her head.

Bull's mood had declined, got blue; he tapped his lips with his fingers. "You been away a long time," he finally said to Kal. "Making your inventions. The Precise X. And your pretty gun. Up there in Canada. Maybe out of touch with the world."

"My pretty gun is all over this war. Or haven't you noticed?"

"Sure. Sure, I notice it all the time. Welsh 70 gets lots of respect around here. Lots of respect. You done very well for yourself, Kal. And I'm glad. An' proud of you. A man's got to look after his famb'ly." To Lilac, "He'll always look after you, little darlin'. You and your ma."

"Lilac is going to be rich."

"I'm going to be a writer," said Lilac, and felt silly. "I mean, I'm—going to work at it."

"That's good, that's fine," Bull said softly. "You got your daddy's brains and your mama's good looks. Just like the song." To Kal, "She's just like the song, Kal. Her daddy's rich and her mama's a beauty. I seen pictures of your mama when your daddy was here in '61. He was proud of you. But he was *afraid* of your mama. You were a skinny little kid. But your mama, she was beautiful. A very fine woman. And now you're all grown up. With a friend who's a Ranger, even if he didn't have to be. You heard he was based in Da Nang?"

Lilac said yes, but she didn't know where he was now. "I'm still hoping he'll contact me," she said. Her eyes darted to Kal.

"Of course he will," said Kal. "He's a good man."

Lilac squirmed. "I'm supposed to be writing a piece on him for the *Tribune*." But her father wasn't listening. The waiter returned with her beer and Kal's cognac. She took a goodly slug and said to

Bull, "I hope he'll eventually see my name in the *Overseas Weekly* and get in touch somehow. For the story. And so we all know he's all right." Bull was making low thrumming noises from his massive chest, his intelligent eyes in that scarred face watching her with kindness, as if he'd like to grant all her wishes. He was like a stained-glass window, colourful, and cut up. She trusted him. "I'd just like to know that Gavin is okay."

"Course you would," said Bull.

"I should go back to Da Nang to try to find him."

Bull shook his head. "Hairy up there these days."

"What happened to your hands?" she asked before she could censor herself. She could feel Kal in his chair, drinking his cognac but still sober enough; he placed his own hands on the table.

Bull said, "Uh." He shifted his body, arranging his legs. He had to lift one leg with his hands and place it, and he winced. "Won't bore you *that* way." To Kal, "We ain't gonna be old vets with a story. Are we, brother." He drank his beer. "Never let the cat outta the bag."

She stared at him. "You were there. When my dad got hurt."

He shrugged. "I was close in the neighbourhood."

She realized that Bull was that "other man standing nearby," an anonymous American injured in the same attack; a blurred figure in her dad's account, not this marvellous giant, a friend who obviously cherished him. In Kal's angry reminiscences, he'd never included Bull in full colour. The proportions of her father's self-interest scared her.

Kal was watching the light shine over his own scarred hands. "Do you think he's still alive?"

"Thanh? Yeah, he's alive," said Bull. "'Less he got his in the last week or so."

When Kal drank off his cognac, Lilac saw him abruptly turn that shade, that shade of drunkenness she dreaded.

Bull said, "He's full military now, you know. Up in One Corps."

"Which side?" said Kal, trying to make a joke.

Bull blinked slowly, and Lilac sensed that he aimed to keep Kal calm. "You know Thanh sides with the South, man."

Kal shook his head. "Why would the ARVN let in a murderous bastard like Thanh?"

Bull gave a deep, heaving laugh and slapped the table. "You take the cake! You take the entire enchilada! We don't want no murderous bastards fighting on *our* side?"

Kal said, "He's in One Corps, you say."

"That's right."

"You're stationed in One Corps."

"Big place."

"Ever run into him?"

"Times." Bull shifted his weight uneasily.

Kal was zoning in. "You've seen him?" When Bull nodded, Kal persisted. "What'd you do when you saw him?"

Bull regarded Kal coolly. "I went about my business."

Kal thought about that for a moment, then observed, "He never got charged. Did he."

"No." Bull shook his big head. "Got to admit, I think about it pretty often. The sight of him. Taller'n any Vietnam dude I ever seen. Tossin' that frag like it was a pineapple at a picnic."

Kal gazed longingly into his empty glass. "He should face judgment."

"Can't hold a grudge, Kal. Thanh's people were bullied by both sides, us and the VC. Humiliated and boxed in. It's their country, man. We barged in and now we can't get out."

"He tried to kill us."

"Yeah. This here's a war."

"You forgive him?"

"No. But I had to let it go, Kal. I had to get on with my life."

Lilac said, "I'm going to the bathroom," and left them staring at each other.

22.

When Lilac returned, the Welsh Stalker Model 80 was seated on the white tablecloth. A replenished glass of cognac and two half-bottles of beer now sat on a table nearby. She and Kal and Bull were the only customers.

The waiter lurked at the door to the kitchen, watching, his hands in the pockets of a shiny tuxedo, his legs crossed at his ankles. He wore shiny black shoes. A black moustache thin as a pipe cleaner accentuated his upper lip.

Kal's new model leaned on its bipod. That mutant ant. She had a weird sense that when she looked at it, she was looking at herself. She approached it, reached out one hand, and touched the cool steel of its thorax. It was almost like a reunion. She marvelled as her mood subtly lifted; she remembered herself more fully, seeing the gun here, her name stamped on it.

Bull leaned heavily on his cane, sniffing at the gun, examining its action. "It's got no happy switch? No switch for automatic?"

"It's semi-automatic. Sniper. It uses the Browning fifty."

Bull shook his head. "Browning fifty would break a man's collarbone. Snap it like a wishbone." He raised his eyes to Lilac. "Machine gun ammo. Can't use it in a rifle."

Lilac tensed up. She wanted Bull onside, to agree that Kal's invention was ingenious. If Bull were to consider her father off the rails, it would leave her alone with him, it would make him seem crazy, and she didn't want to be the sidekick to a crazy man. She wanted her father to be brilliant.

Kal was explaining the rifle's action, much of it beyond Lilac's understanding. "It's got a free-floating barrel," he told Bull. "The barrel absorbs much of the force, see? It drives in, like so, toward the receiver. I put springs in, here." His voice was strained with excitement. "The springs store energy, and release it."

"It's a heavy motherfucker," said Bull, then winced at Lilac. "'S'cuse my French, darlin'."

Kal winced too—because he was worried about the weight. "No problem. See, the barrel is fluted so it reduces the weight. And it cools better. The muzzle brake reduces recoil, too. See?" His enthusiasm kept mounting. "I use some of the recoil energy to push back the block and cycle the action. Cocks the firing pin. And loads a new round. That's the system. The recoil actually cycles the action." When he stood straight, he was flushed. He tossed back his cognac with a victorious flourish.

Bull said to Lilac, "Give him a lemon, he makes a cool million in lemonade." Leaning on his magnificent cane, he walked around the thing, pulling the chairs out of the way to get a better look.

The waiter uncrossed his ankles and said something over his shoulder to someone in the kitchen, then stood sentry again, watching closely. Lilac hoped that her father wouldn't pick up the gun. She imagined the waiter taking a pistol out of his tuxedo pocket and hitting the floor, shots ricocheting off the tiles, divots in the pink plaster.

She said, "Where are you staying, Dad?"

Kal looked up at her as if she'd made some kind of barking noise. "What?" he asked sharply.

"Where are you staying? It's getting late."

"It *is* gettin' late," said Bull. "I need my beauty sleep."

"I've had thirty built," Kal declared to Bull. "In Connecticut. First run. I placed an ad in *Shooting Times*. Now we'll see who comes to the table."

Lilac said, "Thirty? Already?" It was supposed to be a prototype. "What about the field trials you talked about?"

"Your daddy wants to put a flag up the pole, an' see who salutes." Bull handed him the leather bag. "Now, let's see how quick your big gun disappears."

Kal grabbed the bag, put it on a chair, and, resentfully, began to disassemble the rifle. "You think my fifty-cal won't work."

Bull sighed. "You're a fine man, Kal. With a turbo-charged brain. But it's late, and I got to be on deck early."

"How about we go out and test it somewhere tomorrow? I can show you how clean it fires."

"Tomorrow, I'm due back in Quang Tri. Left my 'lil enterprise with an underlink."

Lilac asked Bull, where's Quang Tri, and he told her it was north of Da Nang. Far. North of Hué.

"I went to Quang Ngai," she said. She was waving a red flag at her dad, inviting his anger, letting him know what risk she'd taken. She wanted him to listen. "Quang Ngai was supposed to be dangerous, but it was okay. I was okay."

Bull's big orange face was apprehensive. "Quang Ngai? It's a petting zoo compared to Quang Tri where I live. Quang Tri is jus' too far north for comfort. Nothin' but a dusty, sandy, hotter'n hell, uglified army base. No fun for nobody." Glancing at Kal, he said, simply, "Tet." When Kal didn't seem to hear, he added, "Tet Offensive. We lost control for a while there. Got real hairy."

Kal zipped the gun into its black leather jacket and heaved it off the table. "We'll come with you," he said.

"It's gettin' bad again," said Bull.

"We'll be coming along," Kal repeated. "Going to take my gun to the action." The leather case weighed him crookedly.

"That's not a nice idea, Kal, much as I enjoy your company. *Definitely* a bad idea for your child." To Lilac, "I'd love to have you along, little darlin', but I want you to stay *well*."

Kal claimed impatiently, "She wants to go."

Bull moaned, "No way, man," while Kal's eyes roved the room, passing over her.

Lilac saw her father's trick at the same moment she succumbed to it. He needed to make his desires become her desires. She wondered if all fathers do this. Make out like they're only taking care of their family, while they go after whatever they want. But she did want to go. She felt a delicious release, a sweet whiff of self-destruction in this merging of her will with his. Surely he wouldn't let anything bad happen. Plus, she'd get a story out of it. The newspapers would publish it for sure. A story from Quang Tri, which Bull says is even farther north than Quang Ngai, would sure impress the *Tribune*, and entertain the *Loving Couch*. She said to Kal, "Yeah. Let's go." But she added, "We'd better tell Mum."

Bull chimed in, "I don't think your mama would like it. I bet she wouldn't like it one bit."

"Ruby begged me not to let Lilac out of my sight. I'll honour my promise."

"I want to go on this trip with my dad," Lilac told Bull. Then, to Kal, she said, "And I have a friend who'd want to come along."

"Oh, now," said Bull.

"Larry Donovan."

"Who's Larry Donovan?" Kal asked. Then, "The photographer? The journalist? Larry Donovan. Him? You know him? How'd you get to know him?"

"He's been helping me. He knows Bull too."

Bull said, "Larry knows jus'bout everybody. He's an old hand. A good man. But *curious*! He's got the curiosity bug." His huge, brilliant frame pivoted on the cane and he loomed over Kal. "Larry's even curious about *you*, Kal! Only the Lord knows why. Just a genius gunsmith flushed outta the bush in Canada. You don't want to be his story, now, do you?"

Lilac said, "He's curious about your Stalker."

Kal would have seen Larry Donovan's work in *Life* and *Time* and pretty well everywhere. "Is he? Well, he'll see it in action. Up at Quang Tri. Can't imagine a better field trial. This is a God-given opportunity." Then, decisively, "If Larry Donovan wants to come along, that's okay by me."

Bull was shaking his head. "Turbo-charged, Kal Welsh. I don't think *nobody* ever stopped you." He turned heavily to make his way to the front door of the restaurant, his cane clicking on the cracked tiles. Lilac thought how exhausting it must be for Bull to carry around all that glory. Kal was throwing money on the table. The waiter eased himself toward the money on his shiny black shoes.

23.

The intense traffic seemed to come from everywhere, out of the dark. Eerie cowboy-in-the-orient music leaked from the cars to drift over bustling sidewalks. How do you pack six elephants into a Volkswagen? Lilac tried to remember the solution to that joke, squeezed into the back of the taxi between the two men, Kal exhaling cognac like a fire-breathing dragon and Bull sitting with his knees around his ears, crammed so tight beside her. When the cab pulled up at her hotel, he jumped out like a jack-in-the-box, springing Lilac free.

Kal leaned across the seat to talk to Lilac through the open door of the cab. "Early," he was saying. "Dawn."

"Where are you staying?" she had to ask again.

They would find another hotel.

"Why not here?" she asked. But as she spoke, she thought, Don't stay here, leave me alone, at least for another night.

Bull answered, "We got some talkin' to do, little darlin'. Don't want coupla night owls aggravating your landlord." He embraced her till her feet left the ground, nuzzling her neck. "You g'wan now and put your head on your pillow."

He had a non-creepy way of nuzzling, hugging, palming, flattering, and embracing, and she already loved him. She said good night and turned, dizzy and relieved, toward her hotel. As Bull was folding himself back inside the taxi, her father shouted out, "Seven thirty!" The door closed, the cab sped off.

So it was into the silty light before dawn the next morning that Lilac emerged from a short sleep and descended to the street. In her hands she carried the creased paper with Larry Donovan's address. It wasn't far, ten minutes if she was quick. She began to run, her big feet in their canoe shoes slapping painfully against the pavement.

Larry came to the door of his apartment wearing a plaid bathrobe, his sand-coloured hair in disarray. She apologized for waking him but told him there was no time to lose. "My father is here." In some alarm, Larry glanced over her shoulder. "I mean, my dad's here in Saigon."

"Oh," said Larry. He invited her in and went to another room and closed the door. When he emerged a few minutes later, groomed, dressed in a grey cotton shirt, and smoking a cigarette, he spooned fine brown espresso coffee into a press, his long white wrists twisting the filter into its cast iron cylinder of water, and put it on to boil. When he opened the door to his tiny fridge, Lilac glimpsed his stock of mangoes and pineapples and gin. He selected a pineapple. A trail of ants like a string of tiny black beads traipsed faithfully along the counter toward the sink. From a strip of magnet above the counter, he removed a paring knife and made an incision into the pineapple's core, and another incision beside it.

Lilac said, "There's a lot of urgency in this."

"You will have coffee and some pineapple."

She explained the situation: her father would leave that morning for Quang Tri, and if Larry wanted the story, he'd have to come now to meet him. "Right now at seven thirty," she emphasized. "I'm going along too."

Larry stiffened, lifted the knife from the yellow flesh, and without looking at her said, "Your father is taking you to Quang Tri."

"I'll get a good story out of it, right? It's like Heather Markham going up to the DMZ. I need to get out on the field."

He looked at her now with intimate yet impersonal intensity and repeated, "He's taking you to Quang Tri."

"No. I'm going on my own. With him. This is your chance for you to get *your* story too, right? Your profile of my dad. So? Let's go."

"It's very dangerous."

"Not with him, it won't be." She paused. "I want to go. He's not making me or anything."

"Do you know where Quang Tri is?"

"North of Hué. Heather went. She was all right. We'll be with Bull. C'mon."

He shook his head. "That isn't how I work," he said. "But thank you for the tip." He took the tiny coffee cup from her hands and replaced it with a slice of pineapple, touched her elbow, and ushered her to the door.

Where he hesitated. "Are you sure?"

"About what?"

"Two things. One: Are you sure you want to go to Quang Tri?"

"Of course."

He looked at her again, closely, quick shutter speed, but she didn't know what he was taking in.

"What's the other thing?" she asked.

"Are you sure that you want me to do a story about your father?"

She told him she was sure, and he asked, "Why?"

The pineapple was cold in her hand, she could almost feel its citric freshness entering her blood through her skin. "Because I can't," she said without thinking. She felt suddenly desperate to have Larry's company on this trip. "I thought you were curious about him." *He wants you to write about him, Larry Donovan.* She did not say this. She refrained. She recoiled from the vision of Kal as an opportunist. Even if that's what he was. It was okay for her to feel angrily ambivalent about the man, but it remained essential that others respect him. He belonged to her.

Larry said, "You stick with Bull, if you're hell-bent on going."

"I *am* hell-bent."

His sad smile. "Your self-knowledge is refreshing."

"So you'll come?"

He shook his head. She thought he was saying no. He must've seen her disappointment, because now he was saying yes, he'd meet them in Quang Tri. Then he was giving her the strangest look with his cool-blue eye while he closed his door on her.

She hesitated for a moment in his hallway, then plodded back to her hotel and arrived in a sweat. It was already oppressively hot. The cab carrying Bull and Kal pulled up and she shouted, "Wait!" and raced up to room 214 for her camera and notebooks. She put on her khaki costume with the combat boots and slid a couple of reefers along with her toothbrush into her cotton purse then dashed downstairs to join the men.

24.

Bull proved a gracious guide. Like Larry, he had a knack for catching rides in airplanes by hanging around on the landing strip, and they made it to the air base in Quang Tri in six hours, though Kal had to pay for himself. Only journalists, army, and medical personnel got free rides.

At the air base, they climbed into Bull's black 1967 Buick parked in sun so hot Lilac scorched her fingers on the chrome door handle. The Buick was outfitted with oversized tires on a raised suspension. The car growled through the dusty base, passing US

Army tanks parked in grassy fields. The base was a dispiriting site built of steel and plywood and sandbags pitched into layers of sandy mud. In a watery distance, marshes and fishing boats floated on undulating waves of heat.

Bull kept sticking his head out the window to get a better view of the mountains a few miles away to the west. Lilac worried that he'd drive off the narrow sandy road. Breathing dust in the back seat, she finally asked if anything was bothering him.

"Nope," he said, not taking his eyes from the rocky hills, swerving then correcting himself, and swerving again, "Nothin'. Snakes is sleeping is all." To Kal beside him, he said in a low voice, "I worry about the dear-heart in the back seat."

"God won't let anything happen to her."

Bull laughed while he gave Kal a nervous look. "Might not be up to God, Kal. In a pinch."

Lilac was straining to hear them. "What are you two muttering about?"

"Nothin'," said Bull, then he muttered, "Never took you for a holy roller, Kal."

"I've been doing some hard thinking," said Kal.

Bull's 'lil enterprise turned out to be a vast steel pavilion like a storage shed for farm equipment. The "underlink" was nowhere to be seen. Bull unlocked and opened it up, revealing long rows of picnic tables laden with stuff. Instamatic and Nikon cameras, cans of paint, toothbrushes and Bic lighters, chopsticks, plastic Buddhas, lacquer paintings of Jesus, a Chicom rifle, light bulbs, anchovies, steak sauce, liquor, knives, soap, baby oil, *Playboy*, *Hustler*, tins of oysters, vinyl albums, and thousands of cassettes.

Bull was switching on a fan when he saw Kal pick up the Chicom rifle to examine it, and he said, "That's Chink. It sure was news when the VC got Chinese weapons. There's a bullet hole in the pistol grip, right here. The bolt face been welded shut. Just a trophy some poor grunt gonna take home to show his girl."

"You run this place?" Kal said.

"Doesn't take much to run. I'm on my lonesome with Psyops now. Last couple years, there's not much call for hearts and minds. I'm glad to make myself useful. 'Fraid they'll send me stateside, otherwise."

Toward the back of the pavilion, though, Bull's Psyops equipment was still in working order: an Olivetti typewriter, pens and brushes, bottles of red and black ink. He had a radio transceiver, plus a reel-to-reel tape recorder and a sixteen-millimetre film projector. Kal told Lilac, "Bull's a genius in radio technology."

The space was clean, and what remained of his Psyops work was well-organized. There were shelves in aluminum brackets stacked with cardboard file boxes, everything labelled by day/month/year since 1961, the number of boxes dwindling since 1970.

Bull, dressed in fatigues now, his dazzling silk jacket packed in his duffle bag, had retained the turquoise earring and added a purple paisley silk scarf, knotted around his peroxide ponytail. And the cane. Lilac had to wonder why Bull wasn't sent home when he was injured. He must have been in worse shape than her father was. Why did the army keep him on? Just to run a store?

Bull's private nest had a small fridge, a hibachi, and a Bunsen burner. He bustled around, swinging on his cane, surprisingly graceful. The kitchen was also his bedroom. A twelve-gauge shotgun leaned against a sleeping platform set on sturdy legs and draped in a silk cream-coloured parachute. Beside the bed were two overturned wood cartons stamped *Carnation Milk* on which he kept a turntable, with dozens of LPs and singles stacked neatly beside it. The floor was covered by rattan mats, swept clean. Bull pointed to several nylon lawn chairs set up around a large plastic patio table. "Make yo'selfs comfy." His goodwill was stamped permanently on his messed-up features.

Kal picked up the twelve-gauge.

"She's just an old friend," Bull explained. He doused the charcoal in fuel and tossed a match at the hibachi then lit the Bunsen burner, one stove for the wok, one for the fry pan. When he became aware of Lilac nearby, watching him, he began to show off, horsing around with a couple of knives, playing them like drumsticks against the flaming hibachi. "Learned this in Tokyo," he told her. He spun around and, despite his mass and his game leg, performed some kind of martial dance with the knives, one eye on Lilac to make sure she was watching, telling her, "I'm showing you my samurai moves, girl." He introduced his knives. "Mister Santoku. And Mister Gyuto. They been dyin' to make your acquaintance. Say kon'nichiwa to sweet Lilac, boys." He wasn't even out of breath, but calmly put the knives down and placed a wok on the charcoal as the flame settled.

"You speak Japanese?"

"Just the kwee-zeen lingo. Spent a lot of time in rehab there after—after. When your daddy and me ran into trouble."

Lilac was about to pursue this when someone called out from the front of the pavilion, "Anybody home?"

Kal had been lounging in one of Bull's nylon lawn chairs, drinking from Bull's ample supply of French wine, and he got quickly to his feet, rumpled and off-kilter. Larry Donovan's figure was hard to make out against the low sunlight pouring through the wide-open doors of the pavilion. They heard Larry's sandy voice. "I hope I'm in time for some of Bull's cooking." He came fully into view. "Your squid."

Bull deftly swung his cane like a sword at Larry then embraced him with one massive arm. "Yo'ol'sum'bitch," he declared. Bull was even taller than Larry by several inches.

Kal reached to shake Larry's hand and said, "Seems I have to thank you for looking after my daughter," looking up at the cool-blue eyes behind the aviator glasses.

"I only saw that she got started. She did the rest."

"She was lucky," Kal said.

Bull was returning to his stove. "Another famous dude," he muttered while he attended to the food. "Got a couple o' movie stars here in Quang Tri resort. Should'a had a red carpet for y'all."

Kal started to tell Larry about the work of his that he'd seen in various magazines, explaining to the man himself where his photos and stories had been published and to what effect.

Lilac floated at the edge of the light, watching. She felt like another type of organism, different from these men, barely connected. The Three Wise Men relaxed, drinking now, calm, and calming to a young woman who must rely on their know-how in this place, this uglified air base near the DMZ.

Bull told them all to sit down. Lilac thought at first the noise was only from the chairs as they pulled them up around Bull's plastic table, but when they were all seated, the noise got louder —low, booming explosions followed by a tat-tat-tat of artillery.

Bull twisted, nearly tipping his chair. "What *time* is it?"

Larry said, "Nearly seven."

"Sons a bitches are early," said Bull.

25.

The thudding of mortar strikes outside the perimeter of the base was punctuated by riffs from machine guns far enough away to sound like strings of ladyfinger firecrackers.

Bull heaved a frustrated sigh. "I see the nightly vexations is under way."

The mortars, he told them, were flung from the hills to strike just outside the base. "They don't *normally* do much damage. But *man*, they know how to buzz the nerves! Makes me nearly *crazy* sometimes. You know, sometimes I almost wish the NVA would jus' *hit* something." Then he twitched and nodded to Lilac. "I mean, not while you're my special guest, little honey."

The bombardment went on for another ten minutes. Lilac ground her teeth till her jaw ached. Across the small table, Kal listened angrily, as if the attack was personal.

Bull fastidiously filled their plates. A shell struck closer, Lilac was sure of it. Her father flinched. Bull used ebony chopsticks to serve the food, his big hands twirling the food onto their melamine plates. Everything seemed to break down into atoms and particles. Her skin was slick with sweat. When life gets very *real*, it simultaneously gets very *unreal*.

Bull said, "I suggest you eat up. You got to have the fuel if we need to run."

Larry's eyes lingered on Lilac while he picked up his chopsticks, commenting on the marvellous food, telling her in a casual voice that didn't completely conceal his anxiety, "Listen to Bull, Lilac."

Kal jerkily moved the food around his plate, and when another mortar struck, he shouted, "God!" Lilac saw the looks Bull and Larry gave him.

Then, abruptly, it got quiet. It took a moment for them to realize that the shelling had stopped. Bull said, "So long till next time."

They finished their meal without talking. Larry lit a cigarette. Lilac felt as if she were watching all of them, herself included, from the ceiling, and she wondered if human beings are essentially crazy. While she was helping Bull clear the dishes, she heard someone laugh, passing by. She heard crickets in the grass, the drone of insects in scraggly brush outside. And felt a rush of bliss. The sweet world still existed.

This conclusion of the evening vexations inspired Bull's spirits to soar into gaiety. He clattered four tin cups on his four fingers, clicking them like castanets while raising a bottle high in the other hand. "Give it up—for Mistah—Jack Daniel!"

A minute later, Lilac rolled the booze around her tongue, limbering her stiff jaw. Smoke from Larry's cigarette braided a silky ribbon in oily lantern light. She liked the way Larry sat, his long legs crossed, his thin white wrists with long white fingers laced over his knees, a smouldering cigarette drifting ash. The bourbon chilled and heated her veins. She wondered when Larry would begin to interview her dad. Such nice bourbon.

She'd hear the gunsmith extol the virtues of his Model 70 and his deep-penetration bullet. He'd explain the freakish anatomy of the Stalker 80. Would he boast about his wealth, would he talk about Rough Rock, the beautiful house he'd built there? Would she and her mother figure into his story? He'd probably talk about the powerful new gun only as a marvel of innovation, not—as he had done for Lilac—a fresh source of income, of lifelong wealth. She hoped that her father would be careful about how he talked about himself, hoped fervently that he wouldn't talk about God the wolf king. She knew a bit about these interviews now, how a person might think he's controlling the story and start yakking, while the journalist plays out the fishing line. But Larry was a kind man. Jack Daniel's whiskey was Lilac's new friend. She poured herself a goodly drink, and made a silent prayer. "Please, God. Stay the hell out of this."

Bull said, "You take care, darlin', you mus' weigh less'n a mosquito." He put the bourbon away.

She nestled with her cup of lovely poison and wondered who would win, Larry or Kal, teller or subject. Would Kal be the fool or the king in the story that Larry would tell?

She watched Larry relax into his lawn chair. He had set aside his two cameras on the plywood floor, within reach. He might be feigning uninterest, letting Kal feel safe from intrusion. She'd learned something of this indirection while taking photographs. You pretend that you're under a magic cloak, invisible, posing no threat. His cigarette's long ash coiled and dropped onto his grey shirt and seemed to wake him from reverie, and he stubbed out the butt, flicked away the ash, never letting his eyes stray to Kal, but gazing out, toward the entrance, where light from the pavilion yawned into the night through a fluttering curtain of mosquito netting.

Kal seemed absorbed in a study of his cuticles. Bull cleaned up his kitchen, humming a meandering tune that Lilac couldn't identify. She felt a sideways tilt into dreamland. But then Kal cleared his throat and Larry said, "Pardon?" and Kal said, "I just—" and Larry said, "That would be interesting," and Kal said, "I'll get it," and Larry said, "If you like." Lilac figured that either they were reading each other's minds or she'd fallen asleep. At any rate, the impasse was broken. Kal hauled out the black leather bag. He laid open the upper and lower receiver of the Stalker Model 80, spreading the parts on the floor. She heard the loud click of its assembly.

26.

The scope, the muzzle brake, the bipod with its spiked feet, gave the thing its insistent, predatory look. Such an *obvious* gun, so blatant and horribly ambitious. Sinister. Snide. Smug. "Vicious," she said aloud.

Kal nodded. "It's the most powerful gun ever made." And he began to point out its features, reiterating what he'd described for Bull at the French restaurant. With his choked-up enthusiasm and flushed cheeks, he looked boyish. Larry called it "a breakthrough design," and Kal answered, "Yes. It is. It's accurate at two miles, in the right hands."

Larry said, "Imagine."

"You don't have to take my word for it. I'll demonstrate it. Right, Bull? We'll set up a field trial."

Bull shook his head. "Snakes is sleeping, snakes is sleeping," he chanted quietly.

Larry said, "You plan to get an order for Vietnam? It's pretty late in the game, isn't it?"

From out in the night, there came the distant riff of machine guns. Then it got quiet again. Kal stretched out on the floor beside his gun as if it were a train set, leaning his head in his hand. "Bull will set up a demonstration with Logistics."

"But has there been any actual interest from One Corps?" Larry asked. "I mean, prior to your designing the gun. Any demand for this thing?"

"LWL put out a call. Weapons contractors. You know them?"

"Might."

"Land War Lab."

"Thought it was defunct." Larry sat back and lit a cigarette.

Kal made an effort to hold his casual pose, but he scoffed. "Guess it was a phantom who put out a call for a dynamically improved system. Could have sworn that was an actual person who showed up at my outfit in Connecticut with the R and D call."

"Seems funny, that's all," Larry observed mildly. "Nixon's pulling out the ground troops. Wonder why they'd want a new order now."

"We need a winner. I'll bet you a hundred bucks I walk away with an order."

Larry waved his hand. "Wouldn't want to make a bet that depends on your being disappointed, Kal." He coughed and took a sip of bourbon.

"Vietnam is just the beginning. A testing ground. This gun will be in demand all over the world, everywhere we're fighting for American interests."

"International." Larry nodded.

"Correct. Central America is heating up. Nicaragua. Guatemala. And Africa. Congo, Eritrea. Look at Israel, fighting for its life. Not only military but police. The Soviets are looking for proxy wars. Going after small conflicts. They'll try to pick off America in dozens of small wars so we can't just hit the bastards with our nuclear weapons. This gun, this gun is perfect for the quick, light raids that'll be the war of the future. It'll make the AK-47 look like a peashooter."

"It's not in the same league, though, is it? It's the M16 that's up against the AK-47."

"Shitty rifle." Kal stood up and dusted his hands.

Larry nodded agreeably, seeming to appreciate Kal's mastery of the subject. "Lot of unhappiness with the M16. Even with the chrome improvements."

Kal shook his head. "Sad," he observed, as if he were speaking of a friend gone wrong. "Mistake to put so many of them in the field before the kinks got ironed out."

"So, you're aiming for field trials. This week?" Larry looked at his watch.

Bull had been sitting still, listening intently to this conversation, his form lit by the kerosene lantern in his kitchen, a domestic mammoth. Lilac studied him. Without his comic extroversion, it was evident that he knew much more than he said.

"Bull?" Kal prompted. "You think tomorrow we can gather up some interest in a field trial?"

"It's real sketchy, man."

"Too much trouble?" Kal said with a quick glance at Larry.

"You're never too much trouble, Kal, course not. Only—"

"I can pay for the set-up, if that's a problem."

"Coupla problems. One: it's Logistics, Kal."

"I'll start the ball rolling with Logistics. I won't put it all on you."

"It's not the work makes me skittish. It's the timing's bad, real bad. And the personnel. It's Thanh, man." It sounded like another of Bull's rhymes. "Thanh," he repeated. "Thanh, man."

Kal's lips fell open. Bull gave him a dry, solemn appraisal. Lilac found it especially unnerving to have a funny man turn serious. Her father sputtered, "What'd you say?"

"Captain Thanh," said Bull levelly.

"Captain," Kal repeated.

"Captain Ly Tong Thanh, head of Logistics for One Corps."

Kal froze. "He's head of Logistics? What the hell."

"Thanh's the man."

Lilac watched the colour drain from her dad's face. "Jesus," he said. "A reunion with Thanh. Captain. You sure? Hard to believe he's a captain. You say *head* of Logistics?"

"You got it. Thanh's our man. Up to him, what happens to your big gun." He seemed almost to find this amusing, and put his hand over his mouth, scars on scars.

Larry commented, "Care to talk about it?"

"Old friend of Kal's and mine," Bull answered. He studied Kal for a moment then plunged ahead, speaking to Larry. "Thanh started out a schoolteacher in Can Tho. Kal hired him to translate for us back in '61 in the Mekong, when Kal and me were makin' propaganda shit for Psyops. We made a movie, a real good one, too. But, turns out, we were filming it smack dab on Mr. Thanh's family graveyard. The Vietnamese are farmers, right? And farmers love their land, 'specially when they bury their ancestors in it. That kinda love goes deeper'n six feet. We trespassed on something they call sacred. Thanh got mad."

Kal tried to laugh. "He was mad."

Shame, shame made her father look small while he tried to be offhand. The curtains were drawn closed at the house in Winnipeg when he came home so badly injured. At the time, in a way, she'd felt as if it was somehow her fault—she was just a little girl he had to provide for, a child in his way, passing her with his crutches on the narrow stairs.

"So it was Captain Thanh who threw the grenade back then," Larry observed calmly. Lilac saw his hands flex; she waited for him to write that down, but he didn't.

"Can't blame him," Bull continued. "We were walkin' all over his great-granddaddy. One thing about Vietnamese folk, they care for their dead. Seen their tombs? Bigger than their houses, all painted up and sweet-smelling. Their land's their everything, their soul in*car*nate." He hauled himself to his feet and sighed. "Anyway, nothin' we can do 'bout it tonight. Ya'll be sleepin' here. Larry? You too. It's too late to be skulking around in the dark, get your head blown off."

He produced three hammocks and a bolt of mosquito netting, then flourished his long Japanese knife to deftly slice the netting into three pieces. Kal was unusually obedient, distracted.

After Bull had settled his guests, he laid his body down on his bed as if loading a backhoe onto a barge. Lilac listened to him heave to his side and a moment later came the sound of Marvin Gaye and Tammi Terrell singing "Ain't Nothing Like the Real Thing." When the song ended, Bull lifted the needle and said, "Sweet dreams, angels. An' if you got to piss in the night, don't stray far from the light." He blew out the lamp.

Quiet. Crickets. Larry coughed. From the dark came Kal's voice. "*Captain* Thanh."

Bull said, "Go to sleep, y'all. Beddy-bye."

Kal went on, "*Captain* Thanh is going to put in a big order for my Welsh Stalker 80."

Bull said, "It's somethin' to dream on, Kal."

"Not a dream," said Kal.

Lilac could hear Kal's hammock swinging. Beddy-bye, rock-a-bye. She heard Larry's laboured breathing, the click of his lighter, the sour fragrance of his cigarette.

27.

Early light. Bull was dressed, swinging his cane while he rushed past Lilac, talking to himself. "Those are B-52s. Big ugly fat fuckers." He went outside.

The noise of aircraft screaming overhead. Lilac realized she must have slept. She rolled out of her hammock and went outside to join Bull with her dad and Larry. A formation of three B-52s roared west. Over the shrieking aircraft, Bull shouted, "Each one of those mothers got eight turbojet engines. Seventy thousand pounds o' damage, that's what they carry, that's what they intend to unload out yonder, on the hills, see? Try an' hurt somebody."

The aircraft cut the sky. Lilac covered her ears. Another cell of three B-52s zoomed overhead. Dawn glinted off the bellies of the planes.

Larry walked off with his cameras, saying something no one could hear.

"Snakes been sleeping," Bull said. "It's a bad-luck sign." He went back inside, loudly complaining, Lilac on his heels. "The NVA been piling up in the hills north and west." With hurried patience, he began to unhook the hammocks, rolling them up, neatly scrolling the mosquito netting.

Lilac touched his shoulder, and he jumped and apologized. "We're in the soup now, honey child," he said. "But we're gonna look after you real good." He focused on arranging the parachute over his bed, smoothing every wrinkle.

Her father walked in and said, "They're heading inland. The action's going to be far away. Way the hell inland."

Bull stood straight and turned on him. "You think they'd be so stupid? *Nobody's* going to have another Khe Sanh. Nobody's that dumb. No way they'd go deep west and get strangulated in NVA country again with no hope of supplies. Tell you what's gonna happen." He tugged at his ear with its turquoise stud and gave Kal a questioning, disappointed look. "B-52s are gonna bomb the shit out of the hills nearby, try and give the ground troops some wiggle room. Flush the NVA outta their tunnels and bunkers, where, I tell you, they've been *sleepin'* for weeks. That means they is all comin' down on our *heads*. Which makes this a very perplexing situation to share with you and your famb'ly, Kal."

"I always protect my family."

Bull took a deep breath, trying to calm himself. "In an hour, we're gonna hear the helicopter squads slappin' overhead. They'll aim to land the ground troops *behind* the enemy. Squeeze 'em from behind, see? So where does that push 'em? If all goes correctly, the NVA comes straight into our lovin' arms." He turned and lifted the film projector off its bench and placed it on the floor, removed the reel-to-reel, removed everything, and cleared a space. He unrolled a map, flattening it out on the bench. "We got to be super-smart where we make our move."

"We're moving?" Lilac asked.

"Safer at the coast." Bull's hand, like a massive starfish, his thick fingers tracing a path from the air base northeast to a river, an estuary opening to the sea. "Thạch Hãn river. Not a lot o' cover, but a deep valley. I got a friend up there. And the Marines are sure to be hanging around that area, bein' ugly, playin' an amphibian trick, a false feint, make the NVA think they're gonna come at them by water. We'd have some protection. Maybe we can get Lilac on a lift outta there."

"Sure," said Kal. "If you think it's a good idea, we can go to the coast. After the field trial."

Slowly, Bull repeated, "We get out *right now*." He leaned to speak closely to Kal. "I can't get her on an airlift from the base today. Nobody's gonna want to be in the sky in a shitstorm. We've gotta make a move on our own cognition. This ain't no place for civilian personnel. I never should've let you come, specially with your little darling."

Lilac studied the map. A river draining east toward the ocean. An escape route.

Her father said, "Slow down. Tell me why you think it's safer to be on the move now than it is to stay on the base."

Bull moved methodically to pull the radio transceiver down from an upper shelf and hand it to Lilac. "Hold that, will you?" She nearly dropped it, it was so heavy. Edgily, he asked Kal, "You want proof?" He pushed the map aside then retrieved the transceiver from her, setting it up on the bench. "I'll give you proof."

He fooled with the dials till there was static, broad interference, "Can't get diddly fuck outta this thing sometimes," fiddling with the radio till it suddenly blatted Earth, Wind & Fire funk transmitted from a supply ship off the coast, an R & B tune called "Uh Huh Yeah," then veering up into a whistle and finally into what Bull was seeking: a hijacked frequency from the mountains where the NVA were holed up—according to Bull— stockpiling captured American 105-millimetre guns along with Soviet 130-millimetres, 122-millimetre mortars and rockets, and anti-aircraft weapons. Planning to attack Quang Tri. As the signal came in more clearly, Lilac could hear a voice, Vietnamese, but different from the liquid language she loved. She asked, "Why does that sound so different?"

"North," Bull explained. "North got an uglified accent."

A harsh tongue, less sensual, less melodic. Lilac was afraid. The voice was utterly confident, implacable, authoritarian. This was the enemy.

Lilac looked at Bull. "Do you speak Vietnamese?"

"Been here a long time. Absorbed some."

"Why?" she asked. "Why have you stayed?"

He answered her so gently she knew it wasn't the whole truth. "I just wanta see how the story turns out."

Kal nodded toward the radio. "What's he going on about?"

"Coordinates. Numbers. It'll be codified. Could be false. Fake info."

"Fake info," Kal repeated.

"Yeah. An info game." Bull's anger toward him relented a little. "Like we used to play."

"Let's try it," said Kal.

"Ain't no game."

"It is if you play it. C'mon. Talk to him."

Bull smiled a little. "Won't. No game. You're one crazy dude sometimes. Ain't a Psyops-adviser war, Kal, ain't been for a long time. You know that."

Lilac found it painful to see her dad shrink. Bitterly, he said, "I didn't do anything back in the day, except draw goddamn useless cartoons of bucktoothed Viet Cong."

"You did more'n that," said Bull. To Lilac, "We made movies. Soundtracks. Made some crazy shit happen." Then, to Kal, "Remember the baby?"

Lilac had to ask, what baby?

"Kal and me, we made tape recordings of a little baby, belonged to a girl where we was stationed. That baby never stopped crying. We looped the sound of the baby bawlin', see? And we added some wicked reverb. Even did some subliminal tricks, right, Kal? We got this bass line down real low where you could hardly hear it. *Boom da-da-boom da-boom.* Eerie as all hell. Then we run it through a badass amp and gear it up to twelve so there's distortion. Scariest sound you ever heard."

Lilac asked why'd they do that.

"We give the tape and amp to the pilots, and they play it loud—I mean *loud*—when they fly over the trees where they know the VC is hiding. Then we litter the air with our pamphlets. All's we have to say in our letter is, 'We have your baby.'" He laughed. "'We have your baby.' Kal wrote that part."

Kal began to cheer up a little. The North Vietnamese voice went on with its litany of numbers, while over the implacable directives Bull chanted, "*Boom da-da-boom da-boom. We have your baby.*"

28.

It was as Bull predicted. An hour after the B-52s roared over the base, a squadron of helicopters flew by. Lilac went outside with the men; they watched the sky. The helicopters were twin-rotary contraptions of improbable size.

"Transport copters," Bull said. "Sea Stallions."

"Stallions," Lilac repeated.

"Sea Stallions. And Sea Knights. Wid' a *K*. The Knights are the smaller ones. Sweet machines."

Larry appeared from his wanderings with his cameras, looking dry in the heat. Lilac turned to him and said, "Stallions and Knights," as if that would explain all this chaos, these huge fantasy toys that somehow flew high in the sky.

Bull was saying that the helicopters carried many men. He was specific: forty-five and twenty-four men respectively. "The B-52s are gonna drop thirty, maybe forty tons of explosives on the hills. Then the choppers go in after them and drop off a few hundred grunts with the little stuff. Grenade launchers, M16s." He turned to Kal and added, "A Welsh or two. Then they fight close. Gladiator-style." He watched the air show and muttered, "It's too much like Khe Sanh."

She asked him what he meant.

"Khe Sanh's just over there." He pointed west. "Six months that siege went on. Poor grunts, runnin' out of C rations, runnin' out of ammo and meds, runnin' out of drinking water in a monsoon. They got so damn thirsty they licked the rain off their ponchos and swallowed the snails. Escargot," he said. "Wid'out the butter."

Lilac watched the helicopter squadron fly into the distance, except for one, a straggler, a Stallion moving no more than a hundred miles an hour. She heard what sounded like a gun going off and saw a narrow projectile strike the Stallion. Flames flashed, oily orange and red, and the helicopter swayed. The missile had struck the rear rotary blades. For a moment it looked as if it could still fly. Then it keeled over, and another fire burst from its fuselage, and it was losing altitude, falling in a low arch, leaving a trail of smoke as it went down toward the hills.

Such a sleek manoeuvre, quick and deadly. She stared at the thin trail of smoke. They heard another explosion, and a bigger cloud of smoke rose in the air from behind a low hill.

"Where the fuck did that missile come from?" Kal wanted to know. His face was coated in sweat.

Bull stood marvelling. "Russian-made. That's the second one I seen this year. That was a high-explosive spear with a homing device, shot from the shoulder of a skinny little VC, rode his bicycle, prob'ly home by now slurping up his soup. Thirty, forty men just died." He laid his hand on Kal's arm. "Time to go."

"What about Thanh?" Kal straightened, shoulders back, the sun beating on him, his sweat glistening. The sky was scarred by trails of smoke, forty men dead or dying on the other side of the bluff. He stubbornly waited for Bull to answer him.

Bull asked coldly, "What *about* Thanh?"

"He's head of Logistics? Fine. We take advantage. Right now."

Larry did a double take. "Now?"

Bull moved till he stood close to Kal, towering over him. "You aim to show Thanh your gun. Today. The big Welsh Stalker. Is that the idea, Kal?"

Irritably, Kal peered up at Bull as if trying to understand how anybody could be so dense. "I'm here, aren't I?" he said. "Anyway. Thanh owes me."

"Captain Thanh don't have time to hear your sales pitch today."

There came the pop-pop-pop of small arms fire in the near distance. A light-armoured tank rolled by on the road past Bull's place, eight wheels in a cloud of dry sand, followed by a Sheridan tank on tracks, moving fast toward the downed helicopter. Six Skyhawks flew over low.

Larry said, "Bull's right. It's time to get out."

"We're not leaving till I get a field trial," Kal responded.

"Captain Thanh don't have time for you today," Bull repeated tersely.

Larry looked at each of them in turn, and turned to Lilac to ask, "How are you?"

"Are you going to check out the crash?" she answered. "The Stallion that went down?" Stallions and Knights. She thought she might throw up. She tried to remember who she was. A journalist.

"Because I should go with you." She made a move to fetch her camera.

Bull put his hand on her arm and restrained her. To Larry, "We're in for another Tet-style invasion. A buildup of NVA right close to the north and bearing down. You want to stay for the party, Mr. Donovan, you go right ahead. But I'm getting Lilac out." To Kal he added coldly, "You want to go find Thanh, you go right ahead. But Lilac's coming with me."

Kal said, "Wait." He shoved Bull's hand away from Lilac, braced her shoulders, and pressed his forehead against hers, his hot breath in her face.

"Don't crush me like that," she said. She tried to pull away, but he held her fast.

"You're all right," he said.

"I have to see the crash."

He squeezed her shoulders more tightly. "You have to stay with me. Nobody can protect you like I can." She struggled, but he gripped her, his fingers digging into her flesh, his strong hands like tongs. He said, "This is your chance to stand up for me. And for yourself. We find Thanh. We test the gun. This is what it means to be great. You and me, we rise above."

"Let go!" She twisted free and staggered back.

Six soldiers walked by in combat gear, their helmets netted to their belts along with pistols and knives, their M16s slung over their shoulders. Lilac automatically looked for Gavin. Another two uniforms were hurrying to catch up to their group, and one of them, a young man (even to Lilac he looked far too young to be a soldier), slowed as he approached, looking her up and down, and when he was only three feet away, still striding as if propelled by the steel toes of his combat boots, he peered at her intently. He was a bit cross-eyed. She'd seen little kids like that at home

in Minaki, so young their eyes weren't yet aligned, as if one eye
was still focused on an original innocence. He gave Lilac a wide-
open smile. When he and his squad had almost passed, he turned
around and smiled again, ear to ear, vulnerable, keeping nothing
for himself, then he turned and followed his brothers into the
dust.

"Listen, honey child," said Bull. "We're gonna pack up and
move you to where we can get you outta here." Kal started to
speak, but Bull continued to talk over him. "Don't you concern
yourself. Your daddy's gonna come to his good sense. And there'll
be plenty of action for you to write about when we get you safe.
Everything you just seen? It's gonna be a hellova good story for
your newspaper back home."

His words were erased by a high-pitched whistling sound. The
light strobed, white, red, yellow, white again. She heard a hammer
striking steel. Her heart leapt out through her ears. Something
smacked her to the ground.

29.

The water where Lilac lay reeked of gasoline. The ground felt
hot. She got to her knees. Her father sat nearby, cradling one of his
own boots. She crawled to him. The noise of artillery. And single
shots. Sniper fire. Rockets exploded somewhere, close, two then
three rockets in succession. Her dad had a watery trail of blood
under his nose, and she wiped it away with her grimy hand. "I'm
okay," he said. He wiped grit from his eyes. "Are you?" He put his
boot on and stood, lifting her up. "Stand," he said.

The rocket fire stopped. There was sporadic shooting. The air was black with smoke. Debris burned green. Where was the cross-eyed boy with the open smile? She would go look for him. But here was Larry, lying in her path.

Larry, motionless, lay on his stomach, his arms around his head, his fingers laced through his ashy hair. She bent down to touch him. Even now his grey shirt felt dry; it too was coated in ash. She had never before touched Larry's hand, but now she took one of his long white fingers and gave a tug. And as if she'd inflated him or raised him from the dead, he lifted himself on his elbows then pushed to sit upright. His glasses were bent. He removed them and studiously twisted them more or less into shape. When he put them on, they were crooked. "Where's Bull?" he asked. He coughed. And stood up, teetering, peering around, a tourist in hell. Lilac started to cry.

Bull emerged from the smoke, his cane in one hand and an M16 in the other. His orange face was laced in red dust like cracked plaster where the dirt lathed into his scars. "Come and get geared up," he ordered.

Kal laughed. "This is the perfect chance."

"What's that?" Bull turned one ear to him, testily. "What's perfect about it, Kal? De-*fine* it for me."

Kal gestured toward a steel Quonset, sheared in half. "It's one big field trial!" Laughing, then coughing and spitting a ball of phlegm into the dirt. Bull began to pant, truly bull-like, but Kal went on, "The Stalker's going to be battle-proven—right now!"

Lilac stuffed her dirty hand into her mouth to stop herself from sobbing.

"I know why!" Bull suddenly shouted. "I know why Thanh fragged you, man! I see it clear as day!" He waved the rifle. "Now you g'wan and get geared up so's we can get your child to safety, or I'll shoot you myself."

Kal went still. A knot of pain the size of a Ping-Pong ball wedged in Lilac's chest. Her father made a show of laughing at Bull. "Take it easy, why don't you."

Bull glanced quickly at Lilac then made a gesture of surrender and said, "You get me riled sometimes, Kal Welsh."

"Yeah," said Kal. "That's all right. If you want to pack up and run, I'm with you."

Bull's face was hard, but he said, "I wanta run. Tha's fine, Kal. You might jus' as well run along wid me." He turned toward the pavilion.

30.

Except for some damage to one wall, several collapsed tables, stuff in a jumble on the floor, some smashed jugs of cooking oil, the pavilion was mostly untouched by the mortars. The tears dried in the dirt on Lilac's face. She and Kal and Larry followed Bull inside and stood mute while he gave them each a helmet, a flak jacket, and a canteen full of water. He dangled the keys to his Buick on a bottle-opener key chain. "We're takin' the car," he announced, as if it were a Sunday drive. "Get ready."

They waited—for a half-hour, an hour—time quickened and bent erratically. At last there came a lull in the shooting. Then Lilac found herself in the back seat of the Buick with Larry. Her father sat up front beside Bull.

Bull gunned it, spinning dust and sand while he talked loudly over the engine, explaining how the Buick was a hundred times better than a jeep. "Got a lid wid a roll bar," he said, rapping his knuckles on the roof, which was fortified by a metal bar that

Lilac hadn't noticed before. "And special suspension I put in for just this type of occasion." When he twisted around to look at Lilac, the back end of the car kicked sideways and he corrected it without even turning around. "It's a whole lot safer than a jeep, darlin'. Safer than a *tank*." He returned his eyes to the wheel and slapped his palm against the dash as if patting a horse. "Safer than a whole tank *battalion*."

Kal held the M16 across his chest. A grenade sat on the seat between him and Bull. The Stalker was out of sight in the trunk. This had spawned another quick tussle between the two men. Kal had assembled the gun and wanted to stick it out the window "for effect." And Bull had stonily taken it from him, handed him the M16, and told him, "Get in the car."

Now Kal observed, "Thanh'll just have to wait to see my gun." His voice trembled a little, but he was making a show of being witty and casual. "Cool his heels."

Bull glared at him, then he broke into a smile. "Yo some crazy sum'bitch, Kal."

Kal nodded. Lilac realized that he was listening for information about himself, and she thought, He has no clue how to fit into a world he doesn't care about very deeply except as it might please his vanity. She gathered herself to survive him.

They drove northeast through the base, past rows of barracks and out toward open country. The road got rougher, red gravel and sand with brush either side. Beside her, Larry took a photograph with a telephoto lens through the open car window. In a brief clearing the downed Stallion's central rotary was visible, poking up from behind a grassy dune, like a broken windmill. A sustained lull — no planes, no missiles, no artillery — though if anyone chose to blow up the Buick, she and her companions would be the last to know.

Larry brought his camera onto his lap and changed lenses. Lilac tried to think of something to write down. Everything seemed horribly self-evident. There was no *idea* behind anything. Action thrusts forward mindlessly, mercilessly, in reaction to what went before, careening into the future.

The dust was intense, but they had to keep the windows open for air. Larry's ashy shirt turned purple and the lines in his long face were creased with red dust. They met a heron posted at a leafless tree at a crossroads. The heron was three feet tall, elegant, and Lilac thought it looked a lot like Larry. A chant came to mind, words like spring lines that would keep her from smashing, cracking up. I love Larry, Lilac chanted in her head, I love Larry and I love Bull, and she felt recalled to the world. Bull's paisley scarf was soaked in sweat, he radiated heat. I love Bull, chanted Lilac's brain, I love Larry and I love Bull.

Her father began to speak. He talked at length, as if talking would redeem his dignity. She tuned him out. Till she noticed that Larry was taking notes, and remembered that her father was a story. It was a risky story for Kal now; he didn't seem to realize how much he revealed of himself.

"Vietnam is a casino," Kal was saying. "A fix for the big defence contractors. Guns are just small fry. The big money is in guided missiles. Aerospace is big, and it's getting bigger. If I had to do it all over again, I'd be an engineer."

"Tell me," said Larry. "Your background is in what's called applied social psychology. Right? I've always been confused by that expression. How do you *apply* psychology?"

"I specialized in social management."

"Propaganda."

"That's right."

"Made you a good fit for Psyops."

"Correct." Kal didn't turn around but watched the landscape with his roving, hunter's eyes. "You calculate how people will behave. Track the crowds. Try to understand what people are willing to do to belong. What they might be willing to give up."

"That sounds pretty *anti*-social," Larry observed.

Kal, distracted, answered, "It's strategic."

Larry wrote that down. Lilac watched nervously. Larry continued, "You live out in the woods in Canada. I guess I can understand that. You study the herds long enough, it'd make you want to run for the hills."

"I like my independence," said Kal agreeably.

"May I assume, then, you apply the same principles to your business? Welsh X bullets and so on, your Model 70. I'm guessing that your new sniper model is going to surprise people. It's highly innovative."

Kal nodded. "Yes, it is."

"Can I ask you a speculative question?" said Larry. "What if Colt's were to come along and offer to buy your Stalker fifty-cal?"

"Welsh Firearms is private."

"Sure. But—hypothetically. What if Colt's were to make you a great offer? Let you retain a degree of control, and pay you royalties till kingdom come. From what I know, you've done very well, you're a wealthy man. But you could be much wealthier. Because you're probably right—after Vietnam, it'll be the Congo, Nicaragua, Israel. Look at Brown & Root, Halliburton, raking in billions. Not just here, but in oil country. They're going to keep building bridges and dams and deep-sea ports, airports and hangars and ice cream factories and barracks. And when Nixon finally gets us kicked out of here, the contractors will go elsewhere. If things ever threaten to get peaceful, big money will scare up a war somewhere. You could expand. Apply your talents to some really big projects. You could be one of the richest men in the world."

Kal seemed to swell a little. "I've thought about it," he conceded. "But first things first." He looked at Bull, unsmiling but with a cocky attitude. "First, I'll sell my fifty-cal sniper rifle to *Captain* Thanh, head of Logistics."

Bull drummed his thumbs on the wheel. "Man, you're a dog with a bone when you sink your teeth into something."

"I'm an idea man," said Kal. "But one thing at a time."

31.

The broken vehicles were occasional at first and gradually multiplied, until the red gravel road was fenced with wreckage. Trucks, bicycles, overturned military reconnaissance trucks and small flatbed trailers that farmers might use to carry produce, a jumble of domestic and military transport that had been raked to the side of the road—it went on for half a mile.

Bull, at the wheel of the Buick, his peroxide ponytail with a green sheen in the dusty light of late afternoon, the paisley scarf tied around his forehead, sweat pouring down his neck and between his shoulders, steered a path toward a grey horizon, and muttered, "NVA been through here, the fuckers."

Figures appeared on the horizon. Two columns were approaching, a wide line of motorized vehicles moving beside a narrower line of people on foot. When they were only thirty feet away, Bull heaved the wheel to the right and the car left the road and bounced over ruts and onto a dried-up field of stunted rice, where he braked. From there, they watched the cavalcade pass, heading south.

Soldiers walked by, wearing the baggy green uniforms of the South Vietnamese army, coated in red dust. Behind them, a heavy military truck with an open trailer was packed with civilians, a few ARVN soldiers in helmets among the throng of refugees wearing straw conical sun hats shining dully in the sun. A woman clutched a big black vase. Bare feet stuck out on all sides; children clung to any adult with enough strength to hold them; teenagers hung on to the sides, dangling over the road. The truck looked as if it might tip over.

More trucks, smaller, wood-framed, crammed with farmers, villagers, people fleeing with the army. Beside the vehicles walked barefoot children and women, thin, malnourished. Women carried their infants and almost no belongings. A grandmother winced with pain as she balanced two straw baskets on a pole over her shoulders. One basket was full of rolled fabric, and in the other, a toddler squatted, balancing himself on his toes, swaying. A small, barefoot boy wearing a sweater with a knitted Christmas tree tried to clutch an old woman's shirt as she plodded ahead. In desperate concentration, his hand reached out, grabbing air.

Every face was rigid with fear, still terrorized by whatever they had witnessed, whatever they were running from. They moved as fast as they could, painfully slow and urgent. The cortege went on and on. Lilac asked where they'd come from and where they were going.

Bull said, "ARVN are quittin' Quang Tri. They're shifting south, I don't know how far, maybe to Hué. Try to regroup there. Everybody's just running now."

Lilac thought, the Buick is headed in the wrong direction. "We're going toward whatever they're running from."

He twisted around to look at her. "Soon as the road's clear, yeah. We're heading north." He sat back again. "A miserable time."

Larry's voice cracked with dust. "This is their only road to Hué."
Bull nodded. "Just the one exit. An' there's a bridge up ahead
of 'em. Two bridges. I don't like the look of things. Exit's too tight.
We're gonna go the other way, north then east a little ways. Get
you to the coast." A fly buzzed around his sweaty neck, and his
hand moved in a blur to catch it.

Larry got out of the car. He walked toward the procession with
his camera. Lilac saw him speaking, probably asking permission,
but the frightened people only stared at him. He began to take
pictures. Lilac opened her car door, but Bull said, "Don't do that."
He looked back at her again. "Please don't do that, honey." She
hesitated. "It ain't safe."

She was sitting with the door open when she saw the plane. A
silver arrow flitting incredibly fast from the west. Another plane
appeared from the north. Together they flew low, very low, a
hundred feet above the road, travelling several hundred miles an
hour.

"MiGs," Bull said. "They got Russian planes. I heard about
them. But I never seen one till now."

Two MiG jets. They played the air close above the heads of the
fleeing crowd and flew up again, twisting as light as paper darts,
shining silver, looping then zooming away, south.

Larry came running to the car and got in. Lilac's door was still
open when Bull gunned it, tearing through the dirt, the tires spinning then finding traction. Larry reached over Lilac and pulled
her door closed. The Buick bucked and rocked over the uneven
ground, racing parallel to the road, and when they'd passed the
last stragglers, Bull yanked the wheel and, maintaining speed,
lurched back onto the crumbling pavement, north.

"They didn't shoot," Bull breathed. "Thank God, they didn't
shoot."

But a mile farther, the road was blocked again by ruined jeeps and ARVN trucks, overturned. The vehicles were destroyed, but there were no people, no bodies. Bull pulled off the road again and forced his car over the muddy field. Sweat poured off his chin and sprayed when he turned his head.

At the rear of the destroyed convoy, a military truck remained upright, with all its windows blown in. Beside the truck was a farmer's cart loaded with burlap bags. In the near distance stood a water buffalo, unmoving, that stolid, placid bulk. Four people lingered around the cart and the truck: three ARVN soldiers, one of whom was very tall, and a tiny old woman, gesticulating down the road at her buffalo, apparently furious, comic, Lilac thought, performing a stuttering dance. Her straw sun hat lay in the mud nearby like a white bowl in the sun.

Bull braked hard. He got out of the car and looked around, then leaned down to speak through the open car door to Kal in the passenger seat. "If you're not the luckiest sum'bitch on the planet, Kal Welsh, I don't know who is."

Kal looked at him blankly.

"It's Thanh," Bull explained. "And I'm guessin' you want to talk to him." He closed the door and started off with his cane, walking toward the strange group on the road, but after a few paces he returned, and leaned down to speak to Lilac through the open window. "You stay put. We don' know when those MiGs might come pokin' around again. Don't you move." He turned again to walk across the broken field toward the road.

Kal got out and went around to the trunk. The sound of the latch, the trunk opening, he grunted as he bent to lift the Stalker from its nest, and then he too hurried toward the road.

Larry was getting out with his camera ready when he stopped and said to her, "I have to get this on film. But you're going to sit here like Bull told you to. I mean it. Sit tight." He began to take photographs even as he walked over the rough ground toward the scene.

Lilac shut her eyes for a moment. She would have liked to have a choice, an alternative to what she knew she had to do. But there was only one way to move and that was toward whatever careened out of the future. She slung her camera over her neck, got out of the car, and followed the men.

32.

At home, Kal's ballistics tests were aimed at a head and chest made of gelatin placed at the end of his makeshift firing range carved out of the bush behind the log house. Now he aimed down a road of mud and gravel, the gun on its two legs propped before him. He was talking. "I'd have preferred to give you a chance to see this baby perform longer range. But this'll have to do."

"Please be quick," said the tall man. Captain Thanh.

Lilac had never before encountered a man more like a machine. The two other ARVN soldiers, standing a few paces behind him, kept glancing nervously into the hot sky, obviously fearful of an attack. But Thanh's reserve seemed impenetrable.

About three hundred yards down the road stood the old woman's water buffalo, immobile, docile, solitary. The woman sat down cross-legged beside her cart and muttered what sounded like obscenities. She had been chewing betel, and her sunken lips were a brilliant red gash around toothless gums, a sinister, clown-like effect.

Lilac was studying the old woman when the gun went off. The

explosion echoed over the fields. One of the soldiers instinctively bucked, bolted before he could restrain himself, then pivoted quickly and returned to his captain.

In the distance, the water buffalo was still standing. Lilac, horrified, thought that her father had missed. But then the animal went down on its knees in an attitude of prayer. It stayed that way for several moments before it wavered and heaved onto its side, sending up a ring of white dust.

Kal rose to his feet as if to take a bow. But he simply nodded and told them all, "Fine penetration. Took it through the shoulder, direct to the heart." To Captain Thanh, "My outfit in Connecticut can have thirty of these weapons in your hands within a week."

One of the soldiers spoke anxiously into his captain's ear, obviously desperate to get out of there, waving his arms up to the sky. Thanh answered him curtly, turned to Kal and nodded again, and without further comment opened the door to his damaged truck. He shouted at the soldier, who ducked hurriedly around him to sweep the glass from the seat of the vehicle, using his bare hands at first, cutting himself then removing his jacket to use as a broom. Thanh's face and bearing were unflinching, but he did stoop briefly to look at Kal and give a slight nod of affirmation. Lilac watched as her father received Captain Thanh's blessing, quite possibly an order for his Stalker.

The truck came to life in a cloud of purple diesel fumes. She became aware of the clicking shutter of Larry's camera, and realized that she should be taking pictures.

Bull was saying something in Vietnamese, while he put some money in the hands of the tiny woman then pulled her to her feet as if she were a hankie. He lifted her till she was trailing her toes in the dirt, and deposited her in the bed of the truck, staring down the anxious soldier who appeared to be complaining about taking a civilian passenger.

Thanh got into the truck and it rumbled off, south. Bull, already walking toward his Buick, said, "Business done. Now I get you back to the land of the living."

33.

Clear water flowed over pebbles of limestone and gypsum, white as quartz. From a distance, the winding river looked emerald. They'd approached it abruptly. The car had been climbing steadily, but on such a gradual incline the valley appeared suddenly like the dream of a valley, the forest a dream of green in richly humid air. A path, worn down by carts and water buffalo, ran eastward beside the river.

Bull stopped the car, the engine ticking, and they all got out and walked down in long, low sunlight toward the diamond light of rushing water. Lilac went to the riverbank, where she kneeled in the grass. Intensely green, green as an aphid. She was shocked by this evidence of purity; she'd so entirely forgotten purity. Bull came to sit in the grass beside her.

Her eyes sought out her dad. He was sitting a ways off, staring into the swift, glittering current. If it wasn't her dad she was looking at, if it was somebody she didn't know, she'd say he looked bored, she'd guess that nothing here interested him.

Bull said, "We're gettin' to the losing end. Communists are going to take over this country. Brutal folk."

They could stay here only a few minutes, Bull said, before they had to move on to the coast, where a friend of his was waiting for them. "My friend's got a nice boat, a smooth little cruiser, cruise down south to Da Nang. Lot safer there. Then you fly back to Saigon."

"You can just set something like that up?"

"I radioed a buddy in MAB. That's the amphibian battalion, honey. Told him I got some famous guests need escort."

Lilac asked him what he'd do with his car.

Bull looked at her blankly.

"At the coast. When we go away in the boat."

"Drive home," he said.

"Oh," she said, "I forgot. You're in the army. You can't leave."

Bull reached out and tucked a strand of her hair behind her ear. His intelligent eyes observed her from that massive, chipped face.

"Why have you stayed in the army all this time, Bull?" she asked. "Even after you got hurt. You stayed. Knowing that the Thanh man tried to kill you. You're strong. I mean, I don't know how you have the strength to put up with so much hate and craziness."

Bull said, "I went out."

"Out of where?"

"Out of the military. I moved sideways," Bull said. "I work in information."

"Are you a spy? Like, with the CIA?" She remembered Heather Markham's speculation about the pilot with the red bandana. She was certain Bull wasn't a drug trafficker.

He smiled, and gently tugged at the camera around her neck. "You take pictures. You know what *parallax* means." He placed his scarred palm over her left eye, then over her right. "Different view, depending on which eye. I try to see out both eyes, to get a full view. Depth of field. That's what I came to see. And stayed to see better."

He let Lilac take his hand while they rested by the river, and she leaned her face into his warm, ragged palm, big as a baseball mitt. In the near distance, the forest, that photosynthetic, light-harvesting green, and the river curling through the narrow valley. Bull said, "It sure is a beautiful place. When it's not scaring the hell outta me." He retrieved his hand—"Come on, darlin'"—and used his cane to push himself to his feet. "Let's go."

She realized they'd have to walk the rest of the way, and asked, "Is it far?"

"You can practically smell the ocean from here." Bull went to the car and pulled a couple of flashlights out of the trunk and handed one to Larry. "Be dark soon," he told him. "Don't use this. Unless you absolutely have to."

Kal hauled out the black leather bag. He had not said a word since his encounter with Thanh. Now he marched behind them all, limping, slowed by the weight of the gun.

She dropped back to walk beside him. He looked at her briefly. She said, "Now that you've made contact with Thanh, you'll probably sell your gun to him, right?"

He nodded dully.

After a moment, she asked him tentatively, "Doesn't that make you happy?"

He didn't answer but trudged on.

She heard the ocean breathing before she saw it. They crested a rocky slope and looked down on white sand and silver surf, the waves luffing in a light breeze from the east. The sun dropped into the sea just as a red crescent moon emerged from it. A small inboard cabin cruiser was beached below, and they walked down. Bull stumbled when his cane slipped on a rock. Lilac touched his arm. "My dancin' days is over," he said.

The boat was like a holiday vessel that she might see moored at Minaki with wet bathing suits hanging from its flagpole. It was unmarked. No flag. Like the unmarked airplane that had taken her to Quang Ngai with Heather. On the beach beside the cruiser stood a grizzled Westerner in rumpled civilian clothes. He greeted Bull warmly. "Knew it was you from fifty yards. There's nobody like you, Bull," the man said. "You're one of a kind."

Larry hung back, a long shadow against the white sand. Lilac went to stand by him while her father walked on, wading into the surf to the stern of the boat. Kal raised the leather bag to his chest and heaved it over the gunnel. She heard it thud against the deck, and said to Larry, "Bull says this guy will take us all to Da Nang." She watched her father standing up to his thighs in water, staring out at the purple horizon.

Larry said, "You be careful in Da Nang. This offensive might push that far south."

She took a breath. His glasses were crooked. "You're not coming with us, Larry?"

Larry glanced back at the stony cliff. "There's a story running wild out there." He gave her one of his sad smiles. "I'd better hang around and see how this dirty yarn plays out."

She was embarrassed by how badly she wanted to get away. And relieved that Bull wouldn't have to make the journey alone, back to his 'lil enterprise. Larry coughed.

"You have to see a doctor," she told him.

Larry said, "Roger that." He surprised her with a kiss on her cheek.

Lilac said, "I'll see you in Saigon. Get out of here soon. Right?"

Larry said, "Go home."

"Sure. But I'll see you there."

"Go *home*." He abruptly wrapped his arms around her, and in the sough of the surf his voice was barely audible. "Go on home, darling one."

She was looking over Larry's shoulder when a movement caught her eye, a form, a man, walking toward them, his dark shape against the moony white sand. It was a soldier, she thought it was Gavin, a shadow; he walked past her and onward, passing them all, and when he walked into the white shells of surf, into the sea, he seemed to multiply till he was many Gavins, dark shapes against the waves, entering the water, and disappearing.

She wasn't going to cry or anything. She put her hand against the dry cotton of Larry's shirt. "Please don't stay long at Quang Tri."

He said, "Won't be long."

"I'll watch for you." She turned from him and went to Bull and threw herself into his chest.

"Hey, honey child." Bull dropped his cane, lifted her in both arms, and waded into the water to the boat. The cabin cruiser had a gunnel about a foot and a half wide, and he set her down there.

PART THREE

1.

The cabin cruiser left the estuary where the Thạch Hãn river drains into the China Sea and churned south along the coast. Lilac's father fastidiously placed his knapsack and the leather bag containing his rifle in a space beneath the companionway then took a seat at the stern, staring out at the starry sea. If it was as Bull predicted, if the Marines would feign an amphibian attack to draw the attention of the NVA, there was no sign of it now. Lilac wondered if there were ships out there, navigating in the dark. Her father looked exhausted, ashen. Lilac asked if he felt sick, but he claimed that he was fine. She stood beside Bull's friend, a guy called Dave, in his tall captain's chair at the wheel, until the drone of the engine and the swells of the calm sea almost put her to sleep on her feet, then went below and slept for most of that night-long journey to Da Nang.

Lilac and Kal spent the next day at the Da Nang Air Base. The North Vietnamese offensive kept advancing, pushing the ARVN south in an attempt to capture Hué. Da Nang was chaotic, crowded with frightened civilians, and soldiers striding with great purpose, and the noise of airplanes and Chinook helicopters moving howitzers, and medevacs dropping off injured men and body bags. Here, Kal established himself in an oily corner of a hangar and barely nodded when she told him she was going to search for a flight. When she returned to inform him that she hadn't yet found anything, she saw the whites of his eyes when he looked up at her, absorbing her update with barely a flicker. Again, she asked him if he was ill.

He said, "Why do you keep asking me that?"

"I mean—aren't you happy about the sale to Mr. Thanh?"

He barked, "Happy?" He studied her closely, searchingly, but she sensed that he was trying to see himself. Someone was screaming in pain. They both turned and, through the open doors of the hangar, saw the stretchers being disgorged from a medevac, medics scurrying from one wounded man to the next. When Kal returned his attention to her, he looked so strained she was afraid of what he might say, afraid that she'd hurt him in a way that she hadn't anticipated and would always regret.

"I mean, he'll buy your gun, right?" she stammered.

Kal nodded and said that he thought there would be an order, but it was hard to be sure. "Thanh has other things on his mind," he added, with some of the wry self-assurance she expected from him.

Tentatively, she continued, "So that was the real-life Mr. Thanh, that tall man on the road? That was the same man who talked in the movie you made. The movie with the trees and the weird song." He was distracted again by the hurried movements outside, the urgency of medics and stretchers and moaning wounded men. She added, "You called him a hungry ghost."

"Yeah," he answered vaguely. "That was him. A captain now. Head of Logistics. A big shot."

"It seems amazing."

"Yeah," he said, but she wasn't sure if they were talking about the same amazement. He scrubbed his face with dry, dirty hands. "God help us." Then he stood and announced, "I'm going to find an Air America flight and get us out of this hellhole right now. Wait here."

It took him three hours, but he got them on a plane with about eighty other people headed for what seemed at the time like the ultimate safety in Saigon.

It was dark when at last they arrived at the Tan Son Nhut airport. He had the taxi take them to her hotel. When they arrived, the taxi idling on the busy, narrow alley, he turned to her to say, "I'll be in touch in the morning to let you know where I'm staying."

"You don't want to stay here?"

"I have to work. I need a place with telephones." He kissed her forehead. "You'd better get something to eat and go to bed."

She was confused by her father's...detachment. The word came to her. It made her yearn for his attention as if she were a kid. She hesitated with her hand on the car door, searching for a way to make him tell her how he was feeling about what they'd just been through. "That was quite a trip," she offered.

But her father was looking over the taxi driver's shoulder and saying, "Take me to Thong Nhut Street." He glanced at her as if surprised that she was still there. Whatever had disturbed him about the violence they'd experienced, the danger they'd been in, it all seemed to have passed, and he was on to the next thing, a hotel with telephones so he could work. He seemed to have forgotten that he'd nearly got them both killed. But quickly his expression changed. He looked almost furtive, shamefaced. Then resentful. He gave his daughter such a look of resentment, she backed out of the car as if he'd struck her.

2.

Kal took a suite with a desk and a couch in a nice hotel. Over the next several days, she'd walk over to find him absorbed in his mail from his company in the States, or on the phone.

His hotel room had air conditioning and a bar stocked with Japanese whiskey. Then there appeared, sitting on his desk, a square, grey machine the size of the sixteen-millimetre projector he'd brought to Rough Rock. "It's a Xerox Magnafax," he told her. "You've never seen one of these before? You didn't notice their ads in *Life*?" This contraption sent letters over the phone somehow, by magic as far as Lilac was concerned. He was absorbed, fascinated, while it whirred and ticked. "Right now, it's sending me a letter from Randy in Connecticut. Six minutes. That's all it'll take."

The noise was familiar to Lilac. "Maybe we had them at the *Trib*, but I never saw one up close before." The *Overseas Weekly* certainly didn't have one. Heather Markham mailed their copy and film to be printed and processed in Hong Kong and mailed back to Saigon, a process she said was streamlined compared to four years ago, when they had to mail everything to Germany.

"It's the future," said Kal. "I can work anywhere in the world now."

But the ticking accelerated then turned into loud static. "Damn," he said. "Maybe the phone service isn't good enough."

"Where'd you get it?"

"I had Randy find me one." He was still waiting for it to spit out the letter. The static got very loud. The Machine began to whistle, and rattle, then it stopped.

She wandered around his elegant room, feeling listless, unwell, and almost overwhelmed by a feeling of dread, even fear, as if her body knew terrible things that her mind was working hard to deny. "Have you heard anything from Bull?" she asked. "And Larry Donovan?"

"Nope." He was studying the Xerox machine with frustration but looked up sharply at her. "You're worried," he said.

"Aren't you?"

He seemed to search himself for signals of anxiety. "It's only been a few days. How about we start to worry on Friday?" He smiled as if he'd hoped to make her laugh, and when she didn't, he sobered and said, "You probably wouldn't worry so much if you were working."

He walked to the bed, where a second phone sat on the bedside table. He was dressed differently from the way he would dress at home. He looked like a businessman. When he sat down on the bed, with both hands he tugged his trousers at the knee, a funny gesture she'd seen men in the city do. He picked up the receiver and dialed. "Front desk? Make a call for me, will you? Yes. I'll hold." While he waited, Lilac asked him if he'd found the shirt and slacks he was wearing here in Saigon. He brightened and said, "I found this great tailor on Tu Do Street—" He was interrupted by the front desk letting him know they were ready to connect him, and he put his hand over the receiver while he told Lilac, "I have to talk to Randy." She stared at him, dazed. "I'll be awhile," he said.

She finally took the hint and walked out.

The streets were more crowded than ever now that the Communists were pushing south, the sidewalks crammed with refugees, barefoot, listless with hunger. She made her way toward the *Weekly* office. Maybe her dad was right, maybe she'd feel better if she was working. She'd ask Heather for an assignment. It'd be a relief not to feel so anxious and tired all the time. There was a fried sensation in her chest, and a headache that hadn't quit for the last couple of days. Her body ached all over, and she didn't think she could handle anything more complicated than home-towners here in Saigon—interviews with injured soldiers at the hospitals that she and Heather could sell to the soldiers' home-town newspapers.

She passed a boy, maybe nine years old, seated alone on a piece of cardboard on the busy sidewalk. Spread around him were packets of Bazooka bubble gum. At first glance she thought he was wearing a nylon stocking over his face, his features were obscured. But then she realized that he had no eyes. Where the eyes should have been, there was nothing but a slight dent in the flesh. She put some money into his plastic bowl and murmured, "Here we are."

At the *Weekly*, Heather greeted her cautiously. When Lilac asked for an assignment, she answered, "Frankly, my friend, you look like you could do with some R and R."

Lilac explained, "I've been up at Quang Tri. It was actually pretty intense." Only then did she realize that she'd been feeling so lousy she'd forgotten that her trip north was going to be a great story for the *Weekly* and the *Tribune*, a journalist's coup.

Heather abruptly embraced Lilac. "Good lord. No wonder you look like you've been put through the wringer." She swayed, hugging her as if she were a child. "Thank goodness you got out." Then quickly the reporter's curiosity kicked in and she pulled away to ask shrewdly, "How *did* you get out?"

"By boat."

Heather repeated, "By boat." She released Lilac. "Down the coast? Not by road?"

"No. On a cabin cruiser."

"So, you weren't on the road." Heather breathed out with relief.

Lilac felt a pang of guilt, remembering the terrified people fleeing south. She asked Heather if she'd heard anything about what happened at Quang Tri.

"Well, it's gone," Heather answered. "It fell." She saw Lilac's face and asked, "Who were you with?"

"My father. And his friend Bull. And Larry Donovan."

"Larry Donovan was there?" She mulled this over. Then, "Your father came to Vietnam?" Lilac said yes, and Heather declared, "He was worried about you."

"Sort of. Yes."

"Who's Bull?" Then she figured it out. "Bull Johnson? The Pysops guy?"

"Do you know him?"

"Bull's been here forever," Heather said. "He's famous."

"Bull and Larry didn't get on the boat with my dad and me. They went back."

"Back to where?"

"To the road, I guess. To Quang Tri."

Heather crossed her arms. "Well. They're both smart, both experienced. They'll be okay."

"What do you mean, Quang Tri fell?"

"I don't know much. We don't have all the casualty reports yet. Just the big names. The ARVN leaders who were killed, that's been reported already."

"What ARVN leaders?" She thought of Mr.—Captain—Thanh.

"Well, I'd have to look." Heather went to her desk, where papers were neatly stacked in several piles, and quickly found the report she wanted and read half a dozen names. And yes, Captain Ly Tong Thanh was among them.

Lilac asked her to repeat the name, which she did. Lilac said, "Captain Thanh is dead."

"You know him?" Heather looked puzzled.

"My dad does. Did. I have to go," said Lilac. "Thank you." She stumbled back out to the street.

3.

Kal regarded her as if she was talking nonsense. "Thanh's not dead, Lilac," he told her in the patient voice he used when he was explaining things to her.

"Quang Tri fell," she said.

Her dad held a sheaf of papers. He shook the paper at her. He was beginning to lose his temper. "Thanh is interested in my gun. He was very impressed. I'm sure he'll make an order. Thirty guns. Lowball, I'm guessing twenty."

"He got killed. With a bunch of other officers who died too. Heather showed me the list." She watched him. It was as if his whole body was pushing back against this unwanted information.

"Who told you?"

"Heather Markham. Like I just said." Lilac cast about the hotel room, looking for a glass; she wondered if he'd been drinking, he seemed confused. His resentment was so palpable, she felt like she should apologize. Of course, he would be disappointed by the loss of such an important contact in Logistics, especially since he'd had that occasion on the road to demonstrate the gun's accuracy.

"He's dead?" He sat down heavily at his desk. He looked extremely sad, and she wondered nervously if he'd weep. She'd never seen her father cry. "Thanh is dead?"

"I still don't know about Bull and Larry."

Kal quickly raised his eyes to her. "They'll be okay." He heaved a sigh. "Thanh is dead." He got up and poured himself a shot of whiskey, took a sip, then asked her, "Want one?" She accepted, and sat on his bed to drink it, while he resumed his chair at the desk, placing his hand across some papers there.

"Hard," he said, "it's really hard to fathom." He sat in silence for a moment, then took a sip as if gearing up to say something difficult. He seemed strangely vulnerable. "Thanh's betrayal has been on my mind all these years. Till he got to be, I don't know, almost like a part of me." He tried to laugh. "I think he was even part of my decision to move you and your mother out to Rough Rock. In fact, I'm pretty sure that's why I needed to go live out there. It was as if he'd exiled me." He paused. "So, he's dead? That's what your friend Heather says? Well"—he finished his drink—"he's not dead to me." He stood to pour more whiskey and went to stare out the window at the street below. "He'll never be dead to me."

Lilac tried to understand. She'd never had a personal enemy. The North Vietnamese army would have killed her if they could, along with her dad and Bull and Larry—yet that was impersonal. The war was indifferent to what happened to her, even though maybe she'd never cut herself loose from it. Her dad's enemy, Thanh, was someone he'd trusted, called a "friend," somebody who was supposed to be working with him yet turned on him violently. That must really set the hook in a person. Her father was having another drink.

Lilac leaned back on her elbows, wishing that she felt comfortable enough here to simply curl up and sleep, get rid of this headache. Her hand touched the glossy cover of a magazine lying on the bed. It was a copy of the *Shooting Times*. She thumbed through its pages to a full-page ad with a photo of the new Stalker posed on burlap sandbags, like an offering of farm produce, or like a woman, one of those semi-nudes in the *Overseas Weekly*. Beside the rifle was a soldier's helmet in twine netting, and an American flag stitched rustically. The ad copy read:

> *Introducing the .50 caliber Welsh Stalker 80.*
> *Battle-proven. A revolutionary sniper weapon.*
> *The Welsh Stalker 80 semi-automatic.*
> *The only rifle that can take down a multi-million-dollar jet*
> *with a two-dollar bullet.*
> *A bold weapon. To do bold things.*

"You took out an ad." She was surprised. "It says the Stalker's 'battle-proven.' Like, it's been used in a war already?"

He turned to her with a mixture of pride and embarrassment. "I thought it would be, by the time we ran the ad. It was just the timing put me off."

"It'll take down a jet with a two-dollar bullet?"

"Well. It'll do a hell of a lot of damage." Thoughtfully, he added, "I guess I'll have to find out who will replace Thanh."

"Larry said it was too late for you to sell the Stalker here." Mention of Larry sent a hot dart of pain across her skull. She'd go to the Caravelle when she left here. Surely Larry will be at the bar, safe and sound.

Her father nodded philosophically. "Larry might be right. But you know, Vietnam ain't the endgame, little darlin'." He was mimicking Bull. Then he explained that since the ad came out about a week ago, he'd had inquiries. "I'm already looking at an order for Israel. And India is showing interest. I never even calculated India in the equation. And it gets bigger. There's

Honduras. And Guatemala. God knows, even Chile. Central America is hot, and who knows what's going to happen in places like Chile and Peru. Maybe even Argentina. Look at their oil. It's a hot situation.

"But let's not write off Vietnam just yet," he continued in a more conciliatory tone. "Maybe, as your friend says, Quang Tri *did* fall. But we'll push back. You watch. We'll take it back. This war ain't over till it's over."

Lilac curled on her side. She felt awful. She tucked one of the quilted pillows under her cheek.

"Hey," her dad said tenderly. "You want some soup?" He put down his drink and came to sit on the edge of the bed and put his hand on her forehead. It was kind. But it was also an imitation of the way her mum would make that gesture. He was talking, his words coming through the blur of her headache.

"The CIA caught wind of my new rifle," he said softly, as if his words were soothing. "When Bull gets in touch, we'll know who'll take on Thanh's job in Logistics."

She mumbled, "I have to go see if Larry's at the Caravelle."

He stroked her hair. His hand felt heavy, those strong hands. He began to talk about Rough Rock, speaking gently. "I took some risk to get the Stalker into production, Lilac. A necessary investment. As a matter of fact, I put a lot of money into it. The house, the shop, all the land at Rough Rock, you see, it's all mortgaged now. But we'll all come out fine in the end, don't you worry. It's highly leveraged for the time being. But I'll be moving guns into the field before you know it." He stroked her hair. "Everything's going to be all right."

Lilac opened her eyes. This was news.

He continued in a low voice. "Bull thought I was nuts. He said nobody can build a shoulder-fired rifle with fifty-cal ammo. He said it's impossible. But I've done it, haven't I. The first. And now that he's seen how it performs, well, old Bull is going to be eating crow." He chuckled briefly. "But it's cost me, you know. A million. More. I put everything on the line. But you see, now there's interest from India, and inquiries from Israel. Central America, all of South America will go Communist unless we help them out."

Lilac pushed his hand away and sat up.

"You know how big this is," he said, moving aside to give her room. "You grew up in the business."

"Does Mum know?"

"About what?"

"The mortgage on Rough Rock."

He shook his head. "No sense worrying her." He winced, thinking things through. "It'll be tricky till I can ramp up some commercial sales."

"Commercial?"

"Civilian. Sport shooting."

She drew her knees to her chest. "Why?"

"What do you mean, why?"

"I mean why the *fuck* would anyone other than a sniper want a gun that can shoot down an airplane?"

"Please don't swear like that." He stood up to fetch his drink. "You know we can't survive on military sales to keep afloat. Look at my Welsh 70. It does pretty good here in Vietnam. But do you really think we could survive without our sales to hunters?"

"But the Stalker isn't a hunting rifle."

"I know." He grinned boyishly. "But it'll go down real good with the city-boy target shooters."

"I'm guessing a few wars might pay better than a bunch of wannabes at a shooting range."

"It's more complicated than that." He sounded hurt.

She hauled herself to her feet. "If you're going to lose the house, you should tell Mum."

"Where are you going?" He looked bereft, watching her go out the door.

"To find Larry Donovan."

4.

Lilac went every day for the next week to the Caravelle Hotel, leaving messages with Henri at the rooftop bar, then to Larry's apartment to knock on his door.

She couldn't see straight and tripped over her own feet. The hotelier with the deep-V eyebrows studied her solemnly when she cracked her shins on the low plastic table in the hotel lobby. That evening she returned to find a packet of tea and a porcelain teapot with a delicate cup at her door.

A high-octane blend of restlessness and fear buzzed in her veins, inflaming her dreams. She had vivid aural hallucinations. One day, lost in thought, she was drifting into the path of a fast-moving limousine when she heard Larry's sandy voice say, "Step quick," and leapt back to the curb.

Ruby sent letters from home at least twice a week. These missives were filled with her mother's worries mixed with glimpses of wind or rain or the red furze of spring on birch trees. News from home blended with Lilac's long, hot walks through the streets of Saigon into a delirious splicing of memory and dream.

Other than the official announcement that Quang Tri had fallen, US military briefings did not include specifics of American or ARVN casualties. And of course, nothing was said about the deaths of Vietnamese civilians. There was no word from Larry or from Bull. Meanwhile, the NVA continued to push farther south, approaching Saigon.

Lilac picked up *Life* and *Time* from a newsstand but didn't see any photojournalism by Larry Donovan. Neither did she see a report of his death. She couldn't believe that Larry would be killed. He was careful and didn't carry a gun, he'd been in Vietnam for over a decade, he was a lucky one. She kept going to the Caravelle and to knock on the door of his apartment, and she mailed countless letters to Bull at Quang Tri. At a street vendor, she found a record player and a single of "Ain't Nothing Like the Real Thing" and played it incessantly. The letters mailed to Bull were only a fraction of the number that she wrote.

And she wrote to Gavin McLean, GC TRP, 1st SQDN, USARV, AB, Da Nang. That first letter to Gavin, the one she mailed before she knew anything about this place, was probably lost, or surely he would have responded. Maybe this one would disappear too. A lost lure. Maybe he was dead, a ghost who walked into the sea, but she wrote to him anyway.

Dear Gavin,

I'm sending you a couple of photographs of lichen. I found the film at the bottom of my purse and got it developed here in Saigon. It was totally weird to see pictures from home. You'll probably recognize the blue-green dried leafy stuff you walked on at the island that day we swam together. And the big splash of crusty sienna on the big rock where you lay to dry in the sun. You know, lichen is not a <u>thing</u>, it's a combination of two things, algae and fungus. It can only live in a conversation—it's a combination of two things that are not it. I'm finding this perplexing. It troubles me, because something I love (lichen) exists between. Always between. So in a way, when it's solo, it doesn't exist.

I'm worried about you. I'm here in the city and I hope you contact me. But no matter what happens, our friendship lives in this strange between. Please write back.

Your friend for life,

Lilac

She placed the photos between two pieces of cardboard in a big envelope and mailed it to AB Da Nang.

5.

The crooked beauty of Jack pines, cloud-shadows moving over aspen and birch, wind-ruffled water, these images came to mind while Lilac paced the grubby streets of Saigon, haunted by thoughts of home. Letters from her mother kept arriving. "Please, please come back." Lilac responded carefully, stalling. "Returning in a while, Mum. I'm finishing up a few assignments here."

Ruby didn't seem so insistent on Kal's return. Her letters from Rough Rock were filled with dissatisfaction, but she never complained about missing her husband. In one, Ruby admitted she'd been having some time to think. "I wonder how I got here," she wrote. She did complain, bitterly, about Kal's love for the new gun. "I just can't accept that he wants to build that thing and take it out into the world. And what the hell is this God-stuff anyway? It's getting worse! Sometimes I wonder if I ever really knew him."

Ruby's doubts made Lilac feel more alone than she might have felt if things were fine between her parents. Her dad was busy, here in Saigon, running his business by correspondence from his nice suite near the presidential palace. He'd ordered more clothes from his tailor on Tu Do Street, all the while talking about how he would make their life at Rough Rock financially secure. Lilac wrote a careful letter to tell her mother, "You have to do what you have to do for your own life, Mum." She did not mention that Kal had financed the Stalker by borrowing against Rough Rock.

She walked in dense heat to the post office to mail this letter to Ruby. The air in Saigon was ripe with the scent of food and the suffocating exhaust from scooters and American army vehicles. She yearned for cold lake water, blue and green. The lake was alive, eight thousand miles away. Here in Saigon, peach blossoms and yellow flowers called Mai blew petals that smeared underfoot. Even by Vietnamese standards it was hot midday, the air yellow the way it would get at home when the forest fires got out of control.

Today at the post office she received a fat envelope from the *Tribune*, and she carried it back to room 214. The envelope contained a cheque along with clippings from a section of the newspaper called The World. Here was Lilac's story, THE BUTCHER'S HELPER. Quotations from Claire were mostly in full, with one alteration: "Send the photographs to Trudeau and tell him he's a [expletive]." A horse's ass.

And whoever edited her work had paraphrased Claire's further assessment of Pierre Trudeau (that he was the devil, a hypocrite): "The nurse told this writer that she was of the opinion that our prime minister has not been fully honest with the Canadian people about our nation's involvement in the conflict in Vietnam." The subhead read: CANADA PROVIDING INTEL TO CIA. There was a handwritten note: "Well done. Bravo. Be careful. Give my regards to Larry. Come home in one piece. Sincerely, Martha Mavin."

And here were Lilac's photographs. The cruelty that she had witnessed in full evidence. The boy with the face of ash, the woman with her starving children, the boy with the hole in his shoulder the size of a hockey puck, the baby in a pool of blood. She felt imprisoned in her pride in publishing this stuff.

Lilac had that headache again. She'd told her father that she'd meet him in a couple of hours for dinner at that French restaurant he liked, but she crawled under her single sheet and fell heavily asleep. In a dream, she heard gunshots, loud shots in succession from her dad's new gun. Ten shots—the shooter slowly and relentlessly emptied an entire magazine—echoes fading when he shot again. Lilac drifted in and out of sleep like a boat drifting shy of the dock, scudding toward the rocks. She heard her mother calling Kal. Ruby's voice rising like a crow's, *Kal* became *caw*.

Even in sleep, a scent of mint. The pink heels of her mother's bare feet on wood chips on the path through poplar that led down to the shed where Lilac stored her little hydroplane. The shed's cedar shakes shone silver in the sun. Its back end leaned into peat at the shore and its door opened out to the steel-grey lake. Instead of the hydroplane, her father was stretched out on the boat cradle. Something in his posture, the way his body was splayed on top of his rifle, embracing or smothering it, made Lilac sick. She lurched out of bed to run and vomit into the toilet, trembling with a fever and chills when she crawled back under her damp sheet and fell into the same dream. Her father pressed his cheek to the stock, prepared to squeeze the trigger. She touched his shoulder and he turned on her. He wore a face of pleasure. He was in his own magic. It all belonged to him.

Day passed into evening while Lilac slept and woke to see ghostly figures floating over her darkening room. She grew fretful, anxious that she was supposed to be someplace but unable to get out of bed or figure out how to leave her room. In darkness, she emerged from a dream about swimming in bones, past a grinning skull. A low-flying helicopter slapped the stones and rattled the cages of pigeons on the roof of the hotel. Someone was opening her door. Ruby emerged from the dark and came to Lilac's bed, leaning over her the way she would when Lilac was a little girl, the rustle of her cotton skirt, placing her hand on Lilac's forehead to test for fever. Lilac heard the clear music of her mother's voice asking, "How are you feeling?" and then the voice was replaced by her father's baritone. "Lilac? What's wrong?"

She said, "I'm swimming." She felt his hand on her face.

He said, "You're burning up," and turned on the bedside lamp. She opened her eyes. He told her, "I waited for over an hour — Never mind." He left and she heard water running and then he was putting cold, wet towels around her neck. He disappeared. She fell back to sleep.

When he came back, he had another man with him. She figured it would be okay with them if she didn't keep her eyes open, the headache was so bad, and she swallowed the pills they put in her mouth and drank the water. And slept.

It was day when she next awoke. Her father lay stretched out on the floor beside her bed. He sat up. His hair, normally combed smooth, fell over his eyes and he pushed it back with his fingers. "Your fever broke a couple of hours ago." He stiffly got up off the floor. She heard him washing at the sink, and when he returned, reassembled with his hair combed and his shirt tucked in, he carried a glass of water. He handed her two pills. "Quinine and Aspirin. That doctor said it might be malaria." He pulled her chair up beside the bed and watched her take it. "You scare me sometimes," he said.

"You scare me sometimes too."

He stood up and lurched forward so quickly she recoiled, but he took her face between his hands. "If anything ever happened to you—" His eyes filled with tears. In a more normal voice, he asked, "Do you think you might eat something?"

She said she thought she could. Compared with how she felt last night, or the day before, or really for the last few days, she felt light and glad and birdlike.

"Good." He clapped his hands together and brightly suggested, "You wash up and I'll bring something for you to eat. Something bland, right? I'll see what I can find." He headed for the door, then detoured and came back to where she was still tangled in her sweaty sheets, and he kissed the top of her head and said, "Darling." Then he left.

A few minutes later, Lilac sat in a cool bath. She was still weak and convalescent, which might explain why she was suddenly overwhelmed by a sensation of deep kindness, something like the relief she felt that summer when she got so anxious as a kid and a voice came out of the forest to tell her, "It doesn't matter." This sensation felt like love. At this moment, anyway, love seemed to be a general condition. A gift.

6.

Gavin's fatigues looked too big for him. His army knapsack was on the sidewalk at his feet. He observed Lilac walk toward him, and she sensed a flicker of affectionate interest. His features were more pointed than she remembered, a fox mask. He'd been growing out his hair from the military buzz cut, and the soft, tufted growth contributed to his quizzical vigilance.

His weight was arranged differently, his centre of gravity had torqued. She remembered her father shoving his chest into Gavin's chest, the two men squaring off. Now he was like a house shifted off its foundations. Maybe it was from carrying a rifle, this half turn toward her, as if he needed to see her down the barrel of a gun.

When she reached him, a tinny version of a Christmas carol was whining out of a cracked speaker somewhere nearby. It might have been "Jingle Bells." It was nearing the end of May. When she embraced him, he gripped her too hard, then released. He picked up the knapsack. "Where do you want to go?" he asked. He had a boy's voice, she'd forgotten that. His eyes were red-rimmed and the amber light in them was smudged by exhaustion.

A sense of chaos afflicted Saigon that spring of 1972, as if the war had already been lost yet careened forward, zombielike. For several blocks, she and Gavin waded through crowds of desperate refugees and hawkers, trying to speak above the shrill traffic. He told her that she was taller than he remembered, and she told him that she'd grown. He gave her a kindly, wistful glance. They stopped at a food stall with tiny chairs and bought two coffees. Gavin ate something, a dumpling. Here too the sidewalk was plagued by loud, reedy music from a broken, buzzing amp. Lilac said, "We can go to my place. It's quieter."

He'd lost a lot of weight; she could see his collarbone and sternum jutting beneath his T-shirt. He'd been discharged—his whole company was being discharged. The US was withdrawing more troops. He kept twisting his neck to look around uneasily at the scooters whining past on the sidewalk, wincing at the constant beeping of their horns. "I go haywire with a lot of noise." With one finger he made circles in the air around his ear, a gesture that meant *loco*, crazy. He kept it up, windmilling with his finger as if he'd set something into perpetual motion. She grabbed his hand to make him stop.

They began to walk to her hotel. She told him it wasn't far, and he said, "I don't mind." Her shoulder bumped his, and this contact released a rank scent. He smelled unclean, almost rancid.

She had Pernod in room 214, the strongest liquor she could afford. She was refusing her father's financial help, managing on the money she made with her stories and photos, but the pay had begun to dwindle as readers were growing tired of hearing about this endless war. People back in "the world" wanted opinions, not reportage. They wanted prefab, mix-and-stir consensus; they wanted "feelings" and personal accounts that weren't too disturbing or dissonant.

On the sidewalk, leaning against her hotel, crouched a skeletal old woman. Flies swarmed at her eyes, the insects strutted across her face to feed at the sores in her skin, but she made no move to brush them away. Lilac placed some money on the pavement at her bare feet. The woman's impersonal glance was helplessly enraged. Then it became clear that she wasn't an old woman after all; she was probably younger than Lilac.

Gavin waited with impatient exhaustion, staring indifferently with his cloudy amber eyes. He moved jerkily as Lilac ushered him through the hotel lobby, past the neon fish and the riotous plants. The hotelier stood behind his desk, and she introduced Gavin as "my friend from Canada."

"Canada," the hotelier repeated. "We go to Canada."

The hotelier's son looked up with a hostile face from the motorcycle magazine he had spread on the low plastic table. Lilac's long stay at his family's hotel meant that the family would be marked as sympathizers for the Americans if the city fell—and people now were beginning to believe it was inevitable, despite what that reptile Nixon said about continued American air support. The whole family would have to run somewhere.

Lilac and Gavin walked upstairs to her room, where she put a kettle on the hot plate to brew tea then poured him a milky plastic glass full of Pernod, which he drank quickly. He calmed a little and made a face. "Sweet."

"Licorice," she said. "Aniseed."

He looked around her room, noting the huge green typewriter on the rickety table, her narrow bed, the porcelain teapot. He went to push open the door to the bathroom, checking inside as if casing for a threat. His movements were sluggish, disoriented. She asked, "How are you?"

"Top-notch."

"Where have you been?"

"Central highlands mostly."

"Pleiku?"

"You know Pleiku, do you?"

"No," she said. "A friend talked about it."

He scratched his neck, which was covered in insect bites.

"Would you like to take a bath?" she asked.

"Am I that bad?" He sat on the bed and removed his boots, revealing surprising white socks, and the black stencil of his dirty feet. He took his clothes off unselfconsciously, without pride. Even his underwear was grey with dirt. His ribs showed. He walked naked to the bathroom and closed the door.

Lilac sat at her typewriter because that was where she sort of felt in control, and listened to him run a bath and let it drain and run another.

He emerged in steam, a thin, damp hotel towel around his bony pelvis. Her eyes stung with tears. It had been only nine months since he departed from the bus depot in downtown Winnipeg, and here he was, gaunt and bug-bitten with his new fox-mask face. It felt uncanny, this missing person in her room. He removed a clean shirt and underwear from his knapsack and got dressed. She was struck by his businesslike attitude toward his own body, as if it was gear he had to carry around. She asked him when he planned to leave for home.

"Tomorrow." He told her the army would fly him to San Francisco but then he was on his own. "I'm a write-off after that." He'd have to thumb back to Thunder Bay. He was quickly uninterested in himself, as if trained to be that way. For the first time, he seemed alert to the oddity of Lilac being in Saigon. "What are you doing here, anyways?"

She explained a little about her work for the *Weekly* and added that she'd been getting stories in small American newspapers, and the *Tribune* in Winnipeg, and another "hippie rag," but interest in the war was drying up. "Unless I make out like Jane Fonda and do the protest thing."

He sniffed. "Jane's a pretty girl, but she's fucking stupid." It sounded like a line he got from his mates, one of those ready-made insults. Now he appraised Lilac. "Thanks for your letter. And the picture. It was cool to see that lichen. I thought it was blood at first. Thought you'd gone crazy. You've actually been in Saigon since—when?"

"Eight months, I think. I'm not even sure."

"By yourself?"

"My dad is here."

He gaped around the room, then said, "Fuck! I thought you meant he was *here*. In this *room!*"

Their laughter was a bit forced.

"No," she told him, "he has rooms at an actually nice hotel."

"Why don't you stay there, then?"

She drank off her glass of Pernod and didn't answer.

"Kal Welsh." He said the full name with a tone of wonder. It twigged. "Bet he's selling his fancy gun to the Man." When Lilac nodded, he went on, "Make himself lots of money?"

"He's trying."

He shook his head. "I sure fell for that one."

"For my father?"

He shrugged. "My pilgrimage. Fuck."

"You were young," she offered.

"I still don't get why you're here."

"I'm working." She'd tidied up, anticipating his coming to her room, but without a mess of papers the typewriter looked like a prop. "And I'm waiting to hear from a couple of friends. They've gone missing."

"Missing where?"

"North. Quang Tri."

"Quang Tri is gone."

"No. I mean, yeah, the Communists took it, but we got it back."

He smiled again, but it was his fox smile, as if he and she were no longer of a kind. "We did, did we."

260

"I can't leave without knowing what happened to my friends."
He asked her more gently to tell him about these friends. They
sat on the floor facing each other and drank all the Pernod. She
described Bull and Larry and could sense him relax into a less
antagonistic form of sadness. She reached a tentative hand to his
chest, but he flinched.

When she finally held him, he was a jumble of bones. Outside,
in the streets, a caterwauling parade went on all night, a mournful
carousal. Vietnamese girls shouted insults at their soldiers. Loud
brawls broke out in the alley. The city had become more brutal
with the passing weeks. In this tumult, it seemed almost selfish to
be softly intimate with Gavin. He was thin but strong. He ran his
hands down her spine, and she sensed that he'd learned how to
break it. Once, he put his hands around her throat and she sat up
and demanded loudly, "Don't!"

He looked surprised, then horrified. "You're scared of me."

"Just don't touch my neck."

He caught her eye, his face broke open, and pain spilled out. He
stuttered, "Sorry, I'm sorry."

She lay down again, and whispered, "Don't be sorry," over and
over, and let him hold her and trusted him fully for the remaining
hours of the night.

In the grey dawn, he asked, "What do you want in your
future?" He was running his hand over her bare stomach.

She said she didn't know. It seemed like a trick question.

"You want to go back to your nice life?" he asked.

"Of course not."

"Sure you do. Who wouldn't?"

"Me. I don't. I can't."

"Marry some rich guy. Have a few kids," he said, not listening
to her.

"I don't want to marry anybody. I don't know about having kids."

"Aw, come on. Have some babies. Feed the machine."

She raised herself on her elbow to see him in the dim light. "You mean I'll make soldier babies."

"Beautiful girl making beautiful babies for the war machine." Then he mumbled, "But people with money never fight the wars. Your dad's going to make it rich while the poor folk do his dirty work."

"I'll never be rich."

He looked around her room. "You might dabble at being broke. But you couldn't be poor if you tried."

He was right. And it would be true even if her father had decided to be a professor his whole life. She moved on top of him, trying to forget who she was, but she doubted that this consoled him much. In the morning, when he left, it would be a relief, most likely to both of them. He was too vulnerable; she wouldn't be able to protect him from the comfort that had been bred in her bones. She wanted more room for joy. He was part of her, but she didn't know if she'd ever see him again. She wouldn't write the story of Gavin McLean for the *Tribune* after all. It seemed that the best way to express her loyalty to him was to keep his memory to herself.

7.

The day after Gavin's visit, Lilac was hurriedly transcribing notes from an interview with a soldier waiting to be court-martialled for allegedly trying to kill his platoon sergeant. He'd tossed a grenade, but either it was a dud or he hadn't pulled the pin, because it rolled intact at the feet of his intended victim. He'd been charged with attempted murder anyway.

Lilac's room was so hot she'd left her door open and didn't hear Kal's footsteps approaching because he'd exchanged his boots for a pair of leather-soled loafers. He startled her when he walked in as if they were back at Rough Rock. The empty bottle of Pernod sat on the floor beside her bed, and while Kal strode cheerfully around her room, she kept glancing at it, wishing she could put it out of sight.

He told her he had some great news.

"You've found Bull. And Larry?" She stood up.

Kal lost his ebullience for a few seconds. "No. There's still no word."

She sat down again. It was nearly one o'clock, her deadline was at two that afternoon, and it was a twenty-minute walk to Heather's office. "I've got to finish this story."

"I don't know where they are. Yet." He paused. "But I *do* have some good news." He told her that he'd made contact with One Corps Logistics, and they agreed to look at the specs on the Stalker. "It's not a field trial, like I'd hoped. But with places like Israel and India looking seriously at the Stalker 80 now, there's real momentum."

Lilac glanced at her notes on the table then up at the paper rolled in the typewriter. The soldier facing court martial had talked to her about what he called "personal freedom." The sentence she'd just transcribed from her scrawl was: "The army can't take my soul from me."

Her dad waited with a grin. "That's nice," she said, and, seeing his disappointment, tried harder. "It must be a relief."

"It's more than relief. I'm gaining traction."

"That's good."

"It means I can go home."

"Oh. Of course. When?"

"Tomorrow."

"Oh. Mum will be glad."

"She'll expect me to bring you with me."

"I know. I just have some assignments to finish up first."

"She'll be very disappointed if I show up without you, Lilac."

"Can we talk about it later? This deadline…" Lilac had never revealed to Kal the stuff her mother wrote in her letters, but it was definitely time for him to go home. There was a lot of work to do there in the spring, for one thing. Ruby had taken off the storm windows and she'd been getting the boats cleaned up. She'd even winched the steel boat down into the water, a job that normally took two people. Lilac had mostly finished transcribing the interview with the soldier in jail but needed to revise her opening. He'd described his "inspiration" for tossing the grenade, telling Lilac that the sergeant was "a subtle brand of bully." The jailed soldier was highly articulate and had hoped to get a university degree in physics when he got trapped in the lottery of the draft. He told Lilac that his action wasn't premeditated. "I just snapped." He couldn't even remember whether or not he'd pulled the pin, his memory had gone blank on the incident. She thought how it was funny that Thanh never got charged for trying to kill her father. His Vietnamese mates must have closed ranks, protected him. The physics student was Chinese American.

"I'm sorry, Dad," she said. "I'm just crushed for time right now." She wished she were immune to Kal's feelings and asked him if he'd meet her for dinner later.

"Sure," he said, opening his hands in a gesture that said, *you win*. He looked diminished, embarrassed that she was dismissing him. But he turned at the door to say, "You've got my work ethic."

She called to his retreating back, "I'll come to your hotel at six." Then, more loudly, "I'll miss you when you go."

He returned and stood in her doorway again. "I'm thinking of moving us to the States."

And suddenly she was furious at him for telling her this now, when she didn't have time to talk about it. She stammered, "Where?"

"Michigan, of course. Now that I'm sure the new gun will pay off pretty soon, I think it's time for a new start."

"Have you told Mum?"

"I'll talk to her about it when I get home. University of Michigan is one of the best in the world. It's about time you got a real education. You need to think about your future." He waved. "Finish your task here. We'll talk tonight." And his oddly quiet footsteps withdrew.

She returned to the story lodged in her typewriter. The jailed soldier said, "Hate can come on as sudden as love. Real fast. But deep and for good."

"For christsake," said Lilac.

8.

On July 1, 1972, two South Vietnamese journalists somehow managed to cross a bombed-out railway bridge over the Bên Đá river between Quang Tri and Hué, and discovered hundreds of corpses strewn across the road and in the fields either side. These were the civilians and ARVN soldiers fleeing in terror while Bull drove Lilac and Kal to their escape by boat on the China Sea.

Two thousand people, many of them children, had been gunned down by the PAVN, the North Vietnamese "People's Army."

The bodies had been two months in the sun. It was impossible to distinguish man from woman, boychild from girlchild, except maybe by their clothing. Heather Markham told Lilac this. One of her Vietnamese stringers had read it in a newspaper called *Sóng Thân*, which Heather said means "tsunami." She said there was a huge volunteer effort under way to identify and bury the dead. To put the hungry ghosts to rest.

It was now July 15. Kal had left six weeks ago. Bull Johnson and Larry Donovan were still missing. Lilac doubted that they were among the dead on the road. Bull would have avoided that stretch, which the newspaper now christened "the Highway of Horror." Still, her waiting felt increasingly futile. It was time to leave Vietnam. But she decided not to go back home. There was no home to go to. Her mother was leaving her father.

Ruby left Rough Rock that summer and went alone to live in Winnipeg, in apartment 4B in a brownstone on Assiniboine Avenue. It was what Ruby called a "moratorium" and Kal called a "sabbatical." Neither of them talked about divorce.

From Saigon, Lilac travelled first to Tokyo then inland to the mountains and down to Kyoto and farther south to Nagasaki. In Nagasaki, she saw how quickly buildings and houses are renewed when there's money, how quickly businesses and children spring up, even at the site of an atom bomb. She went on to Thailand, to Bangkok, then to a small village where she waited out another fever before moving on to an island in Indonesia, and on and on. She was a tourist now, and began to write stories of her travels, which made the *Tribune*'s readers happy because these were happier stories, pleasant observations of foreign customs and food, fairly impersonal descriptions of the pleasures of novelty.

She knew about the journalists who were covering the war in Cambodia, she admired them and envied their courage. But she didn't go. Cambodia was too violent and she was too alone. The casual friendships that occurred on her travels were like butterflies. Lovely encounters, short-lived.

During this time Lilac wrote countless letters to her mother, a correspondence that morphed into the journalism that kept her fed and attached her tentatively to the spinning world. She was at a loss, at first, wanting a focus. Then gradually she came more clearly to understand that running under everything was the power of money, or the vacuum of poverty. In places of poverty, she saw a tough beauty, the roots of a sinewy resilience that she began to believe would be relentlessly exploited. Vietnam had illustrated an asymmetry of power that she thought she might see again—though she didn't know if she had the stomach to witness another war up close. From reading the English-language newspapers, she learned that it was as her father had predicted: Central America's tendency for socialism and independence was attracting the attention of the US military. Just like Vietnam.

In her letters to her daughter, Ruby seemed surprised by happiness. "I'm amazed," Ruby wrote, "by the smallest things. The beautiful green moss on the shingles outside my apartment window, I stare at it in the sun and in the rain. It sparkles. It's alive. You're travelling the big world. I'm travelling the small. Even an hour breathes differently now that I'm on my own."

Lilac corresponded with Kal too. He was preoccupied by his struggles to get the Stalker 80 into circulation and wrote to inform Lilac that he'd "try to be patient" while her mother went through her "crisis." The condescending tone was in ratio with his uncomprehending pain over losing Ruby. His letters were distressing to read, with their awkward, forceful optimism. But, as he said, "it's not all doom and gloom." The Stalker had begun to sell all over the world, especially in the "hot" zones where America stepped up to fight what it called Communism.

Lilac was travelling through New Zealand when she picked up the mail that had been forwarded to the post office in Christchurch. There she found a copy of *Rolling Stone*, sent by her mother. The *Stone* ran a story about the famous photojournalist Larry Donovan, who had gone missing in the Easter Offensive of 1972 at Quang Tri, along with his "military guide." The story speculated that Larry Donovan and Bull Johnson had been netted by Viet Cong guerrillas. Lilac could only hope that this was false, that Larry and Bull were not imprisoned in the jungle, that they had not died slowly of disease and starvation. She had to pray that there had been a sniper ambush. Precise and deeply penetrating.

At Thanksgiving 1972, her dad sold the log house and his shop and the land at what he called "a fair price"—to Peter, the Ojibwa man, his "friend." He said that Peter and his extended family planned to run it as a fly-in fishing and hunting camp for wealthy Americans.

Kal moved to Lansing, Michigan. He wrote to Lilac to let her know that he expected her mum to "calm down" and join him there soon. He also said he expected Lilac to go to university there. He found a house where he told her they would all live together. He described their "new home" in reassuring tones, as if Lilac and Ruby suffered from the rupture in the family, as if he was the strong and happy one, offering them solace.

The profile of Kal Welsh might never be written. Later in her life, when Lilac tried to write about her father, she'd wish she had Larry's detachment.

9.

Lilac returned to Canada in late summer, 1973. Her mother was ecstatic to have Lilac with her in Winnipeg. Ruby now worked at various jobs: creating some set designs for two small theatre companies, spending a few days each week refinishing used furniture for an upscale shop, and doing part-time office work for a peace organization that filled her with fury because she said the people running it were so contrary.

It had never occurred to Lilac that her mother had any kind of talent for theatre design or furniture. She'd never thought much about Ruby's way of making their log house look beautiful. Even Ruby's rented rooms here in the city looked really nice, though she'd taken only a few small pieces from Rough Rock. The cashmere throw was here, tossed over one of the smaller couches, not the big leather one, which must have been sold with the log house. Her kerosene lantern sat beside her rocking chair. She said she liked to use the lantern "for old times' sake," adding, "Don't tell anybody, or my landlord will evict me."

Lilac stayed in Ruby's small apartment on Assiniboine for several weeks, sleeping on the couch, fretting over what to do next, drinking a bit too much Pernod at night, and leaving newspapers all over the floor. Her friend the nerd from the *Loving Couch* had moved to Toronto and started another magazine. Lilac found a copy at the newsstand on Winnipeg's Main Street, and wrote to him to say that his new magazine was brave, radical, a big accomplishment. The nerd responded by offering her a retainer if she wanted to "go out in the field again," meaning that he hoped she'd send him stories from a conflict zone. She didn't know if she had it in her to see another war. She wasn't the same girl who'd leapt at the chance to go to Vietnam. And it no longer seemed good enough to fake it as a journalist.

Her father mailed brochures to Ruby's place, a lot of glossy information about Michigan State's School of Journalism. Lilac sprawled beside the newspapers and studied the photos of toothy, chummy students wearing burgundy wool sweaters with tartan scarves. The school claimed to help young people "think outside the box." Kal offered to carry all the costs, and she'd get this great education. She'd probably feel more legitimate if she had a university degree. She was in a box now, living with her mother, stalled and hemmed in.

But she found a great place to sit with a view of the river by climbing out Ruby's living room window onto the roof. Lilac spent a lot of time on the roof, eventually taking her meals out there. She needed time to think, though her brain seemed stuck in neutral.

After four weeks of this, she was surprised to see her mother crawl out the window one morning and sidle over the crumbling red asphalt shingles to perch beside her.

"It's nice out here, eh?" Lilac asked. "The trees and everything."

Ruby sighed. "Darling." She'd tied an orange bandana around her red curls and she wore big hoop earrings and she held her arms in a beseeching attitude of prayer. "Do you know what it's like, trying to be your mother now?"

Lilac hadn't given it any thought.

Ruby said, "I feel like I'm cupping a bee. It's like a bee is buzzing in my hands."

"Oh, Mum, I've been driving you nuts, haven't I?" This was a revelation. She was embarrassed to realize that she'd been crowding her mother out of her own place. And just when her mum had been enjoying what was really her first taste of independence. It was very awkward. "God," Lilac said. "I wish I could fly off this roof right now."

Ruby opened her hands. In her palm lay the keys to her station wagon. "I love you," she said. "Your dad's expecting you. The car's in its spot behind the apartment block. But please take the stairs."

Lilac hugged her mother and left that afternoon. She drove twenty hours, south from Winnipeg and west around Chicago to Lansing, Michigan.

•

Kal owned a four-thousand-square-foot split-level house on fieldstone footing with a red-brick exterior on ten acres of green land beside the Grand River. Lilac found the address and pulled over to the shoulder of the road. The place was huge. When he bought it, he must have been certain that Ruby would live here too, that the family would be reunited, though by now, as far as Lilac knew, he'd stopped asking Ruby to come. He must have been tired of getting turned down. Now his plan was that Lilac would settle in and start university right away, since the term had already begun. At the end of a long driveway that ran beside a white post-and-board fence backed by a row of maple trees, the chrome fenders of two sports cars sparkled in the sun. Either Kal owned two sports cars or he had a visitor. She put the station wagon in gear and drove away.

She cruised around for a while. The houses nearby were all beautiful, mostly old and invariably large, and she soaked in the peaceful beauty, slowing down for a better view of an outdoor stone fireplace beside the turquoise tile of a swimming pool partially concealed by cedar screens. There were porticoes and balconies and solariums. Through her open window, she heard screams of joy from children doing cannonballs into their swimming pools. She didn't think she was hungry for luxury, yet the evidence of wealth eased her body. She inhaled the moneyed beauty and guessed that other people found pleasure in this too. There were lots of Sunday drivers gawking at the lovely homes.

She drove back to the big brick house. It was hedged by cypress and juniper—the tame stuff that grows in cities. A massive stone chimney erupted from the slate roof. The extensive green lawn had been landscaped, there was even a goldfish pond, there were roses with fat pink faces. It was weird to think of her father tending ornamental roses. Did he have a gardener? She drove slowly down the long, smooth driveway.

It was also weird that he now lived in a house with a doorbell. Lilac, nervous, had to suppress a surge of giddy laughter, hearing the bell chime loudly inside. She hadn't seen her dad since they said goodbye in Vietnam almost a year and a half ago. She was excited, and prepared to feel a bit shaken, seeing him after such a long time. She was not prepared for the blonde woman wearing cherry-red capris with matching lipstick and nails. Behind her, Kal was climbing carpeted stairs that led up from a lower level. He hurried to intercept and place himself before the eager blonde. But not before Lilac caught a gem-hard glint in the woman's green eye that quickly dissolved into warmly caressing gasps of pleasure. "You're his daughter! Lilac! Welcome!" She pressed herself to Kal's side while she offered a bony, manicured hand. "I'm Melanie."

Kal gave Melanie a deft, light hip check, and brought Lilac into his arms.

The scent of kerosene was gone, but otherwise he still smelled of gun oil and soap. She kissed him, his cheek soft and closely shaved. He limped just a little while he led her into the house through a tiled entry, past a sunken living room with white wool broadloom and white leather furniture, to a vast, sunny kitchen. The air conditioning was not keeping up with the solar heat from twelve feet of skylight. Melanie padded behind them.

Kal said, "We can't sit in here. It's too fucking hot," and was leading Lilac back toward the stairs to the lower level when he realized that Melanie was following. He turned to say, "Not now."

Melanie looked stricken, but undeterred. "I'll get us a snack, then."

"No," said Kal. "How about I call you Friday." It was not a question.

10.

Kal's shop on the lower level did not resemble his shop at Rough Rock. This one had sash windows looking out at Kentucky bluegrass yielding to a three-hundred-yard shooting range. Smoked-glass bookshelves took up one wall, floor to ceiling. His gun cabinet—bigger than the one at Rough Rock—occupied the opposite wall. His shop at Rough Rock had wide, oily oak floorboards, but the floor in this place was cooled by massive granite tiles. A crystal chandelier dangled above a door that went out to the firing range, spinning spectrums on the walls.

On a butler's tray table sat a photograph of Lilac framed in sterling silver with a black velvet mat. She picked it up. "I remember when you took this." She and her father had been fishing in the canoe, Kal in the stern. A sunny day. Blue and green. Lilac was laughing, twisting around to see him. The summer of 1971, about a week before Gavin arrived and everything changed. "That was a good day," she said.

His workbench had been replaced by a drafting table. A three-dimensional diagram of a rifle was pinned there. "You're working on something?"

He nodded yes, and with a show of grim determination added, "Have to." Then, with more enthusiasm, "I'll tell you about it later. A new idea."

He looked sober. Ruby had told her that when she first left Kal, "he did a few laps of sober-to-drunk, drunk-to-sober, then drunk-to-drunk and back to sober." Lilac didn't blame him for that. "How's your mother?" he asked now, resentful, hurt, curious.

Ruby was fine. Lilac did not say more. They heard the throaty muffler of a well-made car; Melanie was leaving the premises.

Kal said, "There are plenty of desperate forty-five-year-old women living around here."

Lilac said, "They must be."

Kal's eyes strayed right then wavered and met Lilac's, and he smiled. "You haven't lost your cheekiness."

She was tempted to make a cool comment on how he hadn't wasted any time finding another woman. The "sabbatical" or "moratorium" had only come to be called a "separation" sometime around last Christmas. But she refrained. Ruby had taken up with somebody too, a man she'd met in her peace work: Clark, a nice enough person with a high voice, as if he was constantly surprised, and a habit of sitting down on the floor to tie his shoelaces. Insipid, in Lilac's estimation. She never said that to Ruby. Friday nights, Clark would climb the four flights of stairs to Ruby's apartment and present her with a loaf of his homemade whole wheat bread before ushering her down to his Volvo and out to see what he called "a classic" at the repertory cinema.

Clark's existence in Ruby's life had changed things between her and Lilac; Lilac felt their relationship pale a little. Their love remained, she was certain of that, but her mother didn't need her much anymore.

Her parents had become more selfish, maybe because, as they got older, they had to fight harder to be happy. And probably they didn't mind causing each other pain. The separation had been civilized, as far as Lilac knew. Their hostility was civilized. When Kal said "your mother" or Ruby said "your father," they each sounded sympathetic, concerned about the mental stability of the person they'd once been devoted to.

Kal asked Lilac if she wanted help with her "luggage." She told him she'd get her stuff out of the car later. "Tell me about your new idea," she said.

There were several. He'd been streamlining the Welsh Stalker Model 80 so that it would have fewer moving parts. And he was developing a thirty-calibre tactical rifle to sell to police. He said that commercial sales were more important than ever. If he didn't have police and sport shooters to supplement the orders from the US military, he'd "go down."

"The competition is on my heels," he said.

Lilac gave a sympathetic nod. She liked to read profiles in *Business Week*, hoping they'd help her understand Kal better. In business lingo, the competition was always "fierce" and "imprudent." Successful businessmen liked to boast about their amazing status on the one hand while complaining about their dire situation on the other. They were oppressed by regulations and tax. When rich people feel slighted or sorry for themselves, you really have to watch out. Look at how brutally sensitive America is. Canada too, for that matter, while pretending to be demure. Lilac did not say this to her dad. She was thinking about what she would write to her old friend the nerd. In the nerd's magazine she'd read the kind of analysis that was now making this conversation with her father feel like she was doing underground reconnaissance.

She was mad at her father. She was mad at her mother. It felt stupid to be mad at them, so she was also angry at herself.

Kal observed her with that opaque combination of self-assurance and incomprehension. In a strange way, he was unworldly. No matter where her dad was on the planet, he was preoccupied by how he looked. The golf shirt he now wore was finely knit, with a logo on it, a green crocodile. She was unnerved to see a gold cross dangling from a gold chain, nestled in the silver chest hair at his open collar.

Lilac looked him in the eye and said, "Yes. There's tough competition in firearms." Then she stared at the drawing of the assault rifle on his drafting table. She'd keep to herself what he had once called her "left-wing sentimentality." The furniture upstairs was so white, so unused, it made her ache for him. She didn't want him to be fully aware of his own vulnerability. It would be up to her to protect him, to give him the solace of a family. He'd obviously recovered financially from the tough early investment in the Stalker, and had once said to Lilac over the phone that her mother should have had the "wits" to stand by him while he struggled. "She must regret that she bailed too soon," he'd said. And after Lilac's prolonged silence, he added, "That was crass. I apologize."

Lilac sank into a leather slingback chair and let her hand drop idly toward a bamboo magazine rack placed beside it. Her fingers met the slick, familiar paper of a *Shooting Times* magazine, which she pulled onto her lap and unerringly opened to an advertisement for the Welsh Stalker. She'd grown up with her father's ads, which he fussed over and controlled, but this one really shook her. It was a photograph of herself, wearing noise-cancelling headphones and eye protection—lightweight wraparound glasses with pale-yellow lenses—and a black jersey with the Welsh logo, black gloves, her hair in a ponytail, a sadly determined but pleasant expression on her face while she peered through the scope, one hand on the trigger, the other gently bracing the cheek piece, long white nails cut square, a big diamond wedding ring, and Lilac realized that it wasn't her, just a look-alike.

Kal was watching with a satisfied grin, as if he'd presented a successful gift. "Uncanny likeness, isn't it," he observed. He crossed the room to take the magazine from her hands and gaze at the photo with great fondness. "I have to admit, I look at it often. Just imagining."

Imagining the daughter who would go in for sport shooting, the daughter who would live inside Kal Welsh's world, help manage the company, get her nails done, flirt with her competitors at the range, live in a mansion, and wear a big fat diamond ring. Lilac retrieved the magazine from her father's hands and stared at the image of herself in another dimension, as if there were the merest tissue separating her from Kal's perfect child.

11.

Kal cooked steaks on a gas grill embedded in what Lilac learned was an "island" in his kitchen. He poured them each a glass of Campari with soda, which was so bitter it didn't count as a drink. Otherwise, he seemed to be off the booze. They sat down to eat at an enormous table in a cavernous dining room with a picture window, now black with night.

He asked her if she was writing, but she easily switched the topic back to him, to his plans. Was it nice to be living in his home state where he'd grown up? On the table, the ice shivered in her glass. She glanced under and saw that he was jiggling his foot in beige cork-soled shoes, excited. Maybe happy. He was greying perfectly, silvering at the temples, very handsome in a conventional, buttoned-down way. She felt a wave of the unfamiliar, of estrangement, a quality that she'd learned to seek out, even love somehow, as if strangeness was her element.

The house was nearly soundless, except for the hum of the air conditioner. She recalled the scream of mortars falling around Bull's 'lil enterprise in Quang Tri, and the aerobatic MiGs zooming above the heads of the fleeing villagers. In the whir of the fan cooling the house there was a faint buzz, a whine, probably from a loose screw. The terror and suffering of war was reconditioned here, redecorated in white leather.

He said, "I'm more active now. Or I mean, I'm more active politically." He straightened in his chair and patted his trim waist. "It's easy living, of course. Socially—well." He nodded with a kindly air, as if to an absent Melanie. "I'm okay on my own. In fact, I'm probably better off. Especially now that you're here." He brightened. "Bet you never pegged me for a committee man."

Lilac said no, she had never pegged him for a committee man, and studied his clean hands where they rested on his dinner table, the scars smoothed, the nails manicured. She was fascinated by how much he'd changed his style. But then he'd always liked to pose, to dress the part. In some ways he too was a traveller. His twenty-five years in Canada had been a prolonged sojourn and now he'd returned to what might be a more essential self, a version of Kal Welsh that soothed his vanity after losing Ruby. "What's the committee?" she asked.

"It's fairly light. A lot of time on the phone." He grinned. "Imagine me chatting on a phone without having to say 'over.' I'll get soft if I'm not careful." He went on. "I'm chair of the Political Action Committee. PAC." He smacked the word affectionately. "It's a branch of the National Rifle Association. An important branch, I admit. You might have heard of us. We're fighting Johnson's gun control fiasco from '68. The NRA isn't just a gun club anymore, you know. Our work will ensure the future of the Second Amendment."

"Wow."

"I'm serious."

"I know."

"As a matter of fact, you're going to meet my committee tonight. Soon." He glanced at his watch. "Very soon." He rose from the table, waving dismissively at the dirty dishes. "My girl will come in the morning to clean."

He tossed a pink linen napkin across a finger of fat on his dinner plate and was heading toward the kitchen, limping more noticeably now, when Lilac asked, "You have a meeting?"

He turned. He seemed surprised and asked innocently, "You don't mind, do you?"

She said she didn't mind and got up to follow him.

"You'll find it interesting." He opened a cupboard over a massive chrome fridge and took down a bottle of bourbon. While he shuffled around, preparing what looked to be a healthy bar, with heavy crystal tumblers, a silver ice bucket, a bottle of vodka from the freezer, a jar of Spanish olives, assembling all this on a large wooden tray, slicing lemons with almost feminine delicacy, he described the members of his committee in terms of gossipy admiration. It was not merely a monthly meeting, he informed her.

"Normally, we work by fax and phone. This is an emergency powwow to strategize the Supreme Court." There'd been a death, he said, a left-leaning judge had died of a sudden heart attack, opening a seat on the bench that Kal and his committee needed to fill with "somebody in the vanguard, someone who can turn the switch on Johnson's gun control insanity." One of his committee members, he added proudly, was arriving in Lansing by private jet. "Got to get me one of those," he said, tossing a couple of Aspirin into his mouth and chewing. When he saw the look of confusion on his daughter's face, he leaned across his island to chuck her under the chin and say, "Just kidding. I don't have that kind of dough." Then, for he was in a merry mood, he added, "Yet."

The doorbell chimed. She trailed him while he made his way to the front door, permitting the scent of roses into the hall, and about six men. "Take some coats, would you?" he said to Lilac. Together, Lilac and Kal collected coats from the men, who were of various sizes but consistently Kal's age or older. As she received their garments, he introduced her, his voice tremulous with affection. "My girl," he said. "She's a writer. But don't hold that against her."

He ushered them all into the sunken living room, turning on table lamps, moving several ashtrays from the mantel to the side tables, and telling Lilac, "Bring the tray from the kitchen." Then he added, "Darling."

He looked so hopeful and proud. She nodded and went to the kitchen to fetch the tray.

12.

Lilac entertained herself with bourbon while the men talked. She'd often been a lone woman among men, where, even while they ignored her, she sensed that they liked her presence, as if she enhanced or gave shape to their conversation. Tonight was different. Her father's PAC committee truly did not give a damn that she was in the room with them. She was totally irrelevant. It was like standing in front of a train.

It was like standing before a train or under a jet taking off. She was brought to terms. It reminded her of the times she'd fallen ill or run out of cash when she was travelling; the machines of civilization will mow you down without even feeling that little bump under the wheel.

The Political Action Committee had a vision for America. And though her father reigned as chair and host, a successful gunsmith, the men seated on his white leather furniture were uncongenial and divergent in their energies even while they all seemed in accord: the Supreme Court must and will get out of their way.

Lilac was especially fascinated by the yellow gleam of hair on a block of masculine currency, a man named Lee, executive something-or-other of the NRA, full of vim boiling inside the upholstery of his dark suit. He wore bifocals in such fine gold frames they were visible only when light glinted from them, when his eyes blazed like cat's eyes. "...the enemies of freedom..." said Lee, "...a dystopian nightmare where law-abiding citizens will be forced to submit their firearms to be melted down into knitting needles, dog leashes, and sex toys..." The furious slogans extruded from him like body armour. But Lee revealed his domestic side too, in a short summary of his wife's shooting her first lion—and here he paid a percentage of respect to his host, telling him, "With that pretty Welsh 70 of yours. A nice little gun." His eyes, masked by lamplight, suddenly glinted in Lilac's direction as if she were the "nice little gun." She felt that her sex was her only significant distinction, negligible yet treacherous, alien, primitive.

In the nerd's magazine, she'd been reading about the unhappiness of the American government over the tendency of peasants in Nicaragua, Guatemala, and El Salvador to resist military dictatorships. Nixon didn't like to see socialists try to nationalize US-owned industries operating in Central America. The nerd's magazine reported that Nixon and the CIA were satisfied with Honduras's president, and provided arms and tactical training for his death squads' murders and torture and rape of trade unionists, farmers, students, immigrants, street children, and so on.

Lilac shivered. The air conditioning was set too high. The men growled in indignant agreement. They fumed over "bureaucrats and socialists," "dangers to the Second Amendment." They gruffly pontificated for over an hour, the house getting increasingly cold. They said "damn right," "that's obvious," in resentful acknowledgement that they were saying the same things, over and over again. They talked about "liberty" in aggravated tones, as if somebody was asking them to share a personal belonging. Lilac was so cold her hands were turning blue, and she began to shake them vigorously to get the circulation running. This windmill activity distracted the men. One after the other they finished their drinks and set their glasses down in wet rings upon the teak tables and stood to go.

They brushed past, not saying goodbye to her, though one short fellow with reddish hair offered an avuncular nod and said, "Very nice." She waited behind her father as the men buttoned their coats and he ushered them through the door toward a cavalcade of shiny black cars in a haze of cigarette smoke hovering over the patient chauffeurs.

Then Lee of the yellow hair, the last to go out, turned and leaned toward Kal, bending at the knee, for he was taller by six inches, and said, "Green light on Honduras."

Whatever this meant—and Lilac figured there'd be a lucky sale of the new thirty-calibre police weapon—infused Kal with almost cosmic gratitude. "Good. That's good," he breathed, and tightly clasped Lee's elbow.

Kal closed the door, then spun around and smiled at his daughter and clapped his hands. "I'd like a real drink!" He was on his way back to the kitchen when she asked him, could he turn down the AC. He stopped dead. "Damn," he said. "Was everyone cold?"

She followed him to the vault-like dining room, where he went to a thermostat beside the big picture window that looked out on the lawn in darkness pierced by the red tail lights of the departing PAC. "I still can't get used to this fucking thing." He was fooling with the dial. His image, his confident, stocky body, reflected in the glass, was multiplied by the triple panes.

"So, Honduras is going well?" Lilac asked, and saw in the triple reflection her father's sharp eyes dart up to meet hers.

13.

She asked him for a sweater, and he fetched a navy-blue cashmere cardigan for her. They were in the kitchen now, his "real drink" in a fresh tumbler with a single ice cube. "Who exactly was that blond man?" she asked, putting on his sweater, folding herself into his scent. "The one with the wire-framed glasses."

"Lee? He's with Halliburton. Knowledgeable about Central America. And just back from the Middle East. One day, he's going to be secretary of state, that's my prediction."

"Do you trust him?"

"I said he's knowledgeable, didn't I?"

"He's a beast, Dad."

"Yeah," he responded cheerfully. "He can be a pretty tough bastard when push comes to shove."

"You're hanging out with some very high-end brokers."

This pleased him; he looked reassured that she'd been here to witness the degree of power he now wielded. "We're making headway." He nodded. "You hang around me long enough, you'll learn plenty about how things work in the real world."

She stared. He had that thick-necked viscosity of movement as the bourbon was upon him, but he saw her look of scorn, and squared his chest and admitted with a show of transparent baseone honesty, "I never did get you to understand me," adding bitterly, "It's probably my fault."

Lilac barely resisted the impulse to reassure him, to tell him he was faultless. He desired her fulsome admiration. She was very tempted to feign for him—it would be such a simple way to make him happy, to make him feel complete.

His heavy hand landed on her shoulder. With clumsy tenderness, he tucked the sweater up around her throat while he quietly observed, "You're going to like it here." He tugged her arm. "Come on. It's getting late. I'll show you around your new home before shut-eye."

He revealed a pristine laundry room (yes, he admitted, proudly defensive, not only a gardener but a housekeeper, his "girl," three times a week); a spare bedroom with a single bed where he kept a set of weights; his leathery oxblood office; three bathrooms, one of them with a bidet. They came to a closed door at the end of a hall, and he said, "This is your room."

He opened the door to a big bright white space with yet another bathroom. Beneath the window was a beautiful teak desk with an IBM Selectric typewriter, obviously new; its upper carriage was still wrapped in plastic. On the walls were fifteen of her photographs.

"You took them from home," she said, surprised by grief, remembering their life there. And the superfluous number of them, the excessive homage, it disappointed her a little. Growing up with him, he'd always scoffed at excess. "Why does anybody need two of anything?" he would ask. But his solitary life here with satellite Melanie and his PAC committee had affected his style.

Now he regarded her with bashful pride. "I only took what really mattered to me."

The tour included Kal's bedroom. His private space, his personal taste. Huge green plants climbed up a plate glass window. There were more bookshelves, dark-grey walls, three Persian carpets intersecting. A comfortable chair was placed beneath a lamp. Beside the chair, a stack of books—a rather pretty Bible bound in white leather. There was a small colour TV and a stereo system. This was where he lived. This room alone seemed true of him.

A pedestal table, comprising various kinds of wood inlaid to form a mandala, stood beside the king-sized bed. Lilac recognized the table: Ruby had found it all beat up in a used furniture store in Kenora years ago, and she'd taken it apart, sanded, varnished, and reassembled it. Here were another three of Lilac's photographs, in the silver frames with black velvet mat that he seemed to like. They were three portraits of Ruby.

Ruby, with sun illuminating her crazy red hair. In another she is ruddy and content, in the flickering light of winter's hearth. The third was an autumn portrait. Distant whitecaps. The lake is choppy, and Ruby is hunched against a cold wind with her hands tucked into the pockets of her corduroy jacket. Black-and-white film, this one, shades of sorrow, the near but as yet unseen end of her marriage to Kal.

Here was his heart. "This is nice, Dad."

"No thanks to you," he responded. He smiled tightly, blinking slowly. Maybe he hadn't intended to say that out loud.

"What are you talking about?"

He reeled a little on his feet and doggedly continued. "Don't kid yourself. You had a role to play in what went wrong with your mother." Suddenly, he looked deflated, and shrugged, appealing, "Why'd you have to go off to Vietnam, Lilac? Stir everything up. Encourage her."

"For christsake."

"You made her feel like she had to go off and—I don't know— *find herself*, or whatever it is people say now." He held up his scarred, manicured hand. "I know. She didn't like my new gun. Even though it's my best one."

"I think she liked the Welsh 70." She liked you, once, Lilac wanted to say. Ruby will probably always love you, but she doesn't like you very much. "Assault rifles really turn her off."

"A slim distinction."

"No," said Lilac.

"It's a question of style with you, is it? You and your mother get off on the walnut stock on the 70." He took a breath and exhaled that sweet scent of liquor. Lilac liked that smell, her body liked it even when she was repelled by it. "Anyway," he continued, "the damage is done. Let's not argue. I can't even tell you how much I've been looking forward to you living here. I don't want to waste any time arguing." He paused then went on more angrily, "But I need you to know. Because I worry that you really don't understand me. Most people can't handle the Stalker. Lilac? Listen to me. Shooting a fifty-calibre weapon takes training and skill. It's challenging. You have to know what you're about."

Lilac stood close to him. "That's always true with guns, Dad."

"I mean"—his watery eyes were searching her face as if he'd find the words there—"I'm not just acting without thought, without care. I'm not heartless. And I'm not particularly greedy." He gave her a sharp look as if expecting her to argue, and repeated, "I'm not. I could be much richer if it really mattered to me. *You* matter to me. And your mother. Still. My country matters, a great deal. *Freedom* matters." He paused before concluding blearily, "This is the world we find ourselves in. We move with it. Or we die."

"The Stalker has cost you everything," she said.

He seemed startled and began to protest, then reconsidered, pros and cons. He lifted his chin. "I've stayed the course."

"Mum is working for some kind of peace group."

"Yeah." He pulled away. "I gave them a lot of money. I mean, a *lot* of money. Some guy named Clark got hold of me. A persistent little creep." He met Lilac's eye, and admitted, "I recently asked her, again, one last time to come here, to try to work it out. She said she's seeing someone. Clark, I'm guessing."

"I thought he was harmless."

"Nobody's harmless."

He flexed his back, his solid, impenetrable torso, a physical density. She wondered if this was what ultimately had turned Ruby away from him. Maybe Ruby had left Kal partly because she grew to dislike his insistent, absolute physicality, his solid feet, his wilfulness. Probably her mother's final disenchantment was not entirely an ethical rejection of a gunsmith. She got turned off, she turned away. And what of Clark, with his Wallabees and his virtue? Was Ruby again under the sway of another social psychologist? Clark was a vegetarian, except for lean steak, Ruby had told her, laughing.

And now the arms dealer was a philanthropist. Kal Welsh had covered both ends of the spectrum, peace and profit. Giving money to the peace movement had disarmed Clark. The gunsmith had bought out the competition. A perfect implementation of the irrational. Lilac felt dizzied by his manoeuvre.

"I put an extra blanket in the bottom drawer of your bureau," he announced. "I know how you don't like to be cold. Tomorrow we'll drive over to Michigan State together, so you can take a look around before you register. Like I told you, it's one of the best in the world. No cost to you, of course. I'll shoulder everything. I want you to be free of worry while you focus on your studies."

Lilac hesitated. Every time he made his offer, she had this same sensation of vertigo, the sway of submission and acceptance.

He wanted to care for her. Such a life with him seemed like an alternate universe. In a flash, she was very young again, his child, and she leaned toward him, leaned toward his vision of an obedient and loving daughter in his white room. She saw his hope, his injury, his loneliness. His ruthlessness. Beneath the tears of sadness or age, his eyes were stones. Her friend the nerd had told her that he would pay her what he could for her stories from the "covert CIA wars" in Central America. The nerd had a good contact in Guatemala City, a photojournalist who would meet up with her there, and get her started, if she ever found the nerve to take that step.

She said, "I have to go out to my car."

"Yes. Bring in your luggage. I'll make us a nightcap. We can talk about our future." He smiled with a show of humility. "Your long future and my short one."

He accompanied her to the front door, saying, "I'll help you carry your stuff."

The mild night was sweetened by the roses in his garden. Finally, it was the smell of cultivated roses, the hybrid scent of his life here in America, that released her. She turned around to face him on his porch and said, "I love you, Dad." It was true, this tribute, this weight, her lifelong debt. How else could she have come to exist, if not through him?

Kal's mouth opened to speak, and closed, and he nodded silently. He gripped her shoulders and pulled her toward him for a hard embrace. Then he relinquished her. Huskily, he told her, "I'm very proud of you. Darling."

She walked to the station wagon, unlocked the door, and looked back at her father, a dark figure framed in the light of his brick house. She got into the car, backed up, and turned around.

His white fence, illuminated in the headlights, raced beside her in a blur, and when his driveway met the road, she stopped weeping, and headed west.

She would drive to Chicago. She would catch a flight to Guatemala City. If she could get a start in Guatemala, she could develop some work from there. Then she'd move on to Managua. And San Salvador. The salt dried on her face. She would see Central America, and it would not be another Vietnam; the people, not the military, would win. This surge, this future, was rushing toward her, she'd go gladly to meet it. She was driving away from him, the gunsmith, but she'd never escape him, she'd have to take him with her. She was scared and she hurt everywhere, and this excitement felt terrible, terrific, and it consumed her completely.

ACKNOWLEDGEMENTS

Research for this novel began with a flight to Ho Chi Minh City in 2015, where I met up with lawyer and writer Mary-Jane Bennett. I will be forever grateful to Mary-Jane for her brilliant company, her patience and curiosity, and her running commentary on a Canadian federal election while we walked miles in the heat of Vietnam.

I owe a debt of gratitude to my lifelong friend Jake MacDonald, to whom this book is dedicated. Jake directed me to the Barrett M82, a fifty-calibre semi-automatic, recoil-operated rifle, which I handed to my fictional character, the gunsmith Kal Welsh. When Jake died in January 2019, it was a great loss to me and to many people.

I'm grateful to beloved friends who read or listened to scenes and drafts of this novel over the years: Catherine Hunter; Barbara Schott; my brother, Scott Sweatman; and my husband, Glenn Buhr. Many thanks to the University of Winnipeg.

My final thanks go to the talented editor Bethany Gibson, whose notes provoked this work to its current form.

Anyone who has taken an interest in the war in Vietnam will have encountered a rich literature surrounding it. There are many astonishing writers who helped me to discover *The Gunsmith's Daughter*. The short list below includes only the books and articles that more directly informed me while I wrote this novel.

War Torn: Stories of War from the Women Reporters Who Covered Vietnam. Tad Bariums, Denby Fawcett, Jurate Kazickas, Edith Lederer, Ann Bryan Mariano, Anne Morrissy Marick, Laura Palmer, Kate Webb, Tracy Wood. Introduction by Gloria Emerson. Random House, 2002.

Mekong Diaries: Viet Cong Drawings & Stories, 1964-1975. Sherry Buchanan. University of Chicago Press, 2008.

A Rumour of War. Philip Caputo. Henry Holt and Company, 1977, 1996.

The Gun. C.J. Chivers. Simon & Schuster, 2010.

Why Is Canada in Vietnam?: The Truth about Our Foreign Aid. Claire Culhane. Introduction by Wilfred Burchette. New Canada Publications, 1972.

Interview with History. Oriana Fallaci. Trans. John Shepley. Houghton Mifflin, 1977.

Vietnam: A History. Stanley Karnow. Viking Press, 1983.

Quiet Complicity. Victor Levant. Between the Lines, 1986.

"Appeasing the Spirits Along the 'Highway of Horror': Civic Life in Wartime Republic of Vietnam." Van Nguyen-Marshall. In *War & Society*, 37, no. 3 (April 2018): 1-17. Copyright School of Humanities, University of New South Wales.

Achilles in Vietnam: Combat Trauma and the Undoing of Character. Jonathan Shay. Scribner, 1994.

A Bright Shining Lie: John Paul Vann and America in Vietnam. Neil Sheehan. Vintage, 1988, 1989.

Snow Job: Canada, the United States and Vietnam (1954 to 1973). Charles Taylor. Anansi, 1974.

Home Before Morning: The True Story of an Army Nurse in Vietnam. Lynda Van Devanter. Warner Books, 1983.

NOTES

The origins of "Hey Joe," the song that Lilac and Gavin hear in the car on page 44, are convoluted and contentious. Various platforms have credited its writing to Billy Roberts or Dino Valenti, or have suggested that it's based on a traditional song. Thank you, Jimi Hendrix, for your recording in 1966.

While Lilac is zipping around in her hydroplane on page 54, she has in mind a song called "I Feel Like I'm Fixin to Die Rag" recorded by Country Joe and the Fish, words and music by Joe McDonald, copyright 1965, renewed in 1993 by Alkatraz Corner Music Co. Used by permission of Alkatraz, with many thanks.

On page 88, Lilac and Vivian are listening to Neil Young's album *Everybody Knows This Is Nowhere*, recorded with his band Crazy Horse, and released in 1969 on Reprise Records.

On page 91, Vivian and Lilac belt out the title of the song "We Gotta Get Out of This Place," written by Barry Mann and Cynthia Weil. This song was made famous by the Animals' recording in 1965.

On page 96, Lilac is inspired by a story she reads in the *Washington Post*. This material comes from *War Torn: Stories of War from the Women Reporters Who Covered Vietnam* by Tad Bariums, Denby Fawcett, Jurate Kazickas, Edith Lederer, Ann Bryan Mariano, Anne Morrissy Merick, Laura Palmer, Kate Webb, and Tracy Wood. I'm grateful to all the contributors of this astonishing book, which I read often while writing this novel, in awe of their courage and intelligence. Used by permission from Penguin Random House.

Lilac's interview with President Nguyen Van Thieu on pages 122-25 is based on Oriana Fallaci's *Interview with History*. Translated by John Shepley. Liveright, 1977.

On page 128, at the Caravelle Hotel in Saigon, Lilac hears "It's My Life," a song written by Roger Atkins, with music by Carl D'Errico, recorded by the Animals in 1965. I'm grateful to Roger Atkins for so kindly responding to my query for permission. I hope readers will listen to this song in the real world.

In chapters 15 and 16 of Part Two, Lilac goes to a hospital in Quang Ngai (pages 167-71 and page 177). This material is based on Claire Culhane's book *Why Is Canada in Vietnam? The Truth about Our Foreign Aid*. The depiction of Canada as "the butcher's helper" comes from Claire Culhane. I'm grateful to Culhane and to New Canada Publications for their generous permission to make use of her devastating reportage and analysis.

The depiction of the massacre at the Bên Đá River between Quang Tri and Hué (pages 265-66) is substantiated by the comprehensive research by Van Nguyen-Marshall, in an essay called "Appeasing the Spirits along the 'Highway of Horror': Civic Life in Wartime Republic of Vietnam." This essay was published in *War & Society*, 37, no. 3 (April 2018): 1-17. Many thanks to Van Nguyen-Marshall for permission to integrate such difficult research into my story.